PRAISE FOR

Kay Hooper

SLEEPING WITH FEAR

"Readers will be mesmerized." —*Publishers Weekly*

"Hooper's Special Crime Unit novels all have their own unique blend of mystery, suspense and the paranormal laced with a touch of romance. The author is a gifted teller of action-packed stories." —*Romantic Times*

"Suspense just doesn't get better than Kay Hooper's novels . . . it's a one-sitting read that will hold you in its grip from beginning to end." —*Romance Reviews Today*

CHILL OF FEAR

"Hooper's latest may offer her fans a few shivers on a hot beach." —*Publishers Weekly*

"Kay Hooper has conjured a fine thriller with appealing young ghosts and a suitably evil presence to provide a welcome chill on a hot summer's day." —*Orlando Sentinel*

"The author draws the reader into the story line and, once there, they can't leave because they want to see what happens next in this thrill-a-minute, chilling, fantastic reading experience." —*Midwest Book Review*

HUNTING FEAR

"A well-told, scary story." —*Toronto Sun*

"Hooper's unerring story sense and ability to keep the pages flying can't be denied." —*Ellery Queen Mystery Magazine*

"Hooper has created another original—*Hunting Fear* sets an intense pace. . . . Work your way through the terror to the triumph . . . and you'll be looking for more Hooper tales to add to your bookshelf." —*Times Record News*

"It's vintage Hooper—a suspenseful page-turner."
—*Wichita Falls (TX) Facts*

SENSE OF EVIL

"A well-written, entertaining police procedural . . . loaded with suspense." —*Midwest Book Review*

"Filled with page-turning suspense." —*Sunday Oklahoman*

"*Sense of Evil* will knock your socks off." —*Rendezvous*

"Enjoyable . . . thought-provoking entertainment."
—*Calgary Herald*

TOUCHING EVIL

"Following her highly popular Shadow series, Hooper again scores big with this psychic thriller. *Touching Evil* is the first installment in her Evil series involving Noah Bishop's specially talented group of agents. It kept me furiously turning the pages until the chilling climax."
—*Old Book Barn Gazette*

"*Touching Evil* is a full-force, page-turning, suspense-driven read. . . . Hooper provided enough twists and turns to her story that it had this reader anxiously gripping the pages and not leaving my couch for hours on end." —*Mystery Reader*

STEALING SHADOWS

"A fast-paced, suspenseful plot . . . The story's complicated and intriguing twists and turns keep the reader guessing until the chilling ending." —*Publishers Weekly*

"This definitely puts Ms. Hooper in a league with Tami Hoag and Iris Johansen and Sandra Brown." —*Heartland Critiques*

HAUNTING RACHEL

"A stirring and evocative thriller." —*Palo Alto Daily News*

"An intriguing book with plenty of strange twists that will please the reader." —*Rocky Mountain News*

"It passed the 'stay up late to finish it in one night' test."
—*Denver Post*

FINDING LAURA

"Hooper keeps the intrigue pleasurably complicated, with gothic touches of suspense and a satisfying resolution."
—*Publishers Weekly*

"Ms. Hooper throws in one surprise after another. . . . Spellbinding." —*Rendezvous*

AFTER CAROLINE

"Harrowing good fun. Readers will shiver and shudder."
—*Publishers Weekly*

"Kay Hooper comes through with thrills, chills, and plenty of romance, this time with an energetic murder mystery with a clever twist. The suspense is sustained admirably right up to the end." —*Kirkus Reviews*

"Kay Hooper has crafted another solid story to keep readers enthralled until the last page is turned." —*Booklist*

AMANDA

"*Amanda* seethes and sizzles. A fast-paced, atmospheric tale that vibrates with tension, passion, and mystery. Readers will devour it." —Jayne Ann Krentz

"Kay Hooper's dialogue rings true; her characters are more three-dimensional than those usually found in this genre. You may think you've guessed the outcome, unraveled all the lies. Then again, you could be as mistaken as I was."
—*Atlanta Journal-Constitution*

"Kay Hooper has given you a darn good ride, and there are far too few of those these days." —*Dayton Daily News*

"Will delight fans of Phyllis Whitney and Victoria Holt."
—*Alfred Hitchcock Mystery Magazine*

BANTAM BOOKS BY KAY HOOPER

The Bishop Trilogies
Stealing Shadows
Hiding in the Shadows
Out of the Shadows

Touching Evil
Whisper of Evil
Sense of Evil

Hunting Fear
Chill of Fear
Sleeping with Fear

The Quinn Novels
Once a Thief
Always a Thief

Romantic Suspense
Amanda
After Caroline
Finding Laura
Hunting Rachel

Classic Fantasy and Romance
On Wings of Magic
The Wizard of Seattle
My Guardian Angel *(anthology)*
Yours to Keep *(anthology)*

ONCE A
THIEF

KAY HOOPER

BANTAM BOOKS

ONCE A THIEF
A Bantam Book

PUBLISHING HISTORY
Bantam mass market edition published October 2002
Bantam mass market reissue / October 2007

Published by
Bantam Dell
A Division of Random House, Inc.
New York, New York

This is a work of fiction. Names, characters, places, and incidents
either are the product of the author's imagination or are used
fictitiously. Any resemblance to actual persons, living or dead, events,
or locales is entirely coincidental.

Bantam Books and the rooster colophon are registered trademarks
of Random House, Inc.

ISBN 978-0-553-59024-1

Printed in the United States of America

www.bantamdell.com

OPM 10 9 8 7 6 5 4 3 2 1

AUTHOR'S NOTE

About ten years ago, I wrote a series of short contemporary novels for Bantam's Loveswept romance series. That's right—romances.

But a funny thing happened while I was writing those books. Although I enjoyed all the characters, one in particular was, quite literally, difficult to keep offstage when he wasn't supposed to be active in the story. My cat burglar Quinn practically walked off the pages, and even at the time my agent told me that "one day" I'd have to do more with him.

One day came.

Sometimes a writer is lucky enough to be able to look back at older work and be granted the opportunity to rewrite it as she wanted to write it at the time; I was writing series romance then, and there were simply things I couldn't do in the books be-cause of what they were—and when they were. I am very proud of those books, but they were defi-nitely stories written for a particular audience at a particular time.

At the time, I was unable—both because of the length of the books and the genre itself—to make the characters as complex as I wanted, to give them shades of gray, ambiguities of motive and personal-ity. And since I was already, by then, feeling the need to stretch my wings, to write bigger, more complex books, I was very conscious that I was not providing Quinn and some other characters the wider canvas they deserved.

Which brings me to the second reason I wanted to include this note in the "Thief" books: *Once a Thief* and *Always a Thief* are not the books you re-member if you read the original versions. They've been, in a sense, reimagined. I haven't just added a few thousand words here and there—I have re-structured the stories in several ways.

Some scenes remain from the originals, but even those have been shifted, sometimes slightly, to pro-vide a different perspective or provide that wider canvas for the characters. Some characters have ei-ther stepped back out of the spotlight or disap-peared entirely from the narrative, and new ones are introduced. The same goes for some plotlines.

This is Quinn's story, or at least the beginning of it. And since he continued to be a lively presence in my writer's imagination long after his story was supposedly told, I gather he has more adventures in mind. We'll see.

If you've enjoyed my more recent suspense novels, I hope you'll give this one a try. It's not as dark and gritty as the Bishop books, and if there are any psychic elements—well, we'll just have to wait and find out about that—but Quinn is a lot of fun, and he's allowed me to show a lighter, more playful side of my writing.

My agent calls this sort of story a "caper, a bright, fun, witty adventure that holds on to its sense of humor even though there might well be deadly danger lurking about."

Might well be . . . and there is. Because there's a spectacular collection of gems and artworks about to go on display, and more than one person is ready and willing to do whatever it takes in order to possess it. Even kill.

Come meet Quinn, and let me know what you think of him. I like him a lot. And I hope you do too.

PROLOGUE

Outside the penthouse windows, darkness hid the fog that had rolled in and now clung wetly to the city; it was a fairly typical San Francisco night. Inside the penthouse, antique furniture glowed in the soft lighting of several lamps turned low. And in the sunken den, the brisk crackling of flames in the big marble fireplace was the only sound to break the tense silence.

Then the man on the couch, who had been staring into the fire with a frown, spoke without looking at his visitor. "What makes you think you can catch him? So far, nobody's come close. A whisper of a name, that's all he is."

The visitor had prowled about the room as he talked but now sat in a chair that was at right angles to the fireplace. Like his host, his voice was low. "A lesson I learned a long time ago: With the right bait, you can catch anything. And anyone. The bait you have to offer is guaranteed to draw him out."

His host slanted him a look. "I'll grant that. It's guaranteed to draw every thief you could name out of the woodwork. They'll be tripping over each other."

"It won't be as bad as that. Tough security will weed out all but the . . . um . . . serious contenders."

"Tough security?" The man on the couch gave a soft laugh. "We both know that most of the time in most places security's a pretty illusion, even with state-of-the-art technology. They want in badly enough—they'll find a way. Sure, the petty thieves will be discouraged if security looks tough, but it still leaves a fairly large field of hopefuls."

The visitor nodded. "I know, but there really aren't many out there ambitious enough to go after any part of the Bannister collection, no matter what kind of security we surround it with. For one thing, it'd be damned difficult to sell any of it. Virtually all the individual pieces are so well-known they'd make any fence think twice and then opt out. The risk outweighs the potential profit. I really believe the bait would draw a *collector*—not just a thief out for a quick score."

"Some thieves are collectors," his host pointed out.

"Not many. But he's one of them. And look at his track record. Every piece we know he's taken in the last three years was one of a kind and had a colorful past; most had so-called curses attached to them. Just like the Bolling diamond. One whisper that the Bolling is out of a vault on public display is going to make his mouth water." The visitor shifted restlessly and added, "I don't want to risk the whole collection. This madman's greedy enough to take everything if we make it too easy for him."

"I can't display the Bolling alone. It's part of the collection, and I've said publicly more than once I'd never exhibit any single piece alone. If I had a sudden change of heart now, any thief worth his salt would smell a trap."

After a moment, the visitor said, "Dammit, I didn't know you'd said that. If I had, I never would have—I can't ask you to risk the entire collection, it's too dangerous. A single piece we could protect, *I* could protect, but if the collection is always together in one place, and he gets past security, past me . . . he could get it all."

"The bait and the fish gone forever." Returning his gaze to the bright fire, the man on the couch said quietly, "It's taken my family almost five hundred years to assemble the collection."

"I know." There was a long silence, and then the visitor said softly, "It was a lunatic idea. I'll try something else, Max."

Maxim Bannister sent the visitor another look, this one a bit wry. "There's nothing else to try, and you know it. The kind of bait you need is rare;

off-hand, I can't think of another collector who'd be willing to take the risk."

"I can't ask *you* to take it."

"What choice do you have?"

The worn folder contained a number of eight-by-ten photographs in full color. They were pictures that had been printed again and again in books and magazines all over the world. The Bannister collection rivaled the treasures of the Pharaohs in terms of sheer dazzling mystique and public fascination. It was the last great "family" collection of jewelry and artworks, privately owned and displayed only at the whim of its owner. It hadn't appeared publicly for more than thirty years.

He opened the folder with hands that weren't quite steady, and a tight little breath escaped him when the light of the desk lamp fell onto the first photograph. No matter how many times he saw it, the effect on him was always the same. Simply but exquisitely set in a pendant of twenty-four-karat gold, the Bolling diamond was breathtaking. It was a seventy-five-carat teardrop canary, the brilliant yellow hue so vivid it was as if the stone had captured a piece of the sun.

The centerpiece of the Bannister collection, it was flawless and priceless. Like the Hope diamond, the Bolling possessed a colorful and often tragic history; it was supposed to be cursed, but he didn't believe in curses.

He rubbed a finger across the photo, almost able to feel the coolness of the polished stone. Then, forcing himself, he turned the photo over and began briefly studying the others, one by one. They had less of an effect on him individually than the Bolling had, but the splendor of the entire collection made his heart pound almost painfully.

The Black Royal diamond, forty carats, a darkly perfect oval surrounded by brilliant white diamonds; it had, supposedly, been a ransom payment for a kidnapping the history books never mentioned.

The Midnight sapphire, a two-hundred-carat square stone, flawed but beautiful in its rich, deep color; legend had it that the stone—believed to be nearly a thousand years old—had been found, faceted and dully polished, in the ruins of a temple in India almost three hundred years before.

The Talisman emerald, a hundred and fifty carats of oval green fire, engraved with cryptic symbols no one had yet been able to decipher, and set in a wide bangle bracelet of twenty-four-karat gold. In mystical circles, the story persisted that the emerald had been worn by Merlin and had been used to amplify the wizard's powers.

There were also numerous lesser pieces of jewelry—lesser in terms of value, but each stunning. Necklaces, rings, and bracelets of gold set with exquisitely cut and polished gems. From the brilliance of diamonds to the opacity of jade, ivory, and opal, virtually every precious and semi-precious stone known to man was represented at its very best.

No wonder they were calling the exhibit *Mysteries Past*; every major piece in the collection had a mystery attached to it in some way, many of them connected to historical events or people.

In addition, there were figurines, cups, decanters, and religious works of art in gold and gems. Each piece had a story or legend connected to it. Each piece was breathtaking. Together, they would have tempted a saint.

He wasn't a saint.

With trembling hands, he gathered the photographs together and returned them to the worn folder. The exhibit opened in just about eight weeks, and was scheduled to run for only two months in San Francisco. After that, the collection would be returned to the safety and silence of the vaults that had protected it for decades.

Unless someone got to it first.

CHAPTER
ONE

Somebody ought to put *her* in one of the display cases. Talk about an eye-poppin' show."

Morgan West stopped in her tracks to lift an eyebrow at a suddenly flustered workman. "Voices carry in museums," she said gently. "You might want to keep that in mind."

"Yeah. I mean—yes, ma'am. Sorry, ma'am. No offense meant."

"None taken. It's always been my ambition to be a museum display."

He cleared his throat. "Priceless things. That's all I meant. Treasures. Works of art." He eyed her, then sighed. "I'm not gonna win, am I?"

"No, I'm afraid not."

"I'm a sexist pig."

"Pretty much."

"Objectifying women."

"This woman anyway. Yes, I'd say that was what you were doing."

"I apologize, Miss West."

Perfectly aware that the other workmen near enough to overhear this exchange were hiding grins, Morgan knew when it was time to let her prey off the hook on which he'd impaled himself. "Accepted. Have a nice day."

"Yes, ma'am. You too."

Morgan strolled away, knowing that laughter would erupt the moment she was out of sight. Which it did.

She sighed.

Her measurements had been causing her problems since her thirteenth birthday, so by now she should have been at least somewhat accustomed to it.

She wasn't.

There were men who admitted that long, shapely female legs inspired amorous fantasies; there were those who had the same basic response to the rich curves of swaying hips. But men whose primitive instincts were aroused by an ample bust, Morgan had found, undoubtedly outnumbered the rest.

Probably something Freudian about it.

Or something infantile.

At any rate, her centerfold measurements had caused her more trouble than joy. A lot more. Her dates during high school and college had been so entranced by her charms, she often wondered if they knew what her face looked like. Even the Rhodes scholar she'd briefly gone out with—hoping his mind was on a higher plane—had stuttered dreadfully whenever his gaze strayed to her chest.

Which was often.

And that explained one reason why Maxim Bannister had won her intense and total loyalty. He had, to be sure, gulped visibly when she'd first walked into his office, but he had also conducted the hour-long interview without allowing his gaze to stray to her chest—and without making her feel it required all his concentration to avoid staring. And since that time, he had managed not only to make her feel completely comfortable in his presence but had even responded with genuine sympathy when a particularly degrading experience with a date had caused her to unburden herself in an explosion of temper.

She liked Max a lot. He was one of the very few male friends she'd ever had, and she was delighted by the knowledge that, while he was no less appreciative of nature's bounty than the next man, his awareness and interest were detached rather than hormonal. He also had an unerring eye for color and style, and during the months of preparation for the *Mysteries Past* exhibit, she had gradually abandoned her dark-colored, loose blouses and multilayered outfits in favor of more elegant and flattering clothing.

When Max told her she looked good in something, she knew it was the truth. He'd said once that she was a queenly woman, the observation made in an assessing rather than complimentary tone, and Morgan had, quite unconsciously, begun walking without the slump she had just as unconsciously adopted in her teens. In a few short months, he had very quietly and gently and unobtrusively eradicated both Morgan's bitterness and the chip on her shoulder. Thanks to him, she was as proud of her body as she was of her mind.

Well, nearly.

Which wasn't to say it no longer caused her problems. In fact, masculine appreciation of her measurements was, indirectly, to blame for a predicament that was destined to occupy her for quite some time.

But on this mild Thursday afternoon, Morgan was blessedly unaware of the storm clouds building up on her own personal horizon. As the director of the forthcoming *Mysteries Past* exhibit, her mind was entirely focused on business.

"You're frowning," Wolfe Nickerson noted when they encountered each other in the lobby. He was the security expert Lloyd's of London had sent to oversee both the preparations for the exhibit and the two-month showing itself.

"I'm not surprised. Do you believe in intuition?" she asked.

"I've been known to get a hunch now and then. Why? Are you feeling intuitive?"

"Yeah. At least—I guess that's what it is. There's something out of focus, Wolfe. Something not right."

"With the preparations for the exhibit?"

"I don't know. Maybe." She sighed. "God, I hate it when I get one of these feelings. It's like I saw something out of the corner of my eye, you know? Something I didn't look at as closely as I should have."

Wolfe nodded. "Yeah, I've been there. But you know as well as I do that it's pretty much impossible to guard against a threat when all you've got to go on is a feeling. We're doing everything we can to protect the collection."

"Maybe not everything. Would pulling up the drawbridge and flooding the moat be out of order?"

"Well, it might make things a bit difficult for visitors."

Morgan hugged her ever-present clipboard and rested her chin on the top, matching his gravity when she said, "Yeah, but do we really need visitors? They come, they gawk—big deal."

Smiling, Wolfe said, "You really are bothered, aren't you?"

"A little bit, yeah."

"But there's nothing here yet to steal, remember? I mean, none of the collection. All those nice display cases the workmen are building are going to be empty for weeks yet."

"I know, I know."

"But?"

"But . . . something's wrong." Morgan shook her head with a faint grimace. "The place just doesn't *feel* right. I did a walk-through a little while ago, and I could swear I was being watched."

Wolfe eyed her, a little amused. "Well, you usually are."

"No, not that way." Morgan was intent on making sense of her own feelings and hunches. "*Watched.* Almost . . . I was going to say *stalked*, but I don't mean it in the modern way, with some half-crazed guy who thinks he's in love with me dogging my every step."

"How do you mean it, then?"

"More of a . . . predatory thing. As if I was being tracked, shadowed, my strengths and weaknesses sized up."

Wolfe's eyebrows rose, but more in surprise than disbelief. "That's a fairly primitive image. And a very specific threat to feel intuitively."

"I know. That's why it's creeping me out, big time."

He frowned. "All right, Morgan. I'll have the extra guards do a sweep of the building at the beginning of each shift, as well as halfway through the shift. Good enough?"

"I hope so." She shook her head again, obviously annoyed by worries too elusive to put into words, then added, "I'll be in my office. I'm going to go study the museum blueprints again."

"Listen," Wolfe said, "don't let the responsibility of being in charge while Max is off on his honeymoon blow anything out of proportion, okay? Whether you're right about somebody watching you or the preparations for the exhibit, the collection is safe and we *are* doing everything possible to make damned sure it stays that way."

Morgan squared her shoulders and nodded. "You're right. But I still want to study those blueprints."

"Have at it. If you see anything that'll help increase or perfect security, I'll be the first to thank you for it."

"I just want to be sure," Morgan said.

"I know."

"It's not that I'm questioning your competence—"

He waved that away. "I never thought you were. We're both responsible for protecting the collection, Morgan, so don't think you're stepping on my toes by double-checking everything, including your own hunches. I'll do the same."

"Okay. Just so we're clear."

"We are." Wolfe watched her head off toward her office, and added under his breath, "We're also both worried. I know why I am...but why are you?"

* * *

Carla Reeves was still astonished she'd been able to get a job with a security company. And somewhat amused.

Security? Yeah, right.

But unless she wanted to flip burgers or bag groceries, she'd had to take the chance and apply. It was her good luck that Ace Security had been in crying need of a few employees with a security background—and that a guy at her last place of employment had owed her a big, big favor, and had provided a glowing recommendation for her.

Still, you'd think a fucking security company would have at least checked for a police record before they hired somebody.

Thanking the universe for small favors and large ones, Carla settled happily into the new job, and within a number of weeks was feeling quite at home there. She was also trusted and given increasing responsibility, which was another amusement but nevertheless appreciated, since it led to a raise.

Carla liked her job. And she had no plans to fuck things up by doing anything she shouldn't have. She had learned the hard lesson that a one-time big score was seldom worth the risk of getting caught. Besides, she didn't need to do that anymore.

No, Carla's life was progressing nicely. So nicely, in fact, that she had absolutely no suspicion that everything was about to hit the fan.

She left work a bit later than usual that evening, mostly because she'd wanted to earn a few employee bonus points by doing some extra work on a security system being designed for a private home—of a personal friend of her boss.

She walked around the corner to where she'd left her car parked, smiling as she thought of the praise that would be heaped on her in the morning. Bonus points were fun.

She was fumbling in her purse for her key ring with its remote keyless entry gadget when a pleasant voice stopped her in her tracks.

"Hello, Carla."

It wasn't a familiar voice, but Carla had grown up literally on the streets, and she recognized a threat when she heard one. Still too far from her car to make a break for it, she turned very slowly and looked at him.

He was smiling at her. He was also holding an elegant little gun in one gloved hand.

"Oh, don't worry, Carla. I don't have rape in mind. Or even robbery."

She swallowed hard. "Then what do you want?"

"Just a little information, that's all."

"Information?"

"Come now, Carla, let's not pretend. You know what I want. And you know how to get it. After all—you've done it before, haven't you?"

Carla stared at him, understanding everything

he didn't say. "Yeah," she answered dully. "So I do know what you want."

It was Morgan's habit to be at the museum very early each morning, long before it was open for business, and the next morning was no exception. Also as usual, the first thing she did was to conduct her own sweep of the building.

It wasn't that she didn't trust the guards, it was just that she trusted her own eyes and other senses more.

After all the months of preparation for the exhibit, she was very familiar with the cavernous halls and labyrinthine corridors of the museum. So much so, in fact, that she probably could have found her way through with the aid of a flashlight—no mean feat, given the size and complexity of the building.

Until very recently, she had never felt uneasy being alone in any area of the museum. But as her heels clicked against the polished marble floors, she once again had the oddest feeling that she wasn't as alone as she should have been. She stopped several times, gazing around her with a frown, but no one was there. She was sure no one was there.

"Morgan, you're losing it," she muttered finally.

Since this was a museum of historical art, it wasn't nearly as creepy as some she'd worked in.

No stuffed or skeletal beasts loomed, and there weren't any exhibits such as *Prehistoric Man at the Hunt* with figures of man and beast frozen in bloody confrontational poses.

There was statuary, however, and more than once Morgan caught herself frowning uneasily at a manlike figure in a dim corner that she only belatedly recognized as some artist's work in marble or bronze.

"Definitely losing it." The sound of her own voice startled her somewhat, and Morgan quickened her steps, even though she kept searching for whatever was bothering her. And found nothing. Or at least found nothing that looked like anything.

"I don't even know what I'm looking for," she admitted half under her breath.

But as she turned to retrace her steps, Morgan's uneasiness intensified. The place still didn't feel right to her. She tried to focus on what she was feeling, but it was vague and unformed. Just anxiety and an odd sense of apprehension.

Morgan stopped at the entrance of the wing and looked back down the echoing corridors. A little laugh escaped her. "We're about to bring a priceless collection of art treasures into this place," she reminded herself aloud. "*Of course* I'm uneasy about it. That's all. That's all it is."

With those reassuring words, she turned and

headed back for the lobby, her heels once more clicking briskly against the marble floor.

The sounds were fading away when, in a dim corner Morgan had passed by twice, one of those manlike figures stirred and stepped out of the shadows. He stood gazing after Morgan for several moments, then turned and headed deeper into the museum, his movements utterly silent and almost feline in their fluid grace.

If anybody had been there to hear, they wouldn't have heard a footstep. But they would have heard a soft, amused chuckle.

At thirty-six, Wolfe was two years younger than Max Bannister; they were half brothers, raised by their fathers on opposite coasts of the country, and had gotten to know each other well only as adults. But even though their knowledge of each other went back less than fifteen years, there was an unusually strong bond between them. It was one of the reasons Max had specifically requested Wolfe when Lloyd's, which insured the Bannister collection, had insisted on having one of their representatives on the scene during the exhibit and the preparations leading up to it.

One of the reasons. The other reason was that Wolfe was very, very good at his job. Good enough so that he took the worries of the *Mysteries Past* director seriously—even if she didn't think so.

"Morgan, all I said was—"

"All you said was that I'm nuts." She planted both hands on her hips and glared at Wolfe.

"No, that is not what I said. I said we've been over this museum and the guards have been over it, and none of us has found a thing out of order. So—"

"So I'm nuts."

Reining in his own considerable temper, Wolfe silently counted to five, too impatient to make it ten. "Look, I appreciate that you're worried. I'm worried too. But until the new security system is up and running, there really isn't much more we can do."

"We can padlock and bar some of the damned doors and make everybody use the main entrance here," she suggested.

"Some of the rear doors have to be used, you know that."

"But—"

"The safety code, Morgan. We can't block doors that could be necessary exits in an emergency. With only the wing set to house the exhibit closed to the public and the rest of the museum open, we have hundreds of people in and out of the building every day; we have to make certain they could get out in a hurry if they had to."

"Shit," she muttered. "I knew we should have put in a moat. I just knew it."

Frowning, Wolfe said, "All I can do is go lean

on the computer technician to step things up a bit and get the new system on line ahead of schedule. Until we have a better way to monitor the comings and goings around here, we're stuck with the current system. You know that, Morgan."

She knew that. But she didn't have to like it.

Determined to get the last word, she said, "Fine. But in the future, when we recall this moment—and we will—just remember that it was me warning you. Okay?"

"On this day, Morgan warned me she had a bad feeling. Noted."

"Smartass."

He grinned at her, then strode off toward the offices.

Morgan remained where she was in the lobby, absently watching visitors come and go. It was turning into a busy afternoon, and there were a dozen things she should have been doing. Instead, she was fretting and worrying and bothering Wolfe.

And all because she felt . . . What?

There was something wrong. Just . . . wrong.

Still, Wolfe had been right when he'd pointed out that the Bannister collection wasn't even in the building as yet and wouldn't be for weeks. So there was time to fix whatever was wrong. Time to get the new security system up and running, the carefully designed display cases built and wired and installed. Time to plug all the holes in the security net. Time to make sure the *Mysteries Past* exhibit was as safe as Fort Knox.

There was plenty of time.

So why did she have the oddest sensation of time ticking away, and much more rapidly than any clock or calendar would indicate?

Why was she sure they didn't have nearly as much time as they thought?

Ed frowned down at the list and then looked at his boss with lifted brows. "So—what? We walk out with all this? Hell, I don't even know if we can carry it all."

"If you can't, I'll find someone who will."

That uncompromising reply hardly surprised Ed. But to say he was happy about it would have been a serious overstatement. "Look, I know our partnership has been a lucrative one, but you're beginning to worry me. Every job is bigger than the last, more dangerous."

"And you're earning more than you ever thought possible, so don't go soft on me now."

"I'm not going soft, I'm just wondering how long our luck can hold out."

"It isn't luck, I keep telling you that. It's skill, and planning—and balls. Sheer nerve. And with this next job, we'll prove it."

"Why the fuck do we want to prove it?" he demanded. "And prove it to who?"

"To everyone. The police, the other collectors in this town—and anybody else stupid enough to get in our way."

"Christ, all we're doing is making ourselves a bigger target. Your way, we're drawing more and more attention to our operations, which is the last thing we need. Visible thieves end up with their asses in jail, in case you've forgotten that. And we're getting way too visible for my taste. If the jobs get any bigger, we'll need a goddamned semi just to haul away the take. And the security systems are getting harder and harder to get through; the last one was tricky as hell."

"We got through it, didn't we?"

"Yeah, but—"

"No buts. If you don't like the management, go look for a new job."

Ed drew a breath and let it out, holding on to his temper because he'd learned the hard way that it was much safer. "Okay, okay. Let's take a look at the floor plans and technical specs on security."

"I had a feeling you were going to say that."

By the time her day's work was finished and she was ready to leave the museum on Friday night, Morgan had convinced herself that her uneasiness was no more than a natural worry magnified by the ever-approaching arrival of the Bannister collection at the museum. But that didn't stop her from conducting one last sweep of the building herself before leaving for the day.

For no reason she could have explained to herself, she exchanged her heels for the track shoes she kept handy in a drawer of her desk, and this time her steps through the polished marble halls were virtually silent.

And this time, carrying a flashlight, she peered into every dim corner, behind and around every pedestal and display case. She found nothing. Absolutely nothing that wasn't supposed to be exactly where it was.

Morgan hated admitting even to herself that she had hoped to find something, some evidence to explain her apprehension. Not that she had the slightest idea what that might have been, but still.

"All clear, Miss West?"

She returned the flashlight to the guard in the lobby and smiled ruefully. "As far as I can tell, everything's fine. Thanks for humoring me, Chris."

Seriously, he replied, "Knowing what's coming into this place in a few weeks, I don't blame you a bit for being careful. Oh—and Mr. Nickerson called a little while ago and asked me to tell you that he's putting on a few more guards for the second and third shifts, starting tomorrow night."

So Wolfe had taken her worries more seriously than he had led her to believe. She wasn't sure whether that reassured her or only added to her anxiety.

Morgan nodded. "Thanks, Chris. See you tomorrow night."

"Have a nice evening, Miss West."

As she left the building and headed for her car, Morgan told herself that was just what she was going to have. A nice evening. The date originally planned for tonight had been rescheduled for Monday, but after the tensions of the day she was rather glad of that. What she needed was to curl up with a good book or a good old movie on TV and stop thinking about the museum and the exhibit.

At least for tonight.

Still, she paused with her hand on the car's door to look back at the museum. The building was well-lit after hours, and all the dangling banners proclaiming the forthcoming *Mysteries Past* exhibit were very visible. Very impressive.

Very tempting, to a thief.

Shaking off the thought, Morgan got into her car and headed for home, a little surprised to find that as she drove away from the museum, her anxiety lessened. In fact, by the time she got home, she was feeling her usual cheerful and optimistic self.

Which didn't strike her as at all peculiar until much later.

* * *

He waited until the little car was out of his sight before he emerged from the shadows near the museum. He gazed after it, and her, shaking his head unconsciously.

Logic told him she couldn't possibly be feeling or sensing his presence, as she seemed to be. His own honed senses told him that was exactly what was happening nevertheless.

Had he given himself away somehow?

Perhaps. Or perhaps her instincts and intuitions were a lot better than he'd counted on.

Either way, he thought some readjustment of his plans was in order.

It was late Monday afternoon when Wolfe stood in the lobby of the museum listening to Morgan explain why one of the newly built display cases for the exhibit wasn't going to work.

"So we have to go back to the drawing board," she finished, sounding exasperated. "Damn, you'd think at least *one* of us would have realized the thing wasn't going to fit. And now they say redesigning that case might affect the two closest to it."

"Are we going to lose time on this?" Wolfe asked.

"No way. If anyone even suggests we push the

opening back, I'll have his head," Morgan replied firmly.

"Even though you're still feeling uneasy?"

Morgan eyed him. "It's that obvious?"

"Let's just say it's visible. Still nothing concrete you can point to?"

"No. I was here both Saturday and yesterday, and it was a nice, peaceful weekend. No problems at all."

"I thought Max told you to take weekends off."

"Yeah, but it was a choice between staying home and worrying or coming over here and easing my mind. I picked the latter."

"Doesn't look to me like it eased your mind."

Morgan sighed. "Not much, no. But at least now I have something to focus on. Those damned display cases."

Chuckling, Wolfe said, "Then I'll leave the matter in your capable hands." He saw her glance at her watch, and added, "Have a date?"

"For my sins, yes." She grimaced slightly, then laughed a little. "He seems to be a creature of the mind, but we'll see."

Meditatively, Wolfe said, "I've always found that the mind can go only so far in controlling the instincts."

"Well, if he can't control *his,* he'll earn a right cross. Honestly, Wolfe, if I tangle with one more lusting beast hiding behind a puppy-dog smile, I'm going to join a nunnery."

"Keep your chin up," Wolfe advised, smiling. "Somewhere out there has to be at least one man who'll value your brain as much as your body— and you'll probably fall over him while you're looking for something else."

CHAPTER
TWO

She had buried herself in work in recent years, but after Max's healing wizardry Morgan had begun, somewhat tentatively, dating again. It was just bad luck, she told herself, that the young curator who had always treated her with grave respect turned out to have a baser motive lurking under his smiles.

He was perfectly charming during dinner, then afterward asked if she'd like to go to his museum and see the latest Egyptian exhibit, which wasn't scheduled to go on display for several days. It wasn't exactly "Come up and see my etchings," but since she'd recognized the look that went along with the casual offer, it was enough to make her wary.

Still, she wanted to see the exhibit; the hours she put in overseeing her own forthcoming exhibit would make a visit during regular hours somewhat of a problem. And she was confident of her ability to handle an amorous curator. There would be security guards, in any case.

"That's funny," her date murmured as he used his key and let them in a side door.

"What?"

"The security light in this hall should be—"

It should have been on, Morgan knew, but her escort never got a chance to finish his sentence. They had taken no more than three steps into the dark hallway when he suddenly let out a soft grunt and crumpled to the floor.

Morgan was never sure afterward if she *knew* what had happened in that first instant or if, in the thick blackness surrounding her, pure survival instinct had taken over. She didn't reason that Peter's limp body had fallen between her and the door, preventing that exit; she simply whirled and bolted down the hallway.

After half a dozen steps she managed to kick her heels off without losing much speed, and her instantly quieter passage made it possible for her to hear the pursuing footsteps—fast and heavy, and all too close behind. She had the advantage of knowing the museum well; like many archaeologists, she considered the storehouses of ancient treasures as alternate homes and tended to spend many of her off hours losing herself in the past.

That was what she wanted badly to do now—

lose herself in the past. She was making her way with all the speed she could muster out of the warren of offices and storerooms and into the larger rooms of the museum proper. There was a drawback to that action, but she had little choice. Most of the exhibits were individually lighted, which would make her visible to her pursuer unless she could hide before he emerged from the hallway. As she turned the final corner, she could see the dim glow ahead.

The first cavernous room she burst out into was a hall of paintings offering no place of concealment. Barely feeling the cold, hard marble beneath her feet, Morgan darted through one of the two big archways without immediately knowing why she'd made the choice. Then she realized. There had to be more than one of them and they'd be after the most portable valuables, wouldn't they? Jewelry, then—and a large display of precious gems lay in the direction she hadn't chosen.

Along her route were several larger and less valuable—to the thieves—displays of statuary, weapons, and assorted artifacts, many large enough to offer a hiding place.

She made another desperate turn through an archway that appeared to house a room dimmer than some of the others—and found herself neatly caught. A long arm that seemed made of iron rather than flesh lifted her literally off her feet, clamped her arms to her sides, hauled her back against a body that had all the softness of granite, and a big, dark hand covered her mouth before she could do more than gasp.

For one terrified instant, Morgan had the eerie thought that one of the darkly looming statues of fierce warriors from the past had reached out and grabbed her. Then a low voice hissed in her ear, and the impression of supernatural doings faded.

"Shhhh!"

He wasn't a security guard. The hand over her mouth was encased in a thin, supple black glove, and as much of his arm as she could see was also wearing black. Several hard objects in the vicinity of his waist dug into her back painfully. Then he pulled her impossibly closer as running footsteps approached, and she distinctly felt the roughness of wool—a ski mask?—as his hard jaw brushed against her temple.

She didn't struggle in the man's powerful embrace, although she couldn't have said just why. Instead, she concentrated on controlling her ragged breathing so that it wouldn't be audible, her eyes fixed on the archway of the room. She realized only then that she'd bolted into a room with only one entrance. Her captor had literally carried her back into a corner and in the shadows behind one of the fierce warrior statues, and she doubted they were visible from the doorway.

The footsteps in the hall slowed abruptly, and she caught a glimpse of a rather menacing face further distorted by an angry scowl as her pursuer looked into the room. She stiffened, but he went on without pausing more than briefly. As the footsteps faded, she began to struggle; the steely arm around her tightened with an additional strength that nearly cracked her ribs.

Three breathless seconds later, she realized why.

"Ed." The voice, low and harsh, was no more than a few feet down the hallway.

Morgan went very still.

There was an indistinguishable murmur of at least two voices out there, and then the first voice became audible—and quite definitely angry.

"I thought she came this way. Dammit, she could be anywhere in this mausoleum—the place is huge!"

"Did she get a look at you?" Ed's voice was calmer.

"No, the hall was too dark. When I tapped her boyfriend to sleep, she ran like a rabbit. Why the hell did he have to pick tonight to come here? If he wanted romance, he should have taken her to his place. Judging by what I saw of her, she'd have kept him busy between the sheets for a week."

Feeling herself stiffen again, this time indignantly, Morgan was conscious of an absurd embarrassment that the man holding her so tightly against him had heard that lewd comment.

"Never mind," Ed said impatiently. "We're covering all the doors, so she can't get out, and the phone lines have been cut. She dropped her purse back there, right? Check to see if she had a cell phone, and if she did, trash it. Then go back to your post and wait. We'll be finished in another half hour and out of here. She'll be locked in until morning, so she can't do us any harm."

"I don't like it, Ed."

"You don't have to like it. And stop using my name, you fool. Do what I said and get back to your post."

There was a moment of taut silence, and then Ed's unhappy minion passed the archway on his route back to his post, an even more distorted scowl darkening his face.

Morgan heard his footsteps fade into silence; strain as she would, she couldn't hear anything from Ed. At least five minutes must have passed, with agonizing slowness, before her captor finally relaxed slightly and eased her down so that her feet touched the cold floor. His voice sounded again, soft and no more than a sibilant whisper, next to her ear.

"I'm not going to hurt you. Understand? But you have to be still and quiet, or you'll bring them down on us."

Morgan nodded her understanding. As soon as he released her, she took half a step away and turned to confront him. "If you aren't with them, what are you—" she began in a whisper, then broke off as the question was answered.

He was a tall man, at least two or three inches over six feet, with wide shoulders and a wiry look that spoke of honed strength and feline grace rather than muscled bulk. She'd felt that strength. Enveloped in black from head to foot, he had a compact and very efficient-looking tool belt strapped to his lean waist. And from the black ski mask gleamed, almost catlike, the greenest pair of eyes she'd ever seen.

"Oh." She knew, then, what he was doing here. "Oh, Christ."

"Not nearly," he murmured.

Morgan felt a burst of pure irritation at his ill-timed humor but somehow managed to keep her voice low. "You're just another *thief*."

"Please." He sounded injured. "Such a commonplace word. An ugly word, even. I prefer to call myself a privateer."

"Wrong," she snapped, still in a low voice that would have been inaudible a couple of feet away. "This isn't a ship on the high sea, and we aren't at war. You're a common, ordinary, run-of-the-mill *criminal*." She could have sworn those vivid green eyes gleamed with sheer amusement.

"My dear young woman," he said, that same emotion threaded through his soft, unaccented voice, "I am neither common nor ordinary. In fact, I'm one of the last of a vanishing breed in these uncomfortably organized, high-tech days. If you must attach a noun to me, make it *cat burglar*.

However, I'd much rather you simply called me Quinn."

Wolfe hesitated for a long time before he made the call, but when he did, it hardly surprised him that Max Bannister answered on the second ring. He might be on his honeymoon, but few people even had his cell-phone number, and fewer still would have dared to interrupt said honeymoon.

"Tell Dinah I said I'm sorry," Wolfe told Max.

"You lucked out," Max responded, dry. "She's asleep. It's a bit late over here."

Wolfe checked his watch, did a bit of math, and winced. "Sorry."

"Never mind. I was awake, actually. What's up?"

"The hell of it is . . . I'm not sure how to answer that. Morgan's worried, Max, and she has me worried."

"About?"

"I'd like to believe we're both just jumping at shadows, but I think it's more than that. Something's off at the museum. The feel of the place is wrong."

"That's pretty nebulous."

"No kidding. Morgan felt it first, but I'm feeling it now. It's like the place is haunted. If I didn't know better, I'd swear we've had somebody other than security moving around inside after hours."

"Any solid evidence to prove that?"

"Not a shred."

"And nothing's been taken."

"No. Look, Max, you know I'm not an alarmist. But if somebody *is* inside already, then we've got a big problem. There's no way I can authorize the transfer of the collection, not if I have any doubt at all as to the security of the building."

"The new security system isn't in yet, right?"

"No, not yet."

Max was silent for a moment, then said, "It's still weeks before the collection will be moved. I say we get the new security system up and running, which is supposed to be designed to plug any holes in the existing security net. In the meantime, you and Morgan are authorized to take any steps you deem necessary to secure the building. Hire more guards, somebody to do an electronics sweep, whatever it takes. I'll clear it with Ken Dugan and the board of governors."

"You know Dugan will agree to anything if it means he'll have the Bannister collection on exhibit here. Major career points for any head curator."

"The board won't argue either. I'll finance any extra security measures and guarantee that the museum will be better off even after the exhibit closes."

"That's a dangerous guarantee. The city's crawling with thieves, Max."

"So I've heard. Including a new gang the police can't seem to get a line on."

"Yeah, they've looted a couple of places already. If they aren't stopped, I don't doubt they'll target your collection."

Max chuckled. "My money's on you and Morgan."

"Yeah—literally." Wolfe sighed. "I'll talk to Morgan first thing tomorrow morning. Between us, we'll figure out a way to lock the place down tight."

"I know you will. Keep me informed, okay?"

"You've got it. But I promise not to intrude on your honeymoon any more than I have to."

"I'd appreciate that." Max said his good-byes and ended the call, slowly closing his cell phone.

Dinah, who had been wide awake the entire time, said musingly, "I never realized you could be so deceptive."

"I just told him you were asleep. A small white lie to make him feel better."

"It didn't make you feel better. You don't like lying to him, do you?"

"Of course not."

"Especially about the collection baiting a trap."

"Especially that." Max sighed.

"Trouble's coming, isn't it?"

"Yes. Yes, I'm afraid it is. And soon."

Morgan stared at him. Quinn? Quinn. She knew of him. God, of *course* she knew of him. For nearly ten years, the name of Quinn—along with assorted aliases and journalistic nicknames in various languages—had been synonymous with daring, nerveless theft at its most dramatic.

If the newspapers were to be believed, he had smoothly robbed the best families of Europe, relieving them of fine baubles and artworks with a delicate precision and finicky taste that made the *cat* in his preferred noun an apt choice. And in so doing he had bypassed some of the most expensive and complicated security systems ever designed with almost laughable ease.

Also according to the newspapers, he never used weapons, had never injured anyone, and had never come close to being caught—all of which made him something of a folk hero.

"Hell," Morgan said.

"Not yet." He seemed even more amused. "I see that my reputation precedes me. How gratifying. It's nice to know that one's work is appreciated."

She ignored the levity. "I thought you were a European thief exclusively."

"Ah—but America is the land of opportunity," he intoned in a reverent voice.

She didn't know whether to laugh or swear again. With her own love of ancient artifacts and priceless artworks, she had never felt the slightest urge to romanticize the theft of them. And no matter how rapturous certain journalists seemed to be in describing the daring exploits of thieves with taste and without any leaning toward violence, she saw nothing of a Robin Hood-type myth clinging to this one: No one had ever implied that Quinn shared his spoils with the poor.

"What are you doing here?" she demanded.

"I rather thought that was obvious."

Morgan drew a deep breath. "Dammit, I meant—Stop staring at my chest!"

Quinn cleared his throat with an odd little sound, and in a suspiciously pensive and humble tone said, "I have held in my hands some of the finest artworks the world has ever known. Had I but realized a few moments ago that so exquisite a work of Nature herself was so near...May I say—"

"No, you may not," she said from between gritted teeth, fighting a mad urge to giggle.

"No, naturally not," he murmured, then added sadly, "There are certain drawbacks to being a gentleman burglar."

"Oh, now you claim to be a gentleman?"

"What's your name?" he asked curiously, ignoring her question.

"Morgan West." Oddly enough, she didn't even think about withholding the information.

"Morgan. An unusual name. Derived from Morgana, I believe, Old Welsh—" This time, he stopped himself, adding after a thoughtful moment, "And familiar. Ah, now I remember. You're the director of the forthcoming *Mysteries Past* exhibit."

She raised a hand and shook a finger under his nose. "If you *dare* to rob my exhibit," she said fiercely, "I will hunt you to the ends of the earth and roast your gentleman's carcass over perdition's flames!"

"I believe you would," he said mildly. "Interpol itself never threatened me with more resolution."

"Never doubt it." She let her hand fall, then said in an irritable tone, "And you distracted me."

Still mild, Quinn said, "Not nearly as much as you distracted me, Morgana."

"It's Morgan. Just Morgan."

"I prefer Morgana."

"It isn't your name—" She got hold of herself. Absurd. Of all the ridiculous . . . Here she was in a dark museum that was being systematically looted by an organized group of thieves. Her dinner date had been, at the very least, knocked unconscious; she'd been chased through marble halls by a man who probably wouldn't have been nice if he'd caught her; and now she was defending her name preference to an internationally infamous cat burglar who had too much charm for his own good.

And hers.

Doggedly, she tried again. "Never mind my name. If you aren't with those jokers out there, then why are you here?"

"The situation does have its farcical points," he

said amiably. "I'm afraid I dropped in on them. Literally. We seem to have had the same agenda in mind for tonight. Though my plans were, of course, on a lesser scale. Since they outnumber me ten to one, and since they are definitely armed, I chose not to—shall we say—force the issue. It breaks my heart, mind you, because I'm almost certain that what I came here for is now neatly tucked away in one of their boring little leather satchels. But . . . *c'est la vie.*"

Morgan stared at him. "What did you come for?"

Quite gently, he said, "None of your business, Morgana."

After a moment, she said speculatively, "I don't suppose you'd let me see your face?"

"That wouldn't be my first choice, no. Quinn is a name and a shadow, nothing more. I have a strong feeling that your descriptive powers are better than the average, and I don't care to see a reasonable facsimile of my face plastered across the newspapers. Being a cat burglar is the very devil once the police know what you look like."

"All the surveillance systems in the world that include video cameras, and nobody's yet managed to get a shot of you?"

"I have a knack," he explained modestly.

"Yeah, yeah. It's more likely you have a hammer," she said, eyeing his tool belt.

"I never destroy things. Break a window or a

display case now and then, perhaps, but nothing worse than that."

"Stealing priceless things isn't worse than that?"

"Well, I meant along the lines of destruction."

"And I'm supposed to give you points for that?"

"I was rather hoping you would," he replied with suspicious earnestness.

"Oh, for God's sake," she muttered under her breath.

He had been leaning a negligent shoulder against the stone warrior, his pose one of lazy attention, but before she could say anything else, he straightened abruptly. She didn't have to see his face to feel his sudden tension, and when he reached out for her she felt a moment of real fear.

"Shhh," he whispered, drawing her close to him and deeper into the shadows. "They're coming."

Morgan's instant of rigidity was just that brief. The man must have ears like a bat; she hadn't heard a thing but was now aware of the muffled footsteps coming toward them up the hall. A lot of muffled footsteps.

Quinn bent his head until his lips were near her ear and softly breathed, "Their truck's parked by a side entrance; they have to pass this room in order to reach it."

Morgan was definitely nervous about the possibility of discovery, but even then she was aware of a totally extraneous and illogical observation.

Despite Quinn's implication that if he had known about her charms earlier he might have allowed his hands to wander a bit, the hand at her waist remained perfectly still and had not "accidentally" fumbled en route there. It was to his eternal credit as a man, she thought. Or a credit to his detached professionalism as a thief with more businesslike matters on his mind. Or else he had been grossly exaggerating his admiration of said charms. She wasn't sure which.

She wanted to know, though. She very badly wanted to know.

Pushing the insanely inappropriate thoughts aside, she tried to ignore the disturbing closeness of his hard body as they watched almost a dozen shadowy forms file quietly past the doorway. All the men carried leather satchels and were burdened with various tools. Morgan watched them, and it suddenly hit her that the small brown bags contained the museum's treasures.

It was like a kick in the stomach that hurt and made her feel ill. She couldn't just stand here and watch without lifting a finger to stop them—

That was when Quinn quickly and silently clapped his hand over her mouth again, and the hand at her waist held her in an iron grip that defied her to attempt any movement.

She felt very peculiar. How had he known? Surely the wretched man couldn't read minds? No. No, of course not. She must have given away her feelings somehow. Twitched or whimpered or something. She made herself stand perfectly still until he finally—somewhere around ten minutes later—relaxed and turned her loose.

"My ribs," she said temperately, "are cracked. At least three of them."

"Sometimes I don't know my own strength," he apologized solemnly.

She followed as he strolled casually out of their hiding place and into the hall, reasoning from his lazy attitude—and the fact that his deep voice was no longer unnaturally quiet—that he knew the other thieves had gone. "What happened to the security guards?" she asked him in a normal voice.

"It's just a guess," he answered, walking through the hall with more briskness now, "but from the way they were snoring when I checked on them earlier, I'd say they had been drugged. And nicely trussed as well. You heard the charming Ed say that the phone lines had been cut; the alarm system has naturally been deactivated, and none of the outside doors was damaged when they came in—Damn." The oath, uttered with more resignation than heat, escaped him as they stood in the doorway of what had been meant to be the Egyptian exhibit.

Morgan said something a great deal stronger. In fact, she said several violent and colorful things, the last few of which caused Quinn to turn his head and look down at her with a definite gleam in his vivid eyes.

"Such language," he reproved.

"Look at what they *did*," she very nearly wailed, gesturing wildly at the room as the echoes of her bitter cry bounced mockingly back at her. It looked, she thought painfully, like a room after a child's party: messy, depressingly empty, and rather pathetic.

The thieves had been thorough. Into their little brown satchels had gone all the literally priceless jewelry of the Pharaoh as well as everything else they could carry away. Figurines, the gold plates and goblets meant to hold the food and drink of divine royalty in the afterlife, even—

"The mummy case," she gasped. "They took it too?"

"Carted it out before you crashed the party," Quinn answered, still maddeningly calm.

Morgan turned and seized fistfuls of his black turtleneck sweater, rather pleased when he flinched visibly as her nails dug into his chest. "And you didn't even try to stop them?" she demanded furiously.

Quinn looked down at her. "Ten to one," he reminded in an absent tone. "And they had guns. Don't hit me, but you look rather magnificent when you're angry."

She snarled at him and gave him a shove as she

stepped back. The shove didn't budge him, which also, obscurely, pleased her. "You are a soulless man," she told him. "How anybody—anybody at all—could stand here and look at this...this *rape* in total calm passes the bounds of all understanding."

"Appearances," he said softly, "can be quite deceiving, Morgana. If I could get my hands on the man who ordered this done, I would probably strangle him." Then, in a lighter and rather mocking tone, he added, "Such wholesale thievery has a distressing tendency to enrage the local constabulary, to say nothing of persons with valuables to protect. And it's so greedy, aside from the trouble it causes we honest craftsmen."

"Honest?" she yelped.

"I have my living to make, after all," he said in an injured tone. "Can I help it if my natural skills set me in opposition to certain narrow-minded rules?"

She looked blankly after him as he turned away, then scurried along behind him. The floor was cold under her stockinged feet, and it reminded her... "Oh, hell, I hope they haven't killed Peter," she muttered almost to herself as she caught up with Quinn.

"The boyfriend?"

"My date," she corrected repressively. "He's the curator of this place."

"And he brought you here after hours? Let me guess. He wanted to show you his etchings?"

If she could have seen his face, Morgan knew it would have looked sardonic; she didn't have to see his face, because his voice was just the same. But his question was so damned apt that she had a difficult time being indignant.

Finally, sweetly, she said, "None of your business."

"That's put me in my place," he murmured, then added, before she could explode, "I wouldn't worry about your Lothario; professional thieves tend to avoid murder."

"Does that go for you too?" she asked nastily.

He was unruffled. "Certainly. The judges of the world, by and large, look on robbery with severe eyes—but not nearly so severe as those regarding murder."

Morgan couldn't manage anything but a sneer, which was wasted because Quinn was rapidly surveying the rooms they were passing through. Interested despite herself, she asked warily, "Are you looking for something?"

"I hate wasted efforts," he explained absently.

She almost tripped over a security guard lying on the floor, his hands taped behind his back and—as Quinn had said—snoring gustily. Regaining her balance, she hurried on, catching up to the infamous thief as he stood looking down into a glass case.

"The Kellerman dagger," he said in a considering tone.

She didn't like the tone. "What about it?"

"It's a nice piece. Gold haft studded with rubies. Plain sheath, but what the hell. Fetch a good price."

CHAPTER
THREE

What?" Morgan was so enraged, her voice actually squeaked. "You don't think I'm going to just stand here and let you steal that?"

"No." He sighed. "No, I rather thought you'd have an objection." And then he moved.

Forever afterward, Morgan was unable to explain to her own satisfaction how he managed to do it. He didn't exactly leap at her, he was just *there*, in a flash like a big shadow. She was off balance. That was her only excuse. Off balance and lulled by the sinful charm of the thieving scoundrel.

She found herself, quite unaccountably, sitting on the cold marble floor. She wasn't at all hurt. Her wrists were bound together (snugly but not too tightly) with black electrician's tape, and she was staring at the ornate leg of the display case, which her arms were wrapped around. Effectively immobilized.

She tried to kick him, but he was too agile for her.

Chuckling as he stood just out of her range and removed something from his tool belt, Quinn said admiringly, "Your eyes spit rage, just like a cat's. No, stop trying to kick me, you'll only hurt yourself."

Morgan winced as the glass in the display case shattered under his expert touch. "You're not going to leave me here?" she demanded incredulously, peering up at him.

"Sorry," he murmured.

"You—you *bastard.*"

He might have heard the note of genuine horror in her voice; his head tilted as he looked down at her, and his low voice was more sober. "Only for an hour or so, Morgana, I give you my word. As soon as I'm away, I'll tip the police."

She scowled at him, angry at herself for having shown a moment of weakness. The truth was, she did not at all enjoy the idea of being alone, helplessly bound, in a dim museum with only drugged guards and a possibly murdered Peter for company.

She hadn't realized it until now, but Quinn's insouciant manner and easy strength had been—in some peculiar way she didn't want to think about—more than a little comforting. Even if he *was* a devious, rotten, no-good criminal.

"Is your word any good?" she asked coldly.

He seemed to go very still for a moment, then said in a voice different from any she'd yet heard him use, "My word is the only good thing about me. One must, after all, cling to some scrap of honor."

The overly light tone couldn't quite disguise a much deeper feeling underneath, a seriousness that surprised her. Morgan couldn't hold on to her scowl, but she did manage not to soften toward him. Much.

She watched him lift the dagger from the case and drop it into a chamois bag she hadn't noticed tied to his tool belt. Then a sudden memory made her say, "Ed said I'd be locked in until morning; how're you going to get out?"

"The same way I got in." His voice was his again, careless and somewhat mocking.

"Which is?"

His eyes gleamed, catlike, as he looked down at her. "Which is my little secret. After all—I may use the same trick to get at your exhibit."

Her momentary softening vanished as if an arctic wind had blasted it. "I swear to God, Quinn, if you lay so much as a single finger on any part of Bannister's collection..."

"I know," he said sympathetically when her choked voice trailed off. "It's so hard to rise to glorious heights a second time. The first threat was so marvelously phrased. Let's see—ah, yes. If I tamper with *Mysteries Past,* you mean to hunt me to the ends of the earth and roast my gentleman's carcass over perdition's flames. That was it, I believe?"

She made a strangled sound of sheer rage.

He chuckled. "I must go now, *chérie*. Are you quite comfortable?"

Pride told her to ignore the mockingly solicitous question; the hard coldness of the floor beneath her thin skirt told her to speak up before he disappeared. Common sense won out, but her Cherokee pride made her voice sulky. "No, dammit. The floor's hard. And cold."

"My apologies," he said gravely. "I will try to remedy that." He vanished into the shadows toward another of the rooms.

Morgan had to fight a craven impulse to cry out his name. Museums were unnerving places at night, she decided firmly, squashing the impulse. So . . . so *quiet.* With big, dark things looming in shadows, and the faint, musty smell of age and inexorable decay. She shivered, seeing the remnants of history from a new perspective and not liking it much.

Quinn returned in just a few minutes, carrying a colorful, tasseled pillow he'd gotten from God knew where. Still sulky but curious, she waited to see how he'd manage; her position on the floor was awkward and she couldn't raise herself much. He stepped around behind her, bent, and slid one arm around her waist (again with no exploratory fumbles). Then he lifted her a few inches and neatly slid the pillow underneath her.

"How's that?" he asked briskly.

She looked up at him as he came into sight again. "Better," she said grudgingly. "But the police are not going to believe a ruthless thief took the time and trouble to put a pillow under my ass."

He laughed with genuine amusement. "They will believe it. Trust me. Just tell them you asked for the pillow." The laughter fading, he stood looking down at her for a moment. "And tell them I was here. Don't forget that."

Morgan had the sudden realization that her story was going to sound awfully improbable. She found herself mentally editing Quinn out of the story completely and was so astonished at herself she could only stare up at him bemusedly. "I—I don't—That is, I haven't decided what I'll tell the police."

He was silent for a few beats, then said softly, "Will you lie for me, sweet Morgana?"

"No," she snapped. "For me. In case you haven't realized, any story I tell is going to sound fishy as hell. Running from a group of organized thieves and caught by an internationally famous cat burglar who just happened to be burgling the same museum on the same night? After which, said thief tied me to the leg of a display case and put a pillow under my ass before stealing a lone dagger and making good his escape? Don't forget that Peter and I got in with a key. What's to stop the police from suspecting I was in league with—with you or the other ones?"

"If you know how to play dumb," Quinn said dryly, "the idea will never cross their minds."

"I'll play hysterical," she snarled. "God, the messes I get into. Just because Peter had to show me his etchings. Stop laughing, you monster! Go on—get out of here, why can't you? Fade away into the misty night. Fold up your tent and beat it. Hit the road. The next time I see a black ski mask, I'll kick it in the shin. I hope the next place you burgle has a pack of wild dogs in it. Dobermans. *Big* Dobermans. Big *hungry* Dobermans—who missed their breakfast, lunch, and dinner."

She eyed him resentfully as he leaned somewhat weakly against the display case and continued to laugh at her.

"On the whole," Quinn said unsteadily, "I think I'd prefer the flames of perdition."

"You can count on that. If Interpol doesn't get you, I will."

A last chuckle escaped him as Quinn straightened. "I find myself almost looking forward to that. Good night, sweet—and thank you for enlivening a boring evening."

She held out until he reached a distant, shadowy doorway, then said, "Quinn?"

He hesitated, then turned. She caught the flash of his green eyes.

"You—you will call the police?"

"I give you my word, Morgana," he said steadily. "They'll be here within an hour."

She nodded, and in a moment the shadows were only shadows. It was very quiet and felt curiously desolate. She sat there, bound to the leg of a display case, her stockinged feet growing cold—why hadn't she asked Quinn to find her shoes?—and a thick pillow cushioning against the hard floor.

It occurred to her that she should start weaving a reasonable story for the police. Knit one, purl two. No, that wasn't weaving. Weaving was Penelope picking out the threads of her tapestry by night because she didn't want to marry anyone else even if Ulysses *had* been gone an awfully long time.

What were the odds against running into an infamous cat burglar twice in one lifetime? Remote. Unless, of course, one was the director of a fabulously valuable exhibit. . . .

"Well, officer," she said aloud in the cavernous room, "it happened like this . . ."

By the luminous hands of her watch, the police arrived forty-five minutes later. And Quinn had been right, damn him. They took one look at her and accepted without a blink the notion that a busy thief would take the time to find her a pillow because she'd told him the floor was too hard and cold.

There were benefits to looking like a dumb sex kitten.

Sometimes.

Once in a blue moon.

"I don't like it," Wolfe said, slouching in his chair as he stared broodingly at a police report lying before him. "That makes two museums robbed within two weeks. This new gang is obviously greedy as hell, and I doubt they'll stop now."

"Did you really think they would?" Morgan asked.

"No. No, I didn't."

It was very early, and they were in Morgan's office, since it was the larger of the two.

After a moment, Morgan said, "Neither of those museums has the kind of security being installed here; their systems aren't even as good as the existing system here. They relied on guards and simple door alarms. No lasers or sensors and no backup system in case of electrical failure."

Wolfe shook his head. "That isn't what's bothering me; I'll grant the museums' security was outdated. What I don't like is the *scale*. That gang of thieves came in like an army and stole everything they could carry. According to both your observations and police reports, they were unhurried, methodical, and very businesslike. They didn't leave a fingerprint or a clue, and I can't see they made a single mistake.

"All we have is basic information, and most of that was supplied by you: ten to twelve men, one of them named Ed, who very efficiently stole items no self-respecting fence would touch. That points to a major collector, or cartel of them, being supplied by these thieves. And *that* means nothing stolen is likely to surface again; the police haven't got a hope in hell of finding that stuff."

"The dagger might surface," Morgan murmured.

"What dagger?"

Morgan cleared her throat and met his eyes. "The Kellerman dagger. The thieves—the *group* of thieves—didn't get that. Someone else did."

"Who?" Wolfe asked.

"Quinn."

Wolfe sat up with a jerk, staring at her. "Quinn? He was there last night?"

Nodding briefly, Morgan said, "He was there. I didn't tell the police because...well, because if it hadn't been for him, that gang would have caught me and probably wouldn't have been nice about it."

"I thought they did catch you," Wolfe said slowly.

"No. They knew I was there, and they weren't very happy about it, but they didn't seem too worried either. It was after they'd gone that I was tied up. Quinn did that. I...uh...made a fuss when he decided to steal the dagger, so he tied me to the display case."

"Did you see his face?"

"No, he was wearing a ski mask. He wouldn't tell me what he'd come there to steal originally, he just said that when he discovered he wasn't the only thief in the building—and was outnumbered—he decided to stay out of their way."

Wolfe looked at her steadily for a moment, then said, "You seem to have had quite a conversation with him."

Morgan flushed a little but continued to meet his gaze. "I can't really explain, except that I didn't feel threatened by him. I mean, I wasn't afraid of him at all. He was even sort of charming—and *don't* remind me he's no better than the others. I know that, believe me. It's just that if I'd told the police, it only would have complicated things and, besides, it sounded so improbable. It doesn't make a difference, does it? The only item he took was the dagger, and if he fences that it's bound to surface, so—"

"You know better than that. If the dagger *does* surface, it could well lead the police off on a wild-goose chase. It could indicate to them that all the other items could be fenced as well, so they'd concentrate on the wrong assumption."

"Common thieves versus collectors." Morgan nodded with a sigh. "I know, I know. I obviously wasn't thinking straight."

Wolfe eyed her thoughtfully, then shrugged. "It probably won't make all that much difference in the end. The police have to follow standard procedure in robbery cases, which means they'll keep an eye on known fences. Not really much else they can do without a solid suspect. If the dagger surfaces alone, they'll try to follow that lead as a matter of course—but they won't go off track for long." He paused for an instant, then added, "If you *had* blown the whistle about Quinn being there, it probably wouldn't have made a difference in the way the police work the case. If Quinn's in this country, the police'll know about it soon enough."

"I guess our police would know about him, wouldn't they? But they wouldn't know any more than the information Interpol provides on their watch list."

"Probably not. They'll know his M.O., the alias he uses, the sort of artworks and gems he tends to go after." Wolfe spoke rather absently, his frowning gaze fixed on Morgan's desk.

"Wasn't a journalist in England responsible for that alias? I mean, didn't the journalist start using the name Quinn to describe this particular thief because it meant wise and intelligent, or something like that?"

"If I remember rightly, the journalist claimed he'd received a note from the thief after a big robbery, and it was signed Quinn. The police were never sure it actually came from him, but the name stuck. It was later on that somebody decided he'd chosen the alias because of what it meant."

"Do you think he did?"

"I doubt the note was from him at all. Stupid to claim responsibility for a robbery and give the police a chance to start building a file on him. And I've never heard he was stupid."

"The journalist—or someone else—trying to get more newsprint out of a robbery?"

"Maybe. Probably. In any case, it was the beginning of all the...smoke and mirrors around Quinn and his activities. I always figured the myth got a lot bigger than the man."

Morgan wasn't so sure about that, but wasn't about to say so. Instead, she said, "He is supposed to be good, though. Very, very good at what he does."

"Being active and at large for ten years, he damned well has to be good."

After a slight hesitation, Morgan said, "There haven't been any reported robberies by Quinn in the States until now; I checked. He came here, Wolfe. Straight here, to San Francisco. And he knew I was the director of Max's exhibit. I don't know what he was doing at the other museum last night—but I think we should assume the Bannister collection is his ultimate target."

"Great," Wolfe said a bit grimly. "That's just great."

"It isn't a totally unexpected problem," Morgan pointed out. "We've known all along the exhibit would be a target. And it certainly is a big enough target to tempt even an international thief like Quinn. But it doesn't change anything. You said it yourself; all we can do is make it as difficult as possible for any thief, or group of thieves, to get to the exhibit. And you said Max gave us full authority to do whatever it takes."

"Yeah, but I wish he'd consider canceling. I'm more than a little inclined to call him again and try my hand at persuading him to."

"You know him better than I do," Morgan said. "But from all he's said to me, I don't think it's an option."

"No, probably not."

"Besides, he's on his honeymoon. He'll be back in a couple of weeks, still well before the collection is moved from the vault and long before the exhibit is due to open. Maybe by then we'll have something a little more definite to tell him."

"You *saw* Quinn, Morgan. Talked to him. How more definite could that be?"

"He only told me that's who he was. Maybe he was lying."

"Is that what you think?"

She hesitated, then swore under her breath. "No. I think it was Quinn. But we still don't know for sure that he's after the collection. We can assume, but we don't know for sure. He could decide to take advantage of all the attention being focused on the exhibit to rob somebody else."

"Uh-huh."

"Okay, chances are good he's after the collection."

Wolfe stared at her.

"More than good," she admitted reluctantly.

"I'd say pretty damned certain."

Morgan sighed. "Yeah." She gathered her copies of police reports and various notes and stacked them neatly on her blotter. "Well, I'm getting on the horn to the security company right now. If their bright boys and girls know any tricks we *haven't* planned for security here, I want to know what they are. If we have to, we'll turn this place into Fort Knox."

"I hear that."

Carla Reeves delivered the information he demanded. It didn't take her long, since she had complete access to everything he wanted, and making copies of the schematics was easy. It was also easy to get them out of the office, because she'd developed the sterling reputation of working late and the night guard was accustomed to locking up after her.

She met her blackmailer where and when he'd instructed, and handed over a zip disk.

"These are the most recent diagrams?"

Carla nodded. "Yeah."

"Thank you, Carla."

She eyed him. "So ... we're done now?"

"We're done ... for now."

It was what she'd expected, though it certainly didn't make her happy. "Look, I can't keep nosing around in the system, making copies of stuff for you. There are safeguards built in, firewalls I might not see until it's too late."

"Then if I were you," he said, "I'd be very, very careful."

"Please, I can't—"

"You'd better. And do try not to get caught, Carla. I'm afraid I wouldn't be happy about that. Not happy at all."

Carla Reeves felt a chill and it had nothing at all to do with the cool night air.

Morgan ran into Wolfe just outside the hallway where the office spaces were located, and even though the scowl on his face didn't invite discussion or even greetings, she happily waded in where even angels would have been wary.

"You called Max again, didn't you?"

"Yeah, I called him."

"And he refused to even consider canceling the exhibit."

Wolfe's scowl deepened. "He won't even consider delaying the opening."

"And you're pissed."

Since she was more or less barring his way, Wolfe was forced to reply. "Of course I'm not pissed at Max," he replied.

Morgan lifted an eyebrow.

"All right, so I'm pissed. He's hidebound about keeping his promises, even when it might be better—" Wolfe sighed explosively. "Never mind. It isn't my collection, I just work for the people who insure it."

"Ours not to reason why?"

"Something like that. Anyway, at the moment I'm more ... irritated ... by the computer nerd back there. I think he's in over his head and won't admit it."

"If you keep calling him the computer nerd, I'm not surprised he won't admit anything to you. His name is Jonathan."

"It is?"

Morgan sighed. "Yes, it is. And no matter how young and ... um ... addled he sometimes seems to be, he's an expert."

"Yeah. Supposed to be one of the best Ace Security has, but you can't prove it by me."

"Do you know enough about computers to be sure he's screwing up?"

"I know enough to recognize bravado when I see it. And he's worried too."

"So what're you going to do about it?"

"Not much I can do, for the moment. Max wanted Ace Security, and Lloyd's approved. Ace says this kid is one of their best. Fine. But that doesn't mean I can't demand somebody higher up the food chain than he is come in and check his work."

"You're probably just making him nervous."

"Who, me?"

Morgan grinned at him. "Yeah, you. Mind you, I enjoy the show whenever you're breathing fire and raining brimstone, but I imagine it isn't all that conducive to exacting technical work."

"If he can't take a little heat," Wolfe retorted, "he doesn't belong in the job. Security is not a business for wimps."

"Gotcha. Um . . . Wolfe? You've been in security awhile, right?"

"Ten years, or thereabouts. Why?"

Morgan hugged her clipboard and tried her best to look only mildly curious. "I was just wondering if you'd run into Quinn before now."

Wolfe looked at her steadily, his face peculiarly unexpressive. Then, in a voice that was also rather impassive, he said, "Couple of years ago. I was staying in a private home in London. Got up in the middle of the night looking for something to read, and caught Quinn with his hand in the safe."

"Jesus." That was rather more than Morgan had expected. "What happened?"

With a short laugh, Wolfe said, "Nothing much. He got away. It wasn't what I recall as one of my finer moments."

"Well . . . he's pretty slippery, by all accounts. I mean, you can't blame yourself for not being able to catch him when Interpol hasn't been able to all these years."

"Thanks," Wolfe said dryly.

"Didn't make you feel any better about it, did I?"

"No, but don't worry about it. Morgan . . . if you've got the idea that Quinn is some kind of romantic figure—"

Feeling her face get hot, she instantly said, "No, of course not. I know he's a thief."

"And not a Robin Hood sort of thief," Wolfe reminded her. "He's not robbing the rich to feed the poor."

"I know. I know that. I'm just curious, that's all. Meeting him the way I did . . ."

"I hear he can be pretty charming when he wants to. But think about why he might want to, Morgan. You're the director of the *Mysteries Past* exhibit. The one person who knows just about everything there is to know about it."

"A valuable source of information," she murmured.

"For a thief, the absolute best source. You pointed out yourself that he came straight here, straight to San Francisco. Straight to the future home of Max's collection."

Morgan squared her shoulders and nodded. "Yeah."

"Maybe it's not such a coincidence that you ran into him last night."

That did surprise her. "I don't see how it could have been anything else. He was in the museum long before I got there, he had to be. And no one knew Peter would take me there after hours. *I* didn't even know, until we were in the car."

Wolfe shrugged. "Okay, maybe so. Just keep in mind that there aren't too many coincidences with somebody like Quinn on the scene. From all I hear, he has the knack of manipulating people and events to suit his own purposes."

"I've heard that," she admitted.

"Believe it. He wouldn't have been so successful for so many years if he hadn't learned to turn any situation to his own advantage. And if he's good enough, you'll never know he's pulling the strings. Things aren't always the way they appear to be."

"Does that go for people too?"

Wolfe's smile was wry. "Definitely for people. Most people have their own agenda, you've lived long enough to know that. We both know what Quinn's agenda has to be. All I'm saying is, don't get caught up in the myth of him. At the end of the day, a thief is a thief. Period."

"Yes," Morgan said. "I know."

Several days passed. The slow process of converting an outdated security system continued; Wolfe was in and out, sometimes clearly harassed but usually his rather laconic self, and Morgan dealt briskly with the myriad details of her job.

On Thursday, Wolfe asked Morgan if she would attend a party with him the following evening. It was being hosted by a friend of Max's, a man who was a very influential patron and collector in the art world. The party was a benefit to raise money for a struggling art school in the city, and according to the society pages the elite of San Francisco were expected to attend.

Morgan had done administrative work for another art museum as well as for a foundation based in San Francisco, so she tended to be on the guest list for the benefits and parties connected to the art world, but she had pretty much decided not to go until Wolfe asked her.

If he was interested enough in the party—or the guests—to want to attend, then she wanted to be there as well.

After what he'd said, she was reasonably sure Wolfe was convinced that the gang of thieves led by the charming Ed had behind them at least one art collector, and possibly several of them. So it made sense he'd want to get a good, close-up look at as many collectors as possible, all conveniently gathered together under one roof as if for his inspection.

As for Morgan being his "date," she understood that as well. Not being at all his usual type—long-legged blondes—she wouldn't distract him from business. And if, by chance, he met someone there who did distract him, Morgan would be sure to understand. And take a cab home.

"I even brought the fare with me," she told him cheerfully on Friday evening as he drove them to the party.

"Morgan, I'm not planning on abandoning you."

"Oh, I'm sure you're not. But just in case you decide to later, I thought you should know I'm prepared."

Wolfe shook his head but didn't bother to argue with her. "I want to talk to some of these collectors. It's a purely business evening for me."

"If you say so. Does Leo know you and Max are half brothers?"

"I doubt it." Wolfe shrugged. "Since I wasn't raised here, and Max doesn't really talk about family, I doubt many people know. Not that it's a secret, it just hasn't come up."

"I only know because Max told me why he trusted you more than any other representative of Lloyd's to handle security for the exhibit. He said you'd been raised by your fathers and hadn't gotten to know each other until about fifteen years ago."

"True enough."

"He also said your mother was an amazing woman and that he was terrified of her."

Wolfe grinned faintly. "Also true. She could command armies, our mother. You'd never know it to look at her, but she brings the term 'iron hand in a velvet glove' to a whole new level. And has about five different kinds of charm. I've seen some of the most powerful men in the world following along behind her like besotted idiots."

"Max said your father and his had both remained friendly with her after the divorces."

"Mother never makes enemies, especially husbands."

Morgan had to laugh. "She sounds fascinating. I'd love to meet her one day. Max said she travels?"

"Yeah. Last I heard, she was either in Australia or New Zealand."

"Any chance she might be heading this way?"

"God knows."

Perceptively, Morgan said, "You don't want her here, do you?"

"While Max's collection has the potential to draw every villain in the country to our doorstep? No."

"You know, I hadn't thought about it quite that way."

"I had," Wolfe said, turning his rented sports car into the long driveway of Leo Cassady's Sea Cliff mansion. "I had."

C H A P T E R
FOUR

San Francisco was famous for a number of things, including the Golden Gate Bridge, but since Quinn's interest was professional, what interested him were portable treasures—and the security systems that protected them.

Very good security systems.

It probably wasn't surprising, considering how long the city had housed some very wealthy people, that San Francisco boasted some of the newest and toughest security systems in existence. Leo Cassady, for instance, lived in a mansion whose security system would have shamed most banks.

From his vantage point on the roof of a building nearly half a block away, Quinn watched the cream of San Francisco society arriving. His infrared binoculars gave him a close-up view of everyone, and he caught himself mentally calculating the dollar worth of some of the jewels adorning some of those sleek, well-toned bodies.

The staggering total he arrived at was immensely tempting, but even more so when added to the probable value of what else he knew the mansion contained: Leo Cassady's private collection of artworks and artifacts.

Quinn lowered his binoculars and sighed. A private home stuffed with valuables and playing host to every art collector in the city. Pity one couldn't just throw a net over the whole building.

He laughed under his breath, then tucked the binoculars away in his tool belt and bid a reluctant farewell to all that tempting wealth. For now, at least.

He was on the point of turning away when he stopped suddenly and returned his gaze to the mansion. A low-slung sports car had pulled into the drive and joined others in the circular car park. As Quinn watched, a man and woman got out and joined other guests going into the house.

Quinn didn't reach for his binoculars. He didn't have to. He didn't need his eyes to tell him what his other senses already had.

So Morgan was also a guest. Not that it surprised Quinn; she was very well known among collectors and people connected to museums, aside from knowing Leo Cassady through his friend Max Bannister.

Quinn waited until they vanished into the brightly lit mansion, then turned away. He was frowning a little but didn't hesitate again, leaving his rooftop perch and making his way to the unassuming sedan parked nearby.

He didn't start the car immediately, but instead pulled out his cell phone and made a call.

"Yeah."

"I'm a bit surprised you aren't at the party tonight," Quinn said. "Everyone else is."

"Like you, I have other things to do."

"Any luck getting the technical schematics I asked for?"

"Not so far. I can't just ask for them, remember."

"I don't have to remind you that time is ticking away."

"No, you don't have to remind me. Just as I'm sure I don't have to remind you that this situation is getting more complicated with every day that passes. Security systems are being overhauled right and left, thanks to that gang walking off with everything they can carry. Even if I can get you the schematics, I can't guarantee they'll be up-to-date."

"Let me worry about that."

"You? Worry? Show me that face the next time you're wearing it, will you? Because I've never seen it."

Quinn chuckled. "Oh, I have a few concerns,

believe me. That gang, for one. If their activities aren't stopped, and soon, armed guards are going to be standing elbow to elbow around anything of value in this city."

"And not even you could break through that line."

"Well, let's say I'd rather not have to try." Quinn barely paused. "I'm going to check out a few likely targets and then head back toward the museum. If you get your hands on those schematics, let me know. Sooner is better than later."

"Right."

Quinn ended the call and for a few moments considered his options. Then he shrugged and started the car. If he had learned anything, it was that sometimes the universe had its own plan in mind, and a smart man learned how to go with the flow.

Quinn was a smart man.

Morgan was familiar with the exquisite paintings and other pieces in Leo's impressive collection, but that didn't stop her from wandering through his beautiful house in order to look at them again. She had noted without comment the presence of several unobtrusive plainclothes guards dressed as formally as the guests as they kept an eye on the valuables, and she took it for granted that display cases and paintings were protected by an invisible, but no doubt extensive, security system.

That was a given.

She wound up, finally, back in the big front room where Leo tended to hold court during his parties. He was a very handsome and charming man in his late forties, popular with both men and women alike.

"Where's Wolfe, Morgan?" Leo asked.

"He abandoned me for a blonde," Morgan replied without rancor, and then giggled. "He seems to be irresistibly drawn to them. I suppose I should have reminded him that the one he's dancing with now is a shark with a full set of teeth, but he's a big boy. I decided to let him fend for himself."

Leo smiled at her. "Are you talking about our Nyssa?"

"The very same," she replied promptly. "Not only does she have a habit of snaring my dates without mercy, but she's tried twice tonight to get my promise that she'll be allowed to see *Mysteries Past* even before the private showing to open the exhibit."

Leo lifted a brow. "I should have thought she'd ask Max," he commented.

Morgan grinned. "She's tried everything but blackmail on Max for months and finally admitted defeat. She told me so. So now it's my turn. Lots of sweet smiles and honeyed words." Shaking her head, Morgan added, "She also asked if Max would consider selling any piece of the collection. I thought everyone knew that answer."

"She knows," Leo responded. "She just doesn't give up easily."

"Rabid collectors don't," Morgan agreed with a sigh. "Still, I hope she'll stop wasting her time on me. I have enough to worry about without her pestering me."

"Maybe she'll start pestering Wolfe," Leo said with a grin.

Morgan looked through the wide doorway into the ballroom and chuckled as she watched Wolfe dancing with the tall and stunning blonde. "Maybe she will."

Leo murmured, "And as far as men are concerned, she's also extremely talented in the various arts of . . . persuasion."

"Do you know that firsthand?" Morgan asked with a lurking smile.

In a meditative tone, Leo said, "I turned down an offer of thirty thousand for my Greek chalice." He smiled, said, "Excuse me," and strolled away.

Morgan couldn't help but laugh as she watched her host move away. Nyssa had the Greek chalice, and she had bragged publicly that she'd gotten it for ten thousand. Obviously, she had bartered the rest.

To give the older woman credit, Morgan had to admit that Nyssa was at least honest about her tactics.

Since she was reasonably sure Wolfe could hold

his own with even a rabid collector who also happened to be a gorgeous blonde, Morgan was free to enjoy the party, which she did.

At least until Wolfe got a call on his cell phone.

"We should probably call Max," Morgan said with a sigh as Wolfe's rental car neared her apartment. "He should know how badly Jonathan screwed up."

"How badly *did* he screw up? Do you know? Because I'm not sure."

"Computers aren't my specialty, but from what he told you, I've got the feeling we're talking about a major problem—and a setback of several weeks, potentially. That's assuming he can fix what he messed up without making things worse. Don't you think we should call Max?"

"No reason he has to know until he gets back here," Wolfe pointed out. "There's nothing he could do about it anyway. Nothing any of us can do, for that matter."

"Yeah, but we should tell him."

"Let me see how bad things are first. If there's nothing he could do about it, there's no reason to bother him with it until he comes home."

She eyed him as he pulled the car to a stop at the curb in front of her building. "Okay. Just out of curiosity—are you planning to meet Nyssa later?"

Affably, he said, "Nosy, aren't you?"

"Yes. Are you going to answer the question?"

He sighed. "No, I'm not meeting Nyssa later. As a matter of fact, I'm going back to the museum."

Morgan frowned. "Why?"

"To try to figure out just how badly the computer nerd—excuse me, Jonathan—screwed up. And because your paranoia has infected me." He sounded distinctly irritable about it. "Believe me, I'd much rather spend the night with somebody other than armed security guards, but such is my life at the moment."

"You're going to stay there all night? And do what? Breathe down the guards' necks?"

"I just want to keep an eye on the place." He started to put the car in park, but Morgan stopped him.

"No, you don't have to get out. This building is very safe and has great security. Listen, are you really worried or just humoring me?"

"I could have spent the night with Nyssa. No offense, but humoring you would come in a distant second if those were my choices."

Not at all offended, Morgan said, "Yeah, that's what I thought. You're worried because the technician blew his job? It doesn't affect current security."

"No, but it's an anomaly. I don't like anomalies. I don't trust them. So I'm going to check every door and window in that building personally. And

I'm going to make damned sure all the guards know I'm looking over their shoulders."

"I can—"

"No, you can't. You've spent more time in the museum lately than the exhibits have."

"Very funny."

"Look, Morgan, you've been putting in way too many hours lately. We both know Max won't like it. Besides, there really isn't anything you can do tonight. I promise I won't strangle Jonathan. Hell, I won't even yell at him."

"I'm sure he's gone home by now," she murmured.

Wolfe had to laugh. "Yeah, he probably has. So it'll be me and the guards tonight. You get some rest, and I'll see you in the morning."

Morgan opened the car door. "You can't watch them all the time."

"No, but I can keep a very close eye on them at least until the new security system is up and running."

"Well, I know it won't do much for your social life, but I have to say it makes me feel better that you'll be watching the place."

Moody now, Wolfe said, "Sometimes I hate my job."

Realizing that Nyssa Armstrong must have issued a pretty blunt invitation that Wolfe had refused very reluctantly, Morgan fought to hide a grin. "You're appreciated, believe me. Thanks for the ride—and for letting me wear you on my arm, if only for a little while tonight."

"You're welcome," he said dryly.

Laughing, Morgan got out of the car. She went up the walkway to the apartment building's front door, letting herself in to the well-lit lobby. It was only then that she heard Wolfe pull away from the curb and continue toward the museum just a few blocks away.

She started to take the stairs up to her apartment but hesitated with her hand still on the lobby door. It was the strangest feeling, as though she could—almost—hear someone calling her name. She needed to go back outside. Needed to look for something out there. And she needed to do it now.

Morgan looked down at her sleek gold dress and tiny evening purse, the black jacket that was hardly worthy of the name, and muttered, "This is so stupid."

But she went outside anyway and stood there on the well-lit walkway, looking slowly around. Not much to see, she thought. Couple of big trees casting deep shadows. Other shadows around the shrubbery...

One of the shadows stepped away from the shrubbery.

Morgan felt herself moving toward him even before she made the conscious decision to. He was dressed all in black, just like before, but the black gloves were tucked into the compact tool belt he wore, and the ski mask was rolled up from the bottom so that when she reached him she could see his strong jaw, determined chin—and amused smile.

"What the hell are you doing here?" she demanded, then immediately added, "If you mean to rob this building, you can be sure I'll tell the police *exactly* who did it."

"You cut me to the quick, *chérie*. Would I be so base as to despoil the home of my adored?"

"Very funny," she snapped. "Forget the Don Juan act, because I'm not buying it. As for just how low you'd sink, let me put it this way. I'd hate to have your nerve in a tooth."

White teeth flashed in a brilliant smile as he laughed softly again. "Morgana, you are a delight."

She ignored what sounded suspiciously like a genuine and sincere compliment, because she suddenly realized something. "How did you know I live here?" she demanded.

"Apartment 312," Quinn said lazily. "I followed you home the other day."

Morgan made a strong mental note to pay much more attention to those around her after this. He'd been near—probably unmasked—and she hadn't seen him? "Well, don't do it again," she ordered irritably. "In case you hadn't realized, I don't want to have anything to do with you."

"I'm crushed," he murmured, then added, "You

look stunning tonight, by the way, Morgana. Gold is definitely your color."

She had totally forgotten the rather clingy dress and tried not to feel self-conscious that he had taken notice. "I've been to a party," she said, refusing to thank him for the compliment.

"Yes, I saw the escort leave. *He* didn't want to show you his etchings?"

"He's just a friend," Morgan heard herself say. She scowled at Quinn. "Not that it's any of your business."

"Of course not." He was still obviously amused. "Curiosity brought me here, Morgana. Why didn't you tell the police about my being in the museum the other night?"

Morgan hadn't expected to have to defend that decision to him, and she cast about frantically before coming up with something that would be a sensible answer. "I told you at the time it sounded too damned unlikely to be believed. Besides, what you stole—what I *think* you stole—was nothing compared to what that gang walked out of there with. What does it matter, anyway?"

"As I said—curiosity." In an apologetic tone, he said, "I'm afraid I leaped to a conclusion. Hope springs eternal, you know. However, since you've made your feelings quite plain, I'll retreat to lick my wounds in private."

Morgan found herself hesitating and swore inwardly when she realized it. Keeping her voice dry, she said, "I told you to cut the act. In the first place, you're a thief, which is something I'm not at all in sympathy with. In the second place, I happen to be the director of an exhibit that must be calling to you like a siren song. And in the third place, any woman would need her head examined, by an expert, if she for one single minute believed anything you said."

He was smiling again. "Suppose I were to say it wasn't an act, Morgana. Suppose I denied any interest in *Mysteries Past* and assured you I am to be trusted completely."

"I wouldn't believe you," she said stolidly.

White teeth flashed again as Quinn smiled at her. "Very wise of you, Morgana. Very wise indeed."

Morgan eyed him with more uneasiness than she wanted him to see. "So you are after the Bannister collection."

"I didn't say that, sweet."

"Oh, yeah, like you'd really come right out and tell me the truth about it. Me, the director of the exhibit."

"That wouldn't be at all wise of me, would it?" Quinn said, in a tone of surprised realization. He folded his arms across his chest and made a considering sound. "You're probably right, Morgana. Why don't we pretend the subject never came up?"

"Why don't we pretend it did? Quinn, if you

think I'm going to just stand by and let you get your thieving hands on Max's collection, you're nuts."

"Well, actually, Morgana, you wouldn't be there at the time. Hypothetically speaking, of course."

"I mean—you *know* what I mean." She shook her head. "Why am I even standing here talking to you?"

"My question would be—why did you come *out* to talk to me?"

Morgan stared at him, conscious of a different uneasiness now. "I just . . . I thought I heard something."

"No," Quinn said.

"I did. I thought I heard a noise out here. That's why I came back outside."

"You didn't hear anything, sweet. I was standing here not making a sound."

"I didn't say it was you I heard," she snapped.

Quinn laughed softly. "You aren't going to admit it, are you, Morgana?"

"Admit what?"

"Admit that you feel it when I'm nearby. That you can sense my presence."

"That's ridiculous. I don't—" Morgan stared at him, suddenly remembering her feelings of anxiety at different times in the museum. "Wait a minute. You haven't already found a way into the museum. Have you?"

"Do you really expect me to answer that?" he asked in mild surprise. But before she could respond, he did answer her question, his voice unusually serious. "I've been inside the museum during hours, like any other visitor. As for the night...let's just say I've been keeping an eye on most of the museums in this city."

"Picking your next target?"

"Trying to size up my competition. That gang we both encountered the other night."

"You know who's behind them?"

"No. Not yet."

"And if you find out? What then? You'll tip the police to get them out of your way?"

He chuckled. "That would be the smart thing to do, wouldn't it?"

"Is that what you're planning, Quinn?"

"That," he answered, "depends on who's behind them, sweet."

"Stop calling me that," she said, more or less automatically. "Do you think that gang has targeted the Bannister collection?"

"I think it would be astonishing if they haven't. But it will be weeks yet before you need worry about them, sweet. Or about me, for that matter. The Bannister collection is still safely hidden away in the vaults that have protected it for decades."

"Somehow, that doesn't make me feel better," Morgan said slowly. "I guess it would be...naive of me to expect you to stay away from the collection just because I'm asking you to."

"Can you sense it when I'm near, Morgana?"

She stared up at him, caught by those vivid green eyes, by that half smile that was more beguiling than it had any right to be.

"Can you?" His voice was soft but insistent.

"I...think I can. I don't know how or why, but—but I think I can," she answered finally.

Unexpectedly, Quinn caught one of her hands and lifted it, bending quickly and gracefully so that his lips brushed across her knuckles. Then he released her and stepped back, already blending back into the shadows of the building.

But that white smile flashed again, and he chuckled. "Not naive, sweet. But impractical. Stay away from one of the most priceless collections the world has ever known? What self-respecting thief could do that?"

"Quinn—" But he was gone. She knew it.

She felt it.

Looking down at the hand he had kissed with such elegant charm, Morgan drew a deep breath and then muttered, "Oh, shit."

Carla could have kicked herself for having given in to the blackmailer that first time. Why hadn't she just said no? Why hadn't she said yes and then gone to her employers and confessed all? At that point, she'd only have been fired; the past crime was one she'd already paid for, after all.

She knew why she hadn't done the smart thing. Because she was scared.

By giving in to the blackmailer, however, she had now committed a whole new set of crimes. And once she had started, there really was no going back.

So she was even more scared now. Scared and trapped. One thing growing up on the streets taught you was what a villain really was. And her blackmailer was a villain, a man with so little conscience that he would cut her throat without a second thought.

Carla knew that.

She also knew that it would go on, that he'd demand more and more information from her until he could no longer use her. After that, she probably had the life expectancy of a fruit fly.

She wasn't yet thirty, and Carla Reeves wasn't ready to die.

So she did as she was ordered to do, went to work and did her job and collected information on the security systems designed to protect homes and valuables all across the city, waiting for him to call her to arrange another meeting. She behaved exactly as she should have at work, and all the time, behind her smiling face, her mind was working frantically.

No way to fight him. She didn't know who he

was. In fact, he'd made certain that his face was largely in shadow when they met, so she couldn't even have provided a decent description of his face. Just a man of medium height with a chillingly calm voice—and a lethal gun.

She supposed she could go to the police, even now, but with no proof to offer, she doubted they could or would do anything, including protect her from the blackmailer's wrath.

Could she run? It was possible, but if she tried that Carla knew better than to make any obvious preparations to leave. Which meant she'd be able to take only what she could carry with her. Pretty much just pick up her purse, get in her car, and go. Far away.

She decided that the best time to run would be just after she had given him a disk with information, so that he could expect at least several more days to pass before their next meeting. That made sense, she thought. And just as long as she made damned sure he *expected* another meeting and didn't get the idea he no longer needed her, then it should work.

At least, she hoped so.

He called on Saturday night.

"Carla, add one more security system to the list."

"Which one?" She didn't have to try to make her voice sound shaky, fearful.

"The Museum of Historical Art. Specifically, the

schematics for the security system protecting the upcoming *Mysteries Past* exhibit."

Carla hesitated, her mind working. "That system isn't even on line yet."

"I know that. I also know that the system has been designed, and that the design is on file with Ace. I want it."

She swallowed. "I've told you—museum security systems are harder to get at. There are trapdoors, firewalls, every security precaution possible to protect that information. I don't have the access codes—"

"Then get them."

"Look, I'll try. But only the office supervisor and the manager have those codes, and it's not like they're written down in a Rolodex on somebody's desk."

"I'm not interested in your problems," he said pleasantly. "Just get the design schematics. And do it without getting caught. I wouldn't be pleased if you got yourself caught, Carla. Remember that."

Carla swallowed again, the lump in her throat bigger this time. "All right. I—I understand."

"Good. Now, since I've given you a rather difficult assignment, I'm prepared to offer a bit more time. We'll meet on Tuesday night. Have the disk then."

"But—"

"Don't disappoint me, Carla. Oh—and if you

were thinking of running, I'd advise against it. I will be watching you."

There was a soft click, and then the buzz of the dial tone.

And an overwhelming sense of finality.

CHAPTER
FIVE

Morgan, in Wolfe's office this time, leaned back in his visitor's chair and swore for the third time. "Well, at least now we know how badly Jonathan screwed up."

"Blowing the hard drive," Wolfe agreed, "is definitely what I'd call a screw-up. It might have taken his supervisor a few days to admit the thing was a total loss, but at least he finally did."

"Well, maybe it's a good thing," Morgan said. "As uneasy as we've both felt, maybe starting over with an entirely new security system is the way to go. We are doing that, right?"

"We are. Plus the drive will have to be replaced, and all the basic programming installed again. Which won't be cheap, but Ace *insists* on footing the bill."

"Yeah, Ken Dugan told me he overheard you talking to Ace this morning. Or roaring at them, rather. According to Ken, you used words that were completely original."

"I was upset," the security expert said mildly. "I wanted them to know I was upset."

"Which they undoubtedly do," Morgan murmured. "Along with Ken, all the guards, and the first half dozen museum visitors here this morning."

"Then everybody understands my position," Wolfe retorted.

"I'll say." Morgan grinned, then said, "But the point is—can we stay with Ace?"

Wolfe shrugged. "They're supposed to be the best, in spite of their very red faces at the moment. And their CEO called me about half an hour ago swearing on all he holds dear that there won't be another screw-up. He's even pulling their top computer specialist off a job in Europe to take over for the kid who made a royal mess of things Friday. The replacement should be here by next week."

"And we'll get a brand-new security system?"

"That's the promise. A system designed specifically for us and the exhibit, one that won't be on record anywhere except here in this building. Max and I will have the opportunity to see and approve the entire system and all the schematics before the changeover; only the two of us, you, and the programmer will see the final plans for the exhibit security, and only Ken Dugan will see the security changes for the rest of the building."

"That sounds safe enough."

Wolfe grimaced. "I'm beginning to think nothing's going to be safe enough. But this is the best we can do as long as Max insists on sticking with Ace Security."

"And he does? Even now?"

"Even now."

Morgan frowned, but said, "Still, we have weeks to make sure everything's okay before we bring in the collection. If this new programmer Ace is sending doesn't live up to everybody's expectations, then we can always postpone the exhibit as long as we have to. Or cancel, as a last resort."

"Max won't cancel," Wolfe said definitely.

"Even if you pull your trump card and say Lloyd's won't insure the collection because of inadequate security?"

"I'd have a hard time playing that card as long as Max is using a reputable security company and making every effort to protect the collection."

"But if we keep having these...anomalies? Would you play the card then?"

"Maybe."

"Say you did play it. Would Max cancel?"

"I don't know," Wolfe said. "I honestly don't know. He gave his word the collection would go on display, and he's hidebound about keeping his word. If I were a betting man, I'd bet the collection will go on display sooner or later."

Morgan sighed. "Then that's what we'd better assume."

"Yeah. The *Mysteries Past* exhibit will open. Maybe not on time, but it will open."

Quinn was a thief. Morgan knew that. And stealing was wrong, she knew that too. A part of her even knew he was certainly a dangerous man, entirely capable of ruthlessness and quite probably capable of much worse.

She knew.

But there was something else she knew—and he knew, damn his eyes. Morgan knew there was, somehow, a connection between the two of them. She didn't want to call it affinity, though it probably was, of a certain kind: an affinity of mind and wit, of humor, of swift understanding. Whatever it was, in a single night in a darkened, tense museum, it had very quickly created a bond, and that bond had left behind it an awareness that, try as she would, she couldn't deny existed.

He had made her admit she could sense his presence, and once that admission was out in the open, Morgan found herself trying to do just that. The scary thing was that at least once on Monday morning, she was absolutely positive Quinn was in the museum—and watching her. But it was a very busy morning, and with so many people around, she couldn't pick him out of the crowd.

Not, she thought irritably, that he'd *let* her pick him out of the crowd.

"Morgan, can you—Hey, sorry. Didn't mean to startle you."

She hugged her clipboard and stared up at Wolfe. "It's okay. I was just ... woolgathering."

Eyeing her, he said, "Seemed to me you were looking for somebody."

"No. No, I was just lost in thought. Did you need me for something?"

"Yeah, I need that list you have of all the workmen we have building the display cases."

"Why? They've all been approved by you and Max."

"I know, but I want to run another security check." He shrugged. "Better safe than sorry."

Morgan searched through the thick stack of papers her clipboard held, then produced the list he wanted. "Here you go. I have another copy in my files, so you can keep this one."

"Great, thanks."

She knew she shouldn't ask, shouldn't even bring up the subject, but heard herself saying, "Wolfe ... do you think Quinn really is planning to steal part of the collection?"

"With his nerve, he may well be planning to steal all of it."

"One man couldn't *carry* all of it." She thought about it and felt uneasy. "At least, not without absolutely no guards to worry about and an entire night with the doors wide open. And a big truck."

"Yeah, well, I wouldn't put it past him. We'll just have to wait and see, won't we?"

"I guess so." Morgan watched him head back toward the offices, adding under her breath, "We'll just have to wait and see."

The meeting took place on Monday night and fairly late, as Quinn's meetings tended to do, and if he was something less than his usual cheerful self, the man he was meeting either didn't notice or else simply made no mention of it.

"The new technician arrives next week?" Quinn asked in lieu of a greeting.

"That's the plan."

"All set to design and implement a brand-new security system in the museum."

"Anything less would look suspicious."

"It won't make my job any easier."

"You knew it wouldn't be easy when you signed on. Correct me if I'm wrong, but wasn't that the point?"

"Challenging I bargained for; untenable wasn't part of the deal."

"We have weeks yet to put all the pieces in place. For you, that's an absolute luxury of time."

"Time for too much to go wrong," Quinn said. "There've already been too many surprises."

"Are you saying you want to pull out?"

Quinn shook his head. "I'm saying there have been too many surprises. What good is intelligence if it isn't intelligent?"

"All right. I'll see what I can do about that."

"I'd appreciate it."

"And in the meantime, what do you plan to do?"

"I," Quinn said, "plan to . . . cultivate my own sources."

"Yeah? What's her name?"

The only answer Quinn gave to that was a laugh, and it sounded cheerful. It sounded very cheerful.

By Tuesday night, Carla had once again talked herself out of running. He was watching, he'd said so. She called herself ten kinds of coward, but it didn't help the fear.

So she had obeyed him, and somehow managed to get the information he demanded.

"Well?" He appeared out of the shadows, and suddenly, as usual.

Carla handed over the disk. "This has all the stuff you asked for."

"Including the security system for the museum and the *Mysteries Past* exhibit?"

"Everything I could find."

"You didn't leave any evidence behind, did you, Carla?"

"No. No, I'm sure I didn't. I was careful."

"I hope so."

She drew a breath. "You have everything you asked for. But I thought I should warn you that—that some of the security systems will be updated in the next few weeks. I mean, they always are. To keep the technology current and—and anybody trying to break in off balance. Just so you know."

He laughed softly. "Don't worry, Carla. I'm not quite finished with you yet. As long as you can provide useful information for me, that is."

"I can. I will."

"I know you will, Carla. I know you will."

Morgan sometimes walked to and from work since she lived within four blocks of the museum; it was a relatively safe neighborhood, the street was quiet and well-lit at night, and she liked to think the exercise did her good. Plus, it gave her time and peace to think about things.

Still, she hadn't survived ten years on her own without learning not to take chances: she habitually carried both an earsplitting police whistle (on her key ring) and a purse-sized can of pepper spray.

On this Wednesday night as she walked along briskly, she kept one hand in her purse and the other holding the whistle ready. The precautions were routine; she felt neither nervous nor threatened by her surroundings. Her mind was occupied with speculation about the thieves still at large.

One in particular.

Quite suddenly, she stopped dead in her tracks, all her senses warning her. That uneasy feeling, the building awareness of not being alone, of being watched.

He was here.

The sidewalk leading to her apartment building's front entrance was just a few yards away; on her left was a patch of shadows at the corner of the building where a grouping of several trees provided elegant landscaping.

Morgan turned slowly, searching the shadows. A piece of the darkness moved, stepping toward her but remaining curiously insubstantial. Without thinking about it, she left the sidewalk and crossed the corner of the lawn toward him. As she neared and her eyes adjusted to the dimness, she saw that he was once again wearing a ski mask that was rolled up from the bottom to reveal the lower portion of his face.

"Good evening, Morgana."

He had quite a jaw, she noted. Probably stubborn as hell. And he was smiling.

One more time, Morgan reminded herself of an undoubted, unquestionable truth. The man was a *thief,* for Christ's sake. She really needed to remember that. Reaching him, she said somewhat fiercely, "I have a can of pepper spray in my hand, and I'm not afraid to use it."

Quinn lifted both his hands—ungloved—in a placating gesture and chuckled. "Believe me, Morgana, I have no doubt of that. The last thing I have any intention of doing is to rouse your quite impressive temper." His voice was the one she remembered so vividly—light, insouciant, and somewhat mocking.

"What the hell are you doing here?"

"Just stopped by to say hello, sweet."

"Oh, funny."

"On the contrary, I'm being quite truthful."

"Then I'll go get my ice skates, shall I? Hell must have frozen over."

He laughed.

Not very amused herself, Morgan said, "Just in case you're still planning to rob the exhibit, I thought I'd warn you that we'll have an even better security program than originally planned." Even as the words emerged, she wondered why on earth she was throwing the gauntlet down before him.

Dumb. So dumb. What was wrong with her?

"So I should cross the Bannister collection off my must-have list, is that the idea?"

"If you value that hide of yours—and I hear you do."

"As a matter of fact, sweet, I do."

"Then leave. Get out of San Francisco."

"Now, we both know you don't really want me to do that. Do you, Morgana?"

She should have backed away when he took a step toward her. Or blown her whistle. Or removed the pepper spray from her purse and aimed it at him. However, to her later fury, she did none of those things. What she *did* was to lift her face in the most natural way and melt into his arms as if she belonged there.

She felt his hand at her throat, warm and hard, felt the strength of his arm holding her against him. She saw his eyes gleam down at her with green fire even the darkness couldn't diminish. And then his mouth closed over hers.

It was a peculiarly teasing kiss, without force, yet there was an underlying desire he didn't even try to hide. She was barely conscious of letting go of the pepper spray so she could put her arms around his lean waist, and she only dimly heard the jingle of the keys still dangling from the fingers of her other hand. All she was really aware of was the hard heat of his body against hers and the seduction of that kiss.

She felt ridiculously dazed when he raised his head, and could only stare up at his shadowy, half-masked face in silence. Her heart was pounding and her breathing was unsteady, and she couldn't think at all. He gently removed her arms from his waist and stepped back, releasing her completely. If he was feeling some effect from the embrace, it wasn't at all obvious; when he spoke, his voice sounded, if anything, amused.

"Don't forget me, Morgana."

It sounded like a rather final good-bye, and that impression intensified when he faded back into the shadows. Before she could regain command of her voice or her wits, he was gone.

Just as she had that night in the museum, Morgan felt bereft, as acutely conscious of his absence as she had been of his presence. She wanted to call out his name, and it cost her a severe struggle not to.

Dammit, she didn't even *know* his name! All she knew was the infamous nickname of a conniving thief.

Standing alone in the darkness, Morgan spent a good five minutes cussing herself silently, furious and somewhat chagrined at how easily—how maddeningly easily—he had managed to fascinate her mind and affect her body. It was a typically chilly San Francisco night, but she felt hot, and told herself firmly it was sheer embarrassment. She lifted a hand to tug at the high collar of her sweater, and then froze.

Her favorite piece of jewelry, and the only piece of real value she owned, was a gold pendant she wore suspended on a fine gold chain. The pendant was a heart shape encrusted with numerous small rubies, a piece that could be casual or dressy depending on what she was wearing.

Tonight, it had been casual.

And it was gone.

Morgan let out a sound that couldn't have been heard more than three feet away. Quinn, if he'd been privileged to hear it, would have had no difficulty interpreting it. And the quite lively sense of self-preservation that had kept him alive and at large for ten years would have started warning bells jangling.

If he really hadn't intended to rouse Morgan's considerable temper, he had failed wonderfully.

When Wolfe Nickerson stalked into the museum's computer room in the middle of the following Tuesday afternoon, one look at his face should have warned anyone that he was not in a good mood. Unfortunately, the computer technician who was kneeling half under the main desk couldn't see his face. So his brusque voice and somewhat imperious summons caused her to bump her head—hard—against the underside of the desk.

"Hey—you," he growled, snapping his fingers as he looked around the somewhat cramped room that was filled with various machines, monitors, and control panels.

He heard the thud, and it effectively drew his attention to the desk. Then he saw the top of a rather wild blonde head being rubbed by one small hand, and a pair of fierce green eyes glaring up at him.

In a voice that was every bit as intense as her eyes and held a strong Southern accent, she said, "To summon a cab, you can snap your fingers. To call a forgiving dog, you can snap your fingers. But if you want a printable response from *me,* use my name."

"I don't know your name," he retorted.

She let out a little sigh that sounded aggravated and climbed to her feet, still rubbing her head. Her expression remained somewhat annoyed, though her voice was milder. "That is true, but hardly an excuse. You might at least have said 'Hey, lady,' or 'Excuse me, miss.' "

"I didn't know you were a—woman," Wolfe said. He realized he was being stared at and decided he'd better clarify that statement. "I mean, I wasn't aware that Ace would be sending me a female technician. And I couldn't see you when I came into the room."

"Next time," she said, "knock."

For a little thing, she certainly had an attitude, he thought. He towered over her by nearly a foot, but she was obviously not in the least intimidated. In fact, there was something slightly mocking in her expression. Wolfe wasn't used to being treated with mockery, especially by a woman.

"What *is* your name?" he demanded.

"Storm Tremaine."

He didn't immediately respond to the information, even though he'd asked for it. He wasn't often caught off guard by a person or a situation, but this was one of the rare occasions. When Ace Security had promised to send him their very best computer technician to replace the one who had unintentionally sabotaged the museum's new security system more than a week ago, Wolfe had expected another earnest young man whose language was so technical it hardly resembled English and who probably had no interest in anything except his computers.

What Wolfe had definitely *not* expected was a pint-size blonde somewhere in her twenties with very long and definitely wild hair, big eyes so haughty, fierce, and green any cat would have been proud to claim them, and a small but alive face that wasn't exactly pretty but certainly wouldn't be easily forgotten.

Wolfe had a thing about blondes, but he preferred them tall, sleek, and leggy. This one hardly fit the mold, in more ways than one. In fact, judging by what he'd seen of her temperament, her hair should have been red. He was almost certain it was meant to be red.

He eyed her, not entirely pleased, because she certainly didn't look like his mental image of a crackerjack computer technician. "Your name is Storm?" he asked dryly.

She returned the stare, then put small hands on her hips and looked him up and down slowly and thoroughly—missing nothing along the way—with a total lack of self-consciousness. "Well, as I understand it, yours is Wolfe," she drawled. "So let's not cast stones, huh?"

There was too much justice in that for him to be able to take exception to it, but he was definitely annoyed by her attitude. "Look, in case nobody told you—you work for me."

Without hesitation and in a very matter-of-fact way, she said, "My job is to complete the installation of a computerized security system in this museum. I work for Ace Security first because they are my employers, Max Bannister second because he hired us to do a job, and the San Francisco Museum of Historical Art third because the job is here. Fourth is Morgan West, who is the director of the *Mysteries Past* exhibit. You come in fifth, since being head of security for the exhibit is a narrow area of responsibility. And since Mr. Bannister is away—I believe on his honeymoon—I answer directly to you on any problems concerning security." She smiled. "And I don't need any of you hovering over me. In case nobody told *you*—I'm very good at what I do."

"That remains to be seen," Wolfe said. He felt very irritated at her. And couldn't take his eyes off her vividly expressive face. It was a disconcerting combination of reactions.

She nodded slightly, clearly accepting his challenge. "Fair enough. I'll be quite happy to prove myself. I'll work, and work hard—but, as I said, not with you standing there glowering at me. To coin a phrase, this room's too small for the both of us. Was there a reason you came in here?"

"Yes, there was a reason." He knew he sounded as annoyed as he felt. "I wanted to know how long the door alarms will be deactivated; I need the guards stationed in the corridors, not on the doors, while the museum's open."

Storm sat down in the swivel chair behind the desk, leaned back, and propped her feet up on the desk. She was wearing very small, very scuffed Western boots with high heels.

She *was* little, Wolfe realized, noting that the heels had given her at least three inches of height.

"The door alarms are back on line," she said. "I had to take them off line for half an hour because somebody had screwed up and mismatched four different cables, which was threatening to blow the whole system."

"It wasn't me," he heard himself say, aware of a peculiar urge to defend himself because of the way she was looking at him. At the same time, he was relieved to know that she'd had a good reason for being underneath the desk. That had bothered him on some vague level of his mind.

Storm laced her fingers together across her middle, still looking at him. After a moment she said mildly, "Well, it hardly matters since I fixed it. Anyway, the door alarms will remain on line until the changeover to the new system."

"Which will be . . . ?"

"I had to start all over with a new hard drive, if you'll recall, so all the data has to be reentered, from the operating system on up. Then the new security program has to be written, installed, and integrated. It'll take some time. A week. Ten days at the most."

Wolfe felt his eyebrows climbing. If she could get the new security system on line in ten days or less, they would actually end up ahead of their original schedule. Skeptical by nature, he said, "Aren't you being optimistic about that?"

"No."

Totally against his will, he felt a flicker of amusement. She might be little, but there was certainly nothing small about Storm Tremaine's self-confidence. It was a trait he tended to respect. "Then don't you think you'd better get started?" he suggested dryly.

She nodded toward the main computer terminal atop the desk to the right of her boots. The screen was dark, but the drive system was humming quietly. "I have started. Until the operating system finishes loading, that thing's nothing more than a very stupid, very expensive piece of junk waiting for somebody to tell it what to do. The OS is loading now."

Wolfe wasn't exactly computer-illiterate but, like most people, he just automatically assumed the machine wasn't on if the screen was dark. Before he could either admit his ignorance or come up with a face-saving response, she tossed the subject into the limbo of unimportant things.

"How fast can you run?"

He blinked. "What?"

"Run. The mile, for instance. How fast can you run the mile?"

"About average, I suppose."

She smiled. It suddenly made him *extremely* nervous. "That's good," she said.

Warily, he asked, "Why is that good?"

"I was state champ in college."

Morgan had told herself at least a hundred times that there was nothing she could do to get her necklace back. Max had told her via phone, with his usual courtesy but with emphasis, that there were enough people after Quinn's hide without her involvement.

Well, she knew that.

But. She wanted her necklace back. She had swallowed her pride and explained to Wolfe—with as few details as possible—how Quinn had stolen it from her. Rather surprisingly, Wolfe hadn't given her a hard time about it; he had simply asked Max's police inspector friend Keane Tyler to keep an eye out for the necklace. Without going into much detail as to how the necklace came to be "lost." But if Quinn had sold the thing (the only reason Morgan could think of for him to have taken it—other than sheer devilry, which was admittedly just as likely), it had yet to surface at any fence or pawnshop.

She wanted it back.

That was why, she told herself. That was why she was sticking her nose in where it really didn't belong despite Max's warning and her own common sense. Because she wanted her necklace back. *Not* because she had any desire at all to meet up with that devious thief again.

He was still in the city, she knew that. Still too close by for comfort. At least twice in the last few days, she was absolutely positive he had been in the museum, lost among the crowd of visitors, and close enough to touch.

What she didn't know was whether he'd been casing the joint—keeping an eye on the progress of preparations for the *Mysteries Past* exhibit—or had been hanging around playing invisible merely to annoy her.

He was capable of either motive. Dammit.

She had no idea what his face looked like, and though she caught herself studying several tall strangers with an intentness that had resulted in two indecent propositions and three requests for a date, she was reasonably sure she hadn't actually seen him.

Reasonably sure.

But ever since her last encounter with him, she'd been looking for him. And not just in the museum here. She averaged spending at least a couple of hours every night in her car, parked outside some other museum or jewelry store—any likely target—waiting to see if he would show up. Trying to sense him.

It was dumb and reckless and she knew it . . . but she couldn't help herself.

By Tuesday she was short on sleep and not in the best of moods, so when Keane Tyler called her to report no luck in turning up the necklace Quinn had stolen from her, she vented her feelings in what was a fairly minor explosion.

Keane listened in silence, then said sympathetically, "Well, if it makes you feel any better, Morgan, from all I've heard, Quinn can be a real devil. Not evil the way some thieves genuinely are, but more than sharp enough to cut himself."

Morgan frowned. "What do you mean?"

"I mean he's smart, off-the-chart smart. Wouldn't surprise me to find out the guy was literally a genius. And men like that need challenges, need to push themselves harder than most of us ever will. They find what they need in their work, usually. His work happens to be thievery. So it's not really surprising that he's too good to leave any kind of a trail we might use to find him."

"You almost sound like you admire him."

"I almost do." Keane laughed under his breath. "Look, I deal with the scum of the earth most days. Killers, drug pushers, pedophiles. And, yeah, thieves who don't think twice about killing in the course of a robbery. But a thief like Quinn? He's way down on my priority list of bad guys. He never uses weapons, has never hurt anyone in the course of a robbery—hell, he's never even broken a window as far as I know."

Morgan thought of Quinn's own words on that subject, but all she said was, "Steals from the rich and gives to the poor?"

With another laugh, Keane said, "No, he hasn't gone that far—or if he has, the giving part was anonymous. But he doesn't steal from the poor, doesn't take food out of the mouths of babes, and I count that as at least a point or two in his favor."

Morgan hesitated, then said, "Keane, could you do *me* a favor? Could you find out all the information on Quinn that's available to law-enforcement officials?"

"I figured you'd have researched him by now. I mean, since he's a threat to Max's exhibit."

"I did research him. I read a lot of newspaper

articles written by a whole bunch of journalists gleeful that the rich were getting it in the neck. None of them offered me anything in the way of hard information about Quinn."

"There isn't much, even for us," Keane pointed out.

"Yeah, but can you get me what you have? Maybe there's something that'll help me figure out a way to defend the exhibit against him."

"Maybe—if that new computer technician from Ace knows a trick or two the rest of the world doesn't know."

"Maybe she does. Anyway, I have to give her all the information I can. Will you do me the favor, Keane?"

"Sure. I'll dig up everything I can and get back to you ASAP."

"Thanks." Morgan cradled the receiver, then sat there staring across her office at nothing.

And seeing green eyes filled with devilry.

CHAPTER
SIX

Wolfe wasn't vain enough to instantly assume that Storm had in mind a sexual pursuit—but he couldn't think of any other reason why she'd be comparing their running abilities.

"Are we going to be running somewhere?" he asked.

"That," she said, "depends on you."

"Storm—you don't mind if I call you Storm, do you?" His voice was very polite.

Hers was equally so. "Certainly not. After all, we're both a force of nature—Wolfe."

He crossed his arms over his chest and gazed down at her with what he hoped was an unreadable expression. His curiosity had gotten him into trouble in the past, but he was sure he could handle this diminutive blonde. Without commenting on the comparison of their names, he said, "Storm, are you implying that you'd like to mix business with pleasure?"

"Oh, no, I'd much rather keep the two separate. My business hours—like the museum's—are nine to six. During those hours I fully intend to work. But that leaves a lot of time—and I understand San Francisco has a wonderful nightlife. I don't need much sleep. How about you?"

As he gazed at her vivid face and bright eyes, Wolfe had the sudden wary feeling that there was an underlying guile in her voice or manner that he was missing, and that his instincts were trying to warn him to look beneath the surface. But what she was saying kept getting in the way.

"Somehow, I don't think we'd suit each other," he said finally.

"Why?" she drawled. "Because I'm not five-foot-nine and sleek? You should widen your horizons. To say nothing of your standards."

In a voice that had more than once been termed dangerous, Wolfe said, "I'm going to strangle Morgan."

"Oh, don't blame her—she wasn't the first person who told me about your obsession with Barbie dolls. That's the worst-kept secret in the city—especially since you change them about as often as you change your socks."

He realized his teeth were gritted only because his jaw began to ache. He didn't like feeling on the defensive; it was an unusual and very un-comfortable sensation. Consciously relaxing taut muscles, he said, "Well, we all have our prefer-ences, don't we?"

"That's put me in my place," she said, not no-ticeably discouraged about it. "Most women would view that as a rejection. I'm not most women. And I really do think you owe it to yourself to at least give me a try."

"Why?" he demanded bluntly. He could have sworn there was a fleeting gleam of laughter in her cat's eyes, but her slightly drawling voice remained almost insultingly dispassionate.

"Because a steady diet of *anything* is going to taste awfully bland eventually. If it must be blondes, the least you can do is broaden the range a bit to include those of us who aren't tall even on a stepladder and who don't have blue eyes—which are very common, by the way. Why not put a little spice in your life? I can guarantee you won't be bored."

Before he could stop himself, Wolfe retorted, "That's not what I'm worried about."

A little laugh escaped her. "Afraid I'd cling and be demanding? Happily ever after and a white picket fence? Well, I don't cling, and I tend to ask rather than demand, but as for the rest, I wouldn't rule it out. In fact, small-town Southern girls have that goal drummed into them practically from birth. But I could hardly drag you to the altar bound and gagged, now, could I? And since you're captain of your fate and master of your soul—to say nothing of being considerably larger than me—I imagine it wouldn't do me much good to catch you. Unless you wanted to be caught, that is."

Wolfe had another uneasy feeling, this time that his mouth was open. He was thirty-six, which meant that his interest in females—and vice versa—went back more than twenty years. If he'd wanted, he could have told some colorful stories; he was a scarred veteran of the sexual wars. But this was a first for him.

Was she simply a very honest woman? A woman who was attracted to a man she'd just met and said so without hesitation or any attempt to play games? Somehow, he wasn't quite prepared to buy that. He wasn't that vain—or that gullible. And he was a skeptical man.

So . . . what was she up to?

He frowned down at her, trying to listen to his instincts. "I'm getting a little confused. Are you after a date, a lover, or a husband?"

"Well, that depends on your stamina, doesn't it? At least I assume that's your problem. Judging by what I know of your track record, there must be *some* reason why you haven't been able to go the distance—any distance at all, in fact—with any of your previous blondes."

Whatever Wolfe's instincts were trying to tell him was drowned in the roar of his temper. Biting every word off, he said, "Did it ever occur to you that the *problem* might simply be a lack of continuing interest on both sides?"

Storm pursed her lips thoughtfully. "I suppose it might have occurred to me, but I figure that any man who dates only carbon copies of one type of woman must be sure that he knows what he wants and certainly should know what makes him happy. Assuming that, you must be satisfied with brief, surface relationships—or else you'd make an effort to try something different. Ergo, if there is a problem...it's yours."

Wolfe didn't really follow the logic of her argument, mostly because her drawling voice and dispassionate tone—not to mention her words—were feeding his temper steadily. If she'd set out to make him so mad he would act purely on impulse, she couldn't have done a better job.

Almost growling the question, he asked, "Did you drive here this morning?"

"No, I took a cab."

"Then meet me out front at six."

"You're on," she said promptly.

Wolfe turned on his heel and stalked from the room.

After a few moments, Storm took her boots off the desk and got up. She went to the door and closed it quietly. She leaned against it, gazing at nothing in particular, until a beep from the computer terminal drew her back to the desk. Returning to her chair, she removed a CD from the computer's CD-ROM drive tray and replaced it with another she took from a disk file beside the keyboard. She typed a short command, and the computer began humming softly once again.

Her actions were the automatic and unthinking ones of an expert in her field, and during most of the process she gazed absently toward the door. Finally, however, she leaned back in her chair and peered under the desk.

"Why didn't you come out and provide a little distraction?" she asked in a chiding tone. "It might have saved me from the consequences of my own insanity."

"Yaaah," her companion answered in a voice so soft it was hardly a murmur, then he came out from under the desk to jump on top of it.

The cat was an almost eerie feline replica of Storm. It was very small and appeared delicate; its thick and rather wavy fur was the exact same shade of pale gold as her hair; and its eyes were a vibrant green. Even the small face held the same vivid *aliveness* that was in Storm's expression.

A very superstitious, slightly drunk man had once fleetingly believed that Storm had actually turned herself into a cat. And a good thing too; his brief moment of alcohol-induced terror had given her the opportunity she'd needed to escape.

A close call, that.

Shrugging off the memory, Storm eyed her cat reprovingly. "Don't tell me he scared you."

The cat began to wash a blond forepaw with studied disinterest.

"Yeah, right," Storm said. "Bear, you're almost as good a liar as I am." She frowned slightly. "He's a wolf, you're a bear, and I'm a storm. If any more feral names pop up, I'm going home. It wouldn't exactly be a good omen."

"Yaaah," Bear replied, sounding, as always, the way he looked—like a very small and very meek kitten rather than a full-grown cat who had turned five on his last birthday.

"You're just saying that because you love to watch me walking a high wire without a net."

The cat lifted his chin and half closed his eyes in an expression any cat lover would have recognized. Utter contentment.

"Some pal you are," Storm told him dryly. "It'd serve you right if we find out he's allergic. Then where will you be?" She listened to her cat purr a response and sighed.

If the universe wanted to be kind to her, Wolfe would indeed have an allergy to cats—which would effectively keep him away from Storm.

The problem was, she didn't have much faith in the kindness of the universe. Not this time.

The universe tended not to be kind to liars.

* * *

Carla's nerve broke when she heard through the office grapevine that Jonathan had fucked up his job installing the new security system at the Museum of Historical Art, and that some hotshot programmer was being pulled off a job in Europe and rushed over to patch up Ace's black eye.

And install a totally new security system to protect the building and the upcoming *Mysteries Past* exhibit.

A security system that would not be on file anywhere at the Ace offices.

Carla didn't have to know anything about art or antiquities to know that the Bannister collection was the dream target of every thief that breathed. Including the one who was blackmailing her. And even though he had demanded the design plans of several other security systems, she didn't doubt that getting his hands on the Bannister collection was his ultimate goal. She didn't think he was going to be happy when he discovered that the schematics she'd gotten for him were worthless, and that she couldn't possibly get the plans for the newly designed system.

Carla really didn't want to wait around and find out just how unhappy he would be.

She went to work on that Tuesday as usual, her nerve gone but desperately trying to appear the same as usual even as her mind worked frantically.

Run? Or find something, anything, to placate the blackmailer?

She came within a whisper of going to her supervisor and confessing everything, but the memory of prison stopped her. After all, she couldn't prove she'd been blackmailed, and at least one of the security systems whose diagrams she had copied for him had been breached. Hundreds of thousands of dollars worth of gems had been stolen.

She'd take the fall for that, she knew. An accessory charge or something.

That realization was all it took. Carla was not going back to prison, not if she could do anything to stop it. Running was the only answer. She'd go, just start driving when she left work, and she'd start all over again somewhere else.

She could do that. She could.

It was an hour or so from quitting time when Carla made her decision. After that, she watched the clock and counted down the minutes until she could leave.

Storm was a bit late in leaving the museum, mostly because she had wanted to finish loading the operating system so she'd be ready for the other programs first thing next morning. As a result, she locked the door of the computer room at half past six and found one of the security guards waiting for her at the front door.

"The boss said to wait and let you out," the man said.

She paused to regard him thoughtfully. "Which boss?"

"Ma'am?"

"I'm trying to figure out who runs things around here. So, which boss told you to wait for me?"

"Oh. Well—Mr. Nickerson. He's in charge of security."

Storm found the response interesting. Technically, Wolfe was not, in fact, in charge of security for the *museum*—only for the *Mysteries Past* exhibit. Which wasn't even in place yet. However, it was natural he would be concerned with the museum's security, since the building would house the exhibit. What Storm found interesting was the fact that the guards—and not just this man, because she'd asked a couple of others as well—really did consider Wolfe's word law. Which meant that in an emergency it would be Wolfe the guards would look to, no matter who else was present.

Thoughtful, she nodded to the guard and passed through the door when he opened it for her. She paused just outside at the top of the wide steps, looking down toward the curb.

He was waiting for her, leaning against the hood of a late-model sports car that was, she knew, a rental.

As she started down the steps toward him, she thought about the fact that both he and she were visitors to this city, both living transient lives here. Wolfe had a sublet apartment, she knew; he was set to be here for months while the Bannister collection of artworks and gems was being exhibited at the museum. She, on the other hand, was scheduled to be in San Francisco only a matter of a few weeks, just long enough to get the security system on line and functioning properly; her temporary home here was a small suite in a nearby hotel.

Storm hadn't been granted a lot of time to check out the situation here before she arrived—which was her habit—because she'd gotten her orders on fairly short notice. But she was a resourceful woman, and she'd managed to find out quite a lot, certainly more than Wolfe realized; she'd been most interested in checking him out, since he was head of security. She had found out that the two of them had some things in common—and a number of differences.

Wolfe was based in New York and London; the only place she'd lived for more than a few weeks at a time during the past ten years was Paris, so if she had a base that was probably it. They were both accustomed to living out of a suitcase.

Wolfe had a thing about blondes. That was true enough, and she'd goaded him about it—but she hadn't mentioned one very important point about his seeming fixation. All the blondes he'd dated—for want of a better word—since arriving in San Francisco were in some way involved with foundations, trusts, charities, art societies, museums, or private collections of artworks, gems, and other valuables.

Smart man, she had realized with an inner salute of respect when that pattern became apparent to her. *He* was mixing business and pleasure quite effectively, enjoying the company of his blondes while he picked their brains. In the past months he'd been in and out of San Francisco and, particularly in recent weeks when he'd been living here, he had undoubtedly gathered an impressive amount of intelligence about the close-knit art world in this city—to say nothing of having fun while he did it.

Storm respected that, and she didn't consider it a cold-blooded thing for him to do. She had once or twice dated a man purely because he could tell her something she wanted to know, so why shouldn't Wolfe? (Even if he did take the matter to extremes.) He was a very attractive man—and obviously one with a strong sex drive—who simply looked for his women where their knowledge could help him do his job most effectively.

In fact, she didn't doubt that by now Wolfe had reminded himself of her computer expertise and had come to the conclusion that he might gain some useful knowledge from her even if the first date ended up being the only one.

That also didn't bother Storm; he wasn't likely to waste his charm on her, considering the friction between them, so she wasn't worried about telling him anything she didn't want him to know. Even assuming there was more than this first date, of course, which there probably wouldn't be.

Shouldn't be.

This was not a good time for her to lose her head. And Wolfe, she was certain, was not the kind of man a woman should ever, *ever* lose her head over.

"Nice car," she said when she reached the curb. "But how come men drive either trucks or sports cars?"

"Max drives a Mercedes," Wolfe said, because it was the first thing that popped into his mind.

"Mercedes don't count; they are not cars but works of art. And, anyway, I was asking you personally. So why are you driving something that looks like it belongs in a cage?"

Wolfe had spent quite a bit of time reasoning with himself during the past couple of hours, coming to the conclusion that Storm Tremaine was not only not his type, she was also virtually guaranteed to make his life far more difficult than it needed to be. He had, therefore, very calmly and rationally decided that he was not going to let her get to him during this, their first and last date.

But when he heard that drawling voice laced with mockery and looked into that small, vivid face, he could feel the irritated fascination creeping over him again. He didn't like the feeling one bit— but he couldn't seem to control it.

He also didn't have a good answer for her question. So, in the time-honored tradition, he replied with one of his own. "What do you drive?"

"Something practical," she answered promptly. "While I'm here, I'll probably rent a Jeep."

He eyed her. "So you're a practical woman?" He expected her to bristle a bit or at least instantly deny the horrible accusation; in his experience, no woman wanted to be termed practical. But Storm—and not for the first time—didn't react as expected.

"Oh, it's far worse than that," she said in a solemn voice. "I'm a logical woman."

Wolfe had the notion that he was being warned. "So I should act accordingly?"

Storm shrugged slightly. "That's up to you. Just don't expect *me* to act like one of your Barbie dolls."

"Will you stop calling them that?"

"Are you offended on their behalf—or yours?"

The drawled question brought him up short, because he realized that he *was* offended on his own behalf. That was a sobering realization, so he was naturally annoyed at Storm for having made him face it. "Look," he began, but then broke off abruptly when he noticed something odd.

There was a creature on her shoulder. He wasn't sure what it was, but it had green eyes. That was literally all he could see, since her hair was so thick and whatever was there blended right in.

"What is that?" he asked cautiously.

She didn't need the question clarified. With a practiced gesture, she reached up and flipped her long hair behind that shoulder, revealing a very small blond cat.

"I hope you're not allergic," she said. "Bear goes everywhere with me—except into restaurants, of course."

"Bear?"

"Yes, Bear. He's my familiar."

Wolfe had an odd feeling that she wasn't kidding. And since the little cat looked eerily like her, even to the striking vividness of its green eyes, the idea that there could be something supernatural between the woman and her cat didn't seem as far-fetched as it should have.

"I see," he murmured.

"I doubt it."

He straightened away from the car and stared down at her, instinctively attempting a very old intimidation ploy by making his greater size obvious—and consciously aware that it wasn't working on Storm. Though her chin rose slightly when he loomed over her, she didn't step back and looked, if anything, amused rather than dismayed.

Wolfe nearly snapped the words. "Are you this confrontational with everybody, or is it just me?"

"Lots of people—but not everyone. It must be your lucky day." She smiled. "I forgot to mention: I was also captain of the debate team in college."

Wonderful, Wolfe thought with a reluctant flicker of humor. As a track star she could chase him down, and once she caught him he was never going to win an argument with her.

"This just gets better by the minute," he told her ironically.

"Oh, be brave," she said. "Surely you're not worried about one measly date. Is that why you ordered me to meet you out here, by the way? I mean, are we going somewhere? And, if so, could we get started? In case you hadn't noticed, it's a little chilly out here."

"I know I'm going to regret this." Wolfe opened the car door and gestured for her to get in.

In an interested tone, she asked, "Are you a gentleman born, or is it something you have to work at?"

"Get in the car," he said.

She grinned at him and got in.

By the time Wolfe closed her door with exquisite care and went around to his side, he'd counted to ten at least three times. "Where would you like to go?"

"Well, it was your invitation—at least it was sort of an invitation," she said. "So it's up to you. Since neither one of us is really dressed for it, we'd better rule out someplace fancy. Not that I mind being seen in jeans, but you have your reputation to consider."

If it hadn't been too late to get a reservation for

"someplace fancy," Wolfe would have taken her to the best place in town *and* suffered the indignity of being given a tie by the maître d' just so he could have watched her regret her blithe words. She would have, surely. Even the most self-confident of women would have felt underdressed in jeans and a sweater.

He knew he was letting her get to him, he *knew* it. But he couldn't seem to help himself. Her light mockery grated on his nerves, and something else about her—he wasn't sure what—was affecting his senses in the most peculiar way.

He couldn't decide if he wanted to strangle her or find out if her curiously erotic lips were as soft to the touch as they looked.

"I'm not hard to please," she was saying soulfully in that voice that was driving him crazy. "A crust of bread and a little water—"

Wolfe said something under his breath.

"Such language," she murmured.

He realized he hadn't even started the car. That he was sitting there, staring through the windshield and seeing absolutely nothing. That he was very tense and didn't dare to look at her, because he didn't know which impulse he'd obey if he did—choke her or kiss her. That he wanted a cigarette, and he'd never smoked in his life.

"For Christ's sake," he said, to himself but out loud.

She laughed suddenly. "Look, why don't we

make this easier? Since I'm staying in a hotel, we can go to my suite and order room service. That way, as soon as you get fed up with me, you can walk out, and I'll already be home."

"I never walk out on dates."

"Really?" She sounded very polite. "Then maybe you are a gentleman born. I'll have to reserve judgment on that, though, because they *are* rare beasts."

Wolfe could feel himself tensing even more, despite every effort to relax taut muscles. Why couldn't he respond to her sarcasm with some of his own? Or, at the very least, shrug off the mockery without letting it affect him?

After a considerate pause to see if he had any response to make, Storm said, "If you're not crazy about being seen with me in a hotel—and who could blame you for that?—then we could always go to your place. Just stop someplace for hamburgers or a pizza—already cooked, of course."

"What—you mean you wouldn't cook for me?" he demanded sardonically, risking a glance at her. He looked so quickly that all he really saw was the flash of bright eyes and small white teeth as she grinned at him.

"Now, Wolfe," she said in a patient tone, "you *know* you don't want me to do that. Think of the precedent you'd be setting. It's a very dangerous one, you know. A man's taking his first steps down the road to domestication when he lets a woman cook for him. And a woman's got more than fun in mind when she goes to all that trouble."

He knew what she was saying. And, truth to tell, he'd always looked at it that way, whether it was true or not; he had made sure none of his women had ever cooked for him. But his curiosity, which had more than once led him into trouble, got the better of him. "Can you cook?" he asked her.

"Of course I can." She leaned toward him just a little and added in a conspiratorial tone, "In fact, I can actually cook with a real stove—no microwave required."

"Is there anything you can't do?"

"Along the lines of womanly little talents, you mean? Right offhand, I can't think of anything. I was raised by a very old-fashioned mama who truly believed there was such a thing as woman's work."

Starting the car at last, Wolfe said dryly, "So what happened to you?"

Unoffended, she laughed. "My daddy was a different sort—for which I am most grateful. What with him saying I had a good mind and had to study hard, and Mama teaching me how to make biscuits from scratch, I ended up with a goodly number of diverse talents."

He kept asking questions, prompting her to talk about her background, and her lazy answers led him to more questions. By the time he turned the car into the parking lot of a good (just not fancy)

Italian restaurant half an hour or so later, he had more or less forgotten the friction between them.

"*How* many brothers?" he demanded as he parked the car.

"Six." She chuckled. "So I guess it's no wonder Mama sort of went overboard when she finally got a girl."

"Then they're all older than you?"

"Yeah. Bigger too. I mean, really bigger; they all took after Daddy, and I took after Mama."

"Do they all live in Louisiana?" he asked, since she'd told him that was where she grew up.

"No, we're pretty scattered. Three of my brothers are career military and the other three like to travel, so we're lucky if we can all be home for Christmas." She glanced around, realizing that they'd stopped. "Oh, are we here?"

"Hope you like Italian," he said.

"Very much."

Wolfe had parked the car and automatically got out to go around and open her door. She got out, this time without a comment on his manners, and turned to set Bear in the passenger seat. The little cat looked up at them rather dolefully but didn't attempt to escape the car.

"I hope you're going to lock it up," Storm said to Wolfe as she made way for him to shut the door. "Bear wouldn't appreciate it if he got stolen."

"Any thief is more likely to be after my car than your cat," Wolfe retorted, "so he shouldn't take it personally." But he used the little electronic gadget on his key ring to lock the car. "Will he be all right in there?"

"He'll be fine. Cats are pretty solitary creatures, really, and Bear never minds being alone. Of course, I'd never shut him up in a car if it was too hot or cold, or for more than an hour or so at a time."

Wolfe hesitated, then said, "And what if he has to..."

"He went before we left the museum." Storm smiled up at him. "Since he spends his days with me, I always make provisions for his needs. Don't worry—he won't have an accident."

It struck Wolfe that talking to a woman about her cat's personal habits was not exactly what he was accustomed to, but her smile—surprisingly sweet and warm when it wasn't mocking—made the matter seem unimportant.

And *that* was a fine way to be thinking, he criticized himself as they went into the restaurant.

CHAPTER
SEVEN

If he'd been asked, Quinn would have had a ready answer to explain just why he was spending his evenings watching more than acting, observing the comings and goings of other thieves bent on looting both private homes and other museums.

Sizing up the competition.

"Hell of a lot of thieves around here," he muttered, watching through night binoculars as a skilled pair of burglars gained access to a jewelry store across the street from his rooftop vantage point.

Not quite skilled enough, the burglars set off alarms that began shrieking in the night, and Quinn smiled as he tucked the binoculars into his tool belt and retreated from the edge of the roof.

Like any good thief, he had very quickly become

familiar with the city in which he planned to spend most of his time during the coming weeks. So familiar, in fact, that he moved through the often fog-enshrouded landscape with utter confidence even at night. Within minutes he was some distance away from jangling alarms and the approaching police sirens.

He made his way back across the city, pausing several times to study various buildings he had marked as likely targets. But nothing much was happening on this night, and he reached yet another rooftop vantage point half a block from the Museum of Historical Art hardly more than an hour later.

Morgan's car was parked out front.

Quinn sighed and settled in to watch. He wondered, idly, if Morgan had any idea that their meeting in a dark museum a few weeks previously had not been the first time they had crossed paths. No, probably not; being Morgan, she would have said something if she had known.

The cell phone at his belt vibrated a summons, and he hooked an earpiece receiver and microphone in place before answering with a low, "Yeah?"

"Where are you?"

"Near the museum." He didn't have to explain which one.

"Anything?"

"Couple of overly ambitious burglars got burned

in a jewelry store across town. That's about it. Lot of legit traffic out tonight, so I doubt anything less legit is on the agenda."

"Yours or theirs?"

Quinn chuckled. "Both."

"You do realize the new security system will be up and running within a couple of weeks."

"I do realize that, yes."

"So maybe agendas are changing. Or should be."

"Maybe."

"It's a trap. It has to be."

"The thought had crossed my mind."

"And?"

"And...that just makes it more interesting. More of a challenge."

There was a moment of silence, and then a laugh. "I'll say this for you. You don't lack confidence."

"It's no game for the timid."

"No game for the reckless either."

"Reckless? Me? Perish the thought."

"So what's your next step?"

Quinn trained his night binoculars on the front door of the museum and watched as Morgan came out. She paused on the top of the steps and glanced around, a slight frown drawing her brows together. Then she shrugged and continued down the steps and toward her car.

Smiling, Quinn murmured, "How much do you know about catalysts?"

* * *

"You're frowning," Storm said as she slipped into her chair on the other side of the table.

He looked at her, one brow lifting. "You're imagining things," he told her.

"I'm a logical woman, remember? I don't *imagine* things that aren't there." Before he could respond to that, she was going on in the same lazy voice. "I ran into one of your Barbie dolls in the ladies' room."

"What?" It was the last thing he'd expected, and it effectively took his mind off whether she was being honest with him.

Still smiling, she turned her head a bit and nodded across the room. "That one, at the cozy little table by the window. She was very friendly. She told me—without any prompting from me, you understand—that you liked your scotch with ice and your women wearing nothing at all."

Wolfe turned his head cautiously and immediately spotted Nyssa Armstrong. She was with a bored-looking dark man who didn't appear interested even when Nyssa smiled across the room at Wolfe and wiggled her fingers at him.

He nodded to her, then looked back at Storm. She seemed highly amused. He cleared his throat. "Nyssa isn't a Barbie doll; trust me on that. She's smart."

"She's also very interested in *Mysteries Past*,"

Storm said. "And she knew who I was. Did you tell her I was the new computer technician?"

Wolfe could feel a frown drawing his brows together. "No. I haven't talked to her in days."

"Interesting, huh? It's also interesting to find her here." Storm sipped her wine and then shrugged. "Maybe a coincidence, but not a real likely one. Don't you think? I mean, this is a nice place and all—but I wouldn't guess it was her usual kind of haunt."

He knew he was still frowning, but Wolfe didn't comment on her observation. Instead, he picked up his menu and said, "Why don't we order?"

Storm didn't object, and she gave her order to the waitress a few minutes later. But it was obvious she had no intention of dropping the subject of Nyssa's presence, because as soon as the waitress collected their menus and went away, she said, "A party up on Nob Hill seems more like her usual habitat, I'd say. Am I right about that?"

"That's where she lives," Wolfe admitted, picking up a breadstick and snapping it neatly in half.

There was a slight pause, and then Storm said dryly, "At the moment, I'm less concerned about her interest in you than her interest in the exhibit."

Wolfe looked up quickly. "So am I."

Storm chuckled, a warm, rich sound. "Okay, then stop resisting the subject. Since you and I are both involved in the security for the exhibit, and since I can adapt a computer program to guard against threats—if I know about them—maybe you'd better tell me the lady's story."

"I didn't say she was a threat," Wolfe protested.

One of Storm's delicate blonde eyebrows rose in an expression of mockery. "Let me guess. Chivalry? Once you sleep with a lady you never utter a word to mar her good name? Noted, for future reference."

He could feel the ache in his jaw that told him his teeth were clamped together. It was becoming a familiar sensation. "I knew it was too good to last. You couldn't force yourself to go an hour without getting scornful about something, could you?"

The eyebrow stayed up, and her lips curved to show even more of a taunt. "Certainly not—it's too much fun. You rise to the bait so wonderfully."

"Hasn't anyone warned you about fishing in dangerous waters? You're liable to catch something you can't handle."

"Promises, promises," she murmured, then laughed when his frown deepened. "Oh, stop scowling, Wolfe. I won't ask personal questions about—what was her name? Nyssa? That figures. It's none of my business, at least not at the moment."

He eyed her. "Not at the moment?"

"You never know when something like that could change." Before he could respond to her gentle statement, she was going on briskly, "All I want to know is whatever you can tell me about her interest in the Bannister collection—which you and I are both responsible for protecting."

Wolfe hesitated, but it was a legitimate subject for her to raise—especially if Nyssa had made a point of introducing herself in the ladies' room, and if she did indeed know that Storm was the computer technician at the museum.

"She knew who you were? No kidding?" he asked.

"No kidding. And she didn't just know that I was installing the computer security system—she knew my name. That's the part that set off bells. How could she know my name, Wolfe? You didn't. Nobody at the museum did, until I got there. And even my boss at Ace wasn't sure I'd be able to take the job until yesterday. I packed in a hurry and came over from Paris on the Concorde, so it's not like there was a lot of time for anyone to find out very much about me. So how did she?"

Wolfe sent a quick glance across the room, finding Nyssa and her companion eating their meal and apparently having a casual discussion. "I don't know." He looked back at Storm, a bit unsettled to realize that her brilliant eyes were graver than he'd yet seen them.

Storm shrugged a little, her gaze still locked with his. "Since I like to know what my security programs are supposed to be protecting, my boss filled me in. I had already heard about the Bannister collection. I've even seen all the pictures from

the last time it was exhibited. What was that—
more than thirty years ago?"

"About that," Wolfe agreed. "Lloyd's of London insures the collection—which is why I'm here.
You know that."

She nodded. "You're their top security expert.
That's one reason Max Bannister asked for you.
Another reason, I imagine, is because he knew very
well he could trust you—since you're his half
brother."

It was Wolfe's turn to nod. He wasn't very surprised that she knew about the relationship; he
knew she'd talked to Morgan, and Morgan was
aware that he and Max were half brothers. He
didn't speak immediately, leaning back to allow
the waitress to place his plate on the table. When
she had served Storm and gone, he said, "That's
right. Is it important?"

"That you're his brother?" Storm shrugged
again, beginning to eat almost absentmindedly.
"Probably not, but it never hurts to know these
things. Is Nyssa aware of the relationship?"

He hesitated. "I don't think so. She's never mentioned it, at any rate."

Thoughtfully, Storm said, "It isn't something
that's generally known, so maybe not. Unless she
found out from him. They move in the same circles, I'd guess."

"And you'd be right." Wolfe was watching her
very intently even as he began eating his own meal.

"I don't suppose you'd want to disturb him on his honeymoon?" she ventured.

"I've already had to disturb him a couple of times. I'd rather not do it again, not if I have a choice," Wolfe replied dryly. "Why? To ask about Nyssa?"

Storm picked up a breadstick and nibbled on it for a moment, her eyes abstracted, then shrugged. "I guess it really doesn't matter whether she knows you two are brothers; I don't see how she could use the knowledge. She knows you're in charge of security for the exhibit, she knows what I'm responsible for, and she knows Mr. Bannister; as far as I can tell, she's been pretty blunt about her interest to all of us. True?"

"She's tried for years to persuade Max to let her see the collection," Wolfe said.

Storm waited a moment, then smiled. "And what did she try to persuade you to do?"

The dry tone made Wolfe feel uncomfortable, even though he'd been perfectly aware of Nyssa's aim from the first time they had danced together. Evenly, he replied, "To let her see the collection before the exhibit opens to the public."

"I gather you resisted her blandishments," Storm said in a solemn voice.

"That better not be a question," he said.

Her unexpectedly sweet smile lit up her face. "Perish the thought. Would I cast aspersions on your honesty?"

"Probably."

She chuckled. "Well, I won't." She ate for a few moments in silence, then went on with the original subject. "Since your lady friend has been so open about her wishes, I can't see her as a threat to the security of the collection."

"Neither can I."

"But I still want to know how she found out about me. Granted, I wasn't exactly a secret—but she shouldn't have been able to find out my name."

Wolfe agreed with that. The problem was, he could think of only one way she might have gained the knowledge. Ace Security. Ace's previous computer technician had done a dandy job of wrecking weeks of work, even if it had been accidental.

So what if there was a second strike against Ace? What if Nyssa had bribed or otherwise persuaded someone inside the company to provide her with information? And, if so, what was she really up to? Was her stated desire the true one, that she simply wanted to see the Bannister collection before any other collectors were allowed a glimpse?

Or was she a genuine threat to the collection?

Storm seemed to be following his thoughts with uncanny accuracy. "Does she know anything about computers?" she asked, a glance across the room making it obvious that she was referring to Nyssa.

Wolfe shook his head slightly. "I don't know for

sure—but I'd have to guess yes. She's known to have an outstanding business mind, so it's likely she has experience with computers." He looked across the table to find Storm watching him with something in her eyes he hadn't seen before. There was a shadow there, he thought. A secret.

"Want to set a trap?" she asked casually.

"Why would I want to do that? Risking the collection would be stupid—and definitely not my job," he said.

Storm smiled slightly. "No—but it's always better to take a risk when you can have more control. According to what I read in today's newspapers, this city seems to be crawling with thieves right now. There's a gang nobody can get near, the usual assorted independent thieves who always threaten valuables—and Quinn. Chances are, some or all of them will consider the *Mysteries Past* exhibit a very nice target."

"Undoubtedly," Wolfe said.

"Then why wait for them to come knocking at your door? Why not open the door just a little— and see who can't resist the temptation to come in."

Wolfe pushed his plate away and picked up his wineglass, giving himself a moment. "What kind of trap do you have in mind?" he asked finally.

"Well, let's look at what we have. After the changeover, the museum's security will be state-of-the-art electronics. Now, since there's an independent power supply, which is not accessible from the outside of the building, a thief's best bet would be to control the system with another computer."

Immediately, Wolfe said, "Our system's completely enclosed. There's no modem and no tie-in to the phone lines. So how could anyone outside gain access?"

Storm hesitated, her eyes oddly still. Then she pushed her own plate away and leaned back. "You remember this afternoon, when I was under the desk straightening out cables?"

"Yeah."

"Well, I found something else under there. Somebody had patched in a pretty handy connection to an old, unused phone line in that room. So I'd say that at least one thief has already unlocked the door to the system."

Carla made very sure she wasn't, as usual, the last to leave the office. Instead, she left with the others, laughing and talking as they walked to the nearby car park where they had all left their cars. Carla thought she probably laughed a little too much, both in her efforts to sound normal and in the giddy relief of being almost out of it.

She bid her coworkers goodbye and used the electronic gadget to unlock her car. She got in and immediately hit the door lock. Safe. She was safe now, and—

"Hello, Carla."

For the first time, Carla understood the expression "ice water in the veins." She felt cold. So cold. "I—I wasn't—"

"Running? I think you were. Pity."

In the rearview mirror, she stared at his face, clear to her for the first time. And stared at the gun he was lifting. There was a silencer on the end. "No, please. The security system at the museum—they've sent in a new programmer—I'm sure I can get the plans for the new system—"

"And I'm equally sure you can't." The elegant gun sneezed softly. "But don't worry, Carla. You aren't my only source on the inside. I do have another."

Morgan hadn't planned on spending Tuesday night outside one of the museums or jewelry stores she'd marked as likely targets for Quinn. But when she went home after work, she found herself too restless to be able to settle down, and she knew herself too well to believe she could force it.

So she dressed in dark clothes, took along an auto mug of hot coffee, and went out hunting.

She was still a long way from being convinced that she could, indeed, sense Quinn; since their last meeting outside her apartment building, she had felt several times—both inside and outside the museum—that someone was watching her, but there was nothing to indicate it might have been Quinn.

"This is really dumb," she muttered to herself as she drove toward a jewelry store she had on her list. The scorn in her own voice didn't make her turn back, but when she was almost at the store, something else did.

She found herself stopping the car momentarily, caught herself almost...listening. She didn't hear anything, but something urged her to act, and she turned the car around and headed back the way she'd come. Two blocks later she pulled over to the curb.

In front of a private residence.

Morgan had no idea to whom the house belonged, but it was very large, looked very expensive, and undoubtedly held valuable things that would attract a thief.

It was also behind a high fence.

She sat there in her car for several minutes, frowning toward the house, then got out, closed the car door, and leaned back against it, hands in the pockets of her jacket. One hand grasped the pepper spray and the other her police whistle, but Morgan had a feeling she wouldn't need either.

It was still fairly early, and though the neighborhood was quiet there were lighted windows here and there to indicate that people were up and doing things. Morgan hoped she wouldn't have to wait long.

Just about three minutes later, a patch of

shadow detached itself from the rest at the corner of the high fence and came toward her.

"Morgana, what the hell are you doing here?"

She had to smile at the very polite tone, even as she felt a rush of satisfaction. "Testing a theory," she replied.

Quinn stopped a little more than an arm's length from her, his sigh misting the chill air even through the ski mask. The nearest streetlight was close enough to show her that he was dressed as usual all in black, obviously bent on thievery.

"I knew it was a mistake to make you consciously aware of it," he said. "I should have known you'd come looking for me."

"I thought the great Quinn never made mistakes."

Dry now, he said, "You never heard that from me. I'll only go as far as saying I never make the same mistake twice. Though this one may prove to be quite costly, I'm afraid."

Morgan nodded toward the house behind him. "It will be if you had any intention of robbing them." She pulled the pepper spray from her pocket and held it ready. "This time there's no display case to tie me to, and I'm not exactly unarmed."

"You aren't blowing your police whistle," he noted mildly.

"No need to wake the neighborhood. If, that is, you give me your word you won't be stealing anything at all—at least not tonight."

"Not tonight?" He sounded amused. "What, you don't want me to give up crime for good?"

"I know better than to ask the impossible."

"Then why ask for just one night?" Now he sounded honestly curious.

"Maybe I just want to find out if you really can keep your word."

Quinn laughed softly. "You know, Morgana, you constantly surprise me. I was reasonably sure our next encounter would end with you doing everything in your power to put me behind bars. For taking your necklace, if nothing else."

Morgan was more than a little surprised at herself but tried to keep that out of her expression and voice. "Oh, I'll get you for that eventually," she said. "But I am curious as to why you bothered to take it at all. It's worth nothing compared to your usual loot."

Quinn placed one hand over his heart—assuming he had one—and replied soulfully, "A keepsake."

"Bullshit. You took it to show me you could."

"Well, that too."

"I want my necklace back, Quinn."

"And I would much prefer that you stop testing your theory. It could be a real nuisance, Morgana."

"For me to keep showing up and preventing you from stealing the valuables? Do tell."

Quinn laughed again. "Now, sweet, do you

really think you could have found me if I hadn't allowed you to?"

"Don't tell me you were conducting an experiment of your own."

"Something like that."

Morgan wasn't at all sure she believed him, but she was uncertain enough to say, "So you can stop me from feeling your presence? How, with your cloak of invisibility? With your ability to cloud my mind? With kryptonite?"

"Nothing so heroic, I'm afraid. Just will. My will. I've spent much of my adult life learning how to be elusive, sweet. If I don't want to be found, not even you will find me."

"Why do I get the feeling you're issuing a challenge?"

"Perhaps because I am. Try to find me tomorrow night, Morgana."

She scowled at him. "You're just saying that so I'll let you get away tonight."

"Wasn't that the plan? To test my word?"

Morgan wasn't about to admit that her original plan had been to yell for the police and that she didn't know why in hell she wasn't doing just that. "Are you willing to give me your word? Promise that you won't rob anybody tonight?"

Promptly, he agreed. "Of course I am, Morgana. I give you my word I will not rob any person or place tonight."

She was suspicious but also had to admit to herself, however unwillingly, that she wasn't quite prepared to start yelling for the police. At least, not yet.

Still holding her pepper spray ready, she said, "I don't suppose you'd give me the same promise about the Bannister collection?"

"No," he said simply. "You see, my word does mean something to me. I'll never break a promise to you, Morgana. Which means that I won't steal anything from anyone—tonight. And that's all."

Irritably, she said, "At least give me back my necklace."

"I don't happen to have it on me," he said.

Morgan was tempted. In fact, her finger tightened on the button of the pepper spray. But, finally, all she could do was accept what he said.

"One of these days," she told him, "you'll get what's coming to you. And I want to be there. That's all I ask, that I'm there when you get what you deserve."

"But in the meantime," he murmured, stepping silently away from her and already beginning to blend back into the shadows.

Morgan didn't try to stop him. She just leaned against her car, slowly returning the pepper spray to her pocket, and when she was sure he was gone she muttered into the chill night air, "I am such an idiot."

Then she got in her car and went home.

* * *

By the time they reached Storm's hotel suite nearly an hour later, Wolfe had stopped swearing out loud. But he paced like his namesake caged, barely noticing the room he was in.

Storm bent to allow her cat to transfer from her shoulder to the back of the couch, where he made himself comfortable. Then she sat down at one end. Both she and Bear watched the man moving around the room.

"It had to be the first technician," he said finally.

"It wasn't him."

He stopped pacing to stare at her. "If you're trying to be loyal to Ace—"

"I'm not," she interrupted. "Look, Wolfe, if I or any other decent technician wanted to patch in to a phone line, we could do it without leaving a lot of evidence. What I saw looked like it had been done in one hell of a hurry. Anybody could have gotten into that room at some point during the past weeks, you know that. The hallway isn't guarded, not now when the security system isn't on line. And I'm willing to bet my predecessor didn't spend every minute in there, especially when the machine was loading information and he didn't have anything to do except wait for it to finish."

Wolfe had to admit, if only silently, that he hadn't thought much about the security of the computer room himself. It was as she said—though the machines themselves were certainly valuable, nobody could cart them from the museum unobserved, and the system wasn't vitally important until it was on line, so that hallway had not been the focus of the guards' attention.

"Goddammit," he muttered.

Storm shrugged. "Hey, they've got an unlocked door—not an open one. I can lock it for good by cutting the connection. Or I can stand ready at the door and see who tries to open it."

"We're back to the trap," he said, crossing the room to sit down on the arm of the couch across from her.

"Well, it makes sense to me." Storm wrestled her boots off and then curled up at her end of the couch. "Since the original security program was on file at Ace and would have been potentially accessible to a thief, I was brought in to install a program so new it isn't in anybody's computer. Except this one." She tapped her temple with one finger.

Wolfe nodded. "That's what Max and I agreed to, providing we see the entire program before it goes on line."

"Which you will. But the point is that even if somebody has an unlocked door into the system, getting in won't be easy at all. They'll have to figure out what the access codes are—and I designed tough ones."

"But they could still get in?"

"Oh, sure. Given enough time, patience, and knowledge. They'll have to make a number of attempts, however. So all I have to do is program the system to guard itself; if there's an attempted entry, I'll be alerted."

"Could we find out who was trying to get in?"

"Maybe. We could try tracing the phone line."

"You don't sound too hopeful," Wolfe noted.

She smiled wryly. "If it was me trying to get in, I would have routed the call through so many lines you'd never find me, at least not in the time I'd need to get in and get what I wanted. Any competent technician would do the same."

Wolfe brooded for a few moments in silence, then said, "Then your idea of a trap isn't to catch somebody in the system, it's to lead them to a place where we're waiting for them."

Her smile was quick and approving. "Exactly. If I know they're trying to get into the system, I can have a little subprogram all ready to tell them whatever we want them to know. Like—the system has a weak spot that looks just too inviting for words? No thief worth his—or her—salt is going to pass that up."

What she was saying was reasonable, but Wolfe wasn't quite ready to approve her idea. First, if a thief was after the Bannister collection, he—or she—wouldn't make a move until the collection was in the museum. And second, he wasn't sure that he completely trusted Storm Tremaine. That shadowy, secret expression in her eyes earlier had bothered him.

So he said, "I'll have to think about it. In the morning, I'll want you to show me that phone patch."

"Of course," she murmured. "After all—I might have some nefarious plan of my own. So you'd better give the matter all due consideration."

CHAPTER
EIGHT

Either Wolfe's mistrust had shown more plainly than he'd thought or else she was developing a unique talent for reading his expression; whichever it was, he didn't like it.

"I didn't mean—" he began.

"Oh, don't bother to deny it, Wolfe. I can certainly understand your position. I mean, the exhibit isn't even in place yet, and there have already been so many problems. And I'm sure you'd feel just awful if somebody you were seeing personally—like Nyssa, say—actually turned out to be a thief bent on stealing your brother's priceless collection."

He could feel himself tensing yet again. That drawling voice, dammit. And she had a knack for putting things in such a way that they really did sound insulting.

"I am not seeing her," he said through gritted teeth. "Not now, anyway."

Storm's expressive face took on a look of spurious sympathy. "Yeah, she was another who didn't last long, wasn't she? Have you considered therapy?"

"There's nothing wrong with me!" he practically roared.

She blinked. "No, of course not. Lots of men have a difficult time finding the right woman. But I still say you should broaden your horizons. I mean, you've got to be—what? Pushing forty?"

"Thirty-six," he snapped, telling himself to calm down, because he was positive her eyes were laughing at him.

"Oh, sorry—thirty-six," she said solemnly. "Well, still. You must have been concentrating on your favorite kind of blonde for twenty years now. I'd think that by this time common sense would have told you that whatever it is you're looking for—it isn't there."

Wolfe knew—he *knew*—that he was being deliberately maneuvered. He was even sure that if he stopped and thought about it, he'd come to the conclusion that she had brought up his social preferences every time he had ventured into some area she didn't want to talk about.

"What makes you so damned sure *you've* got what I'm looking for?" he demanded, leaving the arm of the couch to move closer to her. Since she was sitting sideways on the couch with her feet up, his thigh pressed against her hip.

"I didn't say that," she murmured, her ridiculously long lashes dropping to veil the brilliant eyes.

"The hell you didn't. You've been saying it all day. What's wrong, Storm? Didn't you think I'd get curious?"

Her dark lashes rose as she looked at him, and her eyes were quite definitely laughing. Gravely, she said, "Now, don't do anything you'll regret later. We both know I've goaded you into this, and if you let me get away with it . . . I'll always know which buttons to push. Won't I?"

For the second time that day, he said, "I know I'm going to regret this." Then he pulled her into his arms.

What he felt in those first few moments was not regret. She was warm in his arms, slender and almost frighteningly delicate, but all woman. She was a woman he wanted, that's all he felt.

She was a woman he wanted.

Storm wasn't immediately aware that he was going to leave her, and when she did realize, it took her a moment or so to find her voice. "Did I do something wrong?" she murmured, feeling too dazed to consider the question.

His face was very hard, but his eyes were burning like the blue at the base of a flame. "Yeah," he answered, his voice both soft and curiously harsh. "You met me."

Before she could even begin to figure that out, the door closed quietly behind him.

She turned slowly, lowering her feet to the floor, and sat there gazing across the room at nothing. It had been a very long day. She hadn't yet been in San Francisco twenty-four hours, and already she was in trouble.

"Yaah," Bear said, as if he'd read her mind.

"I can handle it," she said, turning her head to look at the little cat. He was sitting on the back of the couch, where he had observed silently. "I won't lose control. It's just jet lag, that's all. That's why I'm imagining things tonight."

Bear chirped softly.

As tired and disturbed as she was, Storm's inner alarm clock reminded her of an appointment that had to be kept. She rose and went into the bathroom and splashed cold water on her face, pausing for a moment to study her reflection in the mirror. Her lips were a little swollen, a deeper red than she was accustomed to, and her eyes were very bright, almost feverish.

"Liar," she murmured to herself, admitting what was gnawing at her painfully. "And the hell of it is—you're getting good at it. Too good."

She dried her face and went back out into the sitting room, trying not to think. Not that she could avoid it. The intensity of desire between her and Wolfe had caught her off guard, the passion it promised a definite complication. It wasn't her job to get involved with a man—and most especially not the man responsible for the security of the *Mysteries Past* exhibit.

She couldn't afford to let that happen, she told herself fiercely. Even if it caused no other problems, her loyalty could be divided. She could let down her guard with Wolfe, tell him things she had no right to tell him.

Even worse, she would be gaining his trust under false pretenses. He was, like his namesake, wary, suspicious of a hand held out; what would his reaction be if they became lovers and he found out she'd lied to him?

"Goddammit," she whispered, unconsciously pacing the sitting room as Bear watched silently from the back of the couch.

A soft knock at the door drew Storm's attention, and she went quickly to the little hallway. She looked through the security peephole and immediately opened the door. Without a word, she stepped back to let him in.

While she was closing the door, he went into the sitting room, looking around him with the automatically searching gaze of a man always wary of his surroundings. Bear spoke to him softly from the back of the couch, and he scratched the little cat briefly under the chin as he passed. He ended up standing to one side of the window, gazing out on the lights of the city.

Storm came back into the room and sat down

on the arm of a chair, watching the visitor. "I don't like lying to him." The statement came out abruptly.

The man turned away from the window, his strange eyes cool and calm. "You don't have a choice," he said.

Quinn didn't linger in the neighborhood where Morgan had found him. Instead, he returned to her neighborhood, the area surrounding the Museum of Historical Art, and from his favorite rooftop vantage point watched the big building.

When his cell phone vibrated a summons, he hooked the earpiece into place and responded with a low, "Yeah?"

"Anything?"

"No. Quiet night."

"Have you been inside the museum?"

"Earlier."

"So they haven't any idea you can come and go as you please?"

"Not yet. But it may well be a different situation once the new security goes on line."

"I think we can safely count on that."

"I'll be able to get inside."

"How can you be so sure?"

"Experience. I don't care how good a security system is, there's always a weak point. Always."

"And you have the knack of finding them."

"It hasn't failed me yet."

"No, but you're pushing it this time. Pushing your luck. Staying too long in the same place. I don't like any of this."

"We've been through this before."

"Look, it's not too late to turn back."

"Yes, it is," Quinn replied. "It's been too late for a long, long time."

A rough sigh came through the earpiece. "You know what I mean."

"Yes. And you know why I can't turn back."

"What I know is that sometimes the price is too high to pay. What good will it do you to get what you want if the cost is your freedom—or even your life?"

"I have nine lives, didn't you know?" Quinn kept his voice light and careless.

"You might have started out with nine, but my reckoning has it down to about two."

Quinn lifted his binoculars and intently studied the side door of the museum. No, nothing... just a shadow. "Then two," he said, "will have to do."

"And if you run out before the job's done?"

"In that case, you'll have to finish for me."

"Christ."

"You will, we both know that." Quinn lowered the binoculars and spoke calmly. "It's late. Go to bed. I'm going to check out a few more possible targets for that gang."

"Just don't get too goddamned close."

"If I don't get close enough to find out who's be-hind them, all this could be for nothing," Quinn reminded. "From what I've seen, they could get the Bannister collection. They could walk off with every last piece of it. I can't let them do that."

"You may not be able to stop them."

Quinn laughed softly. "Watch me," he said.

Storm smothered a yawn with one hand while she used the other to key a brief command into the computer. It began humming busily, obedient to her touch.

"Yarr," Bear commented from his position atop the desk.

"Not so loud." Storm lifted her coffee mug and sipped the steaming liquid cautiously. It was her third cup since arriving at the museum at eight-thirty, and the caffeine was only now kicking in an hour later. Normally, she limited herself to one cup, since caffeine had the peculiar effect of mak-ing her more reckless than usual, but she told her-self that this one time it was more important to wake up and function with something approach-ing a normal efficiency than to worry about being reckless.

A night's sleep had done little to combat her jet lag, and she felt like she was moving through a fog. In addition, she hated mornings just on principle, so her mood wouldn't have been much improved even if she'd been at the top of her form.

She hoped Wolfe wouldn't come into the computer room anytime soon. She hadn't yet seen him this morning, and that was fine with her. If he discovered just how punchy she was first thing in the morning, he was certainly both intelligent enough and ruthless enough to take advantage of it.

She had dreamed about him last night, first an incredibly erotic interlude between them as lovers, and then, in one of those crazy, topsy-turvy changes common to dreams, the scene had turned into something else. She'd been in a peculiar kind of classroom, feverishly writing mathematical formulas on a blackboard draped with glittering gems, while she told herself out loud, over and over, that she had to do her job. Then another change of scene and she was running, hiding, while Wolfe, enraged, hunted her through a creepy jungle filled with computer cables instead of vines; he kept yelling that she'd betrayed him.

Storm had awakened just as Wolfe, turning into his namesake, lunged at her in the dream. She hadn't, as with most nightmares, awakened in gasping, heart-thudding fear. What she had felt was simple pain.

For a moment, as she sat there at her quiet desk remembering the details of the dream, Storm was tempted to just run. But even as the urge occurred, her mind was listing all the reasons why she couldn't.

Having a logical intellect and a strong sense of responsibility definitely had its drawbacks.

Sighing, Storm double-checked the computer to make certain it was loading properly and then reached for the thick cardboard tube leaning against her desk. From this, she withdrew a set of blueprints for the museum, which she spread out atop her desk.

The edges kept trying to roll up, so she used an amiable Bear to weight one corner, a thick manual on the workings of the laser security system to weight another, then propped her telephone and coffee mug on the remaining two corners.

It helped to have something her mind could focus on, and since she had rashly promised Wolfe she would have the computerized security system on line in record time, she had her work cut out for her. After studying the first-floor plans for some time, she got a legal pad from her desk drawer and a handful of sharpened pencils from another. Her favorite bright pink highlighter pen was in the breast pocket of her flannel shirt, and she used that to mark specific points directly on the blueprints.

She left the computer room only once in the next hour, going across the hall to the employees' lounge to refill her coffee cup. She met no one on the way and didn't linger.

It was nearly eleven o'clock when a brisk rap on

the jamb of the open door heralded Morgan West's entrance into the room. The young director of the *Mysteries Past* exhibit looked as elegant as usual, her gleaming black hair worn up today and her astonishing figure simply clothed in a jade silk blouse and black pants.

Storm, dressed in faded jeans and a green plaid flannel shirt worn open over a black turtleneck sweater, felt a pang of rueful envy for the other woman's effortless sense of elegance.

"Hi," Morgan said as she breezed in.

"Hi, yourself," Storm responded. "What's up?"

Amber eyes bright with interest, Morgan rested a hip on one corner of the desk, automatically scratched Bear under the chin, and said mildly, "Wolfe's acting like he got one paw caught in a steel trap."

Storm frowned down at her most recent note and began to erase one word. "Yeah?"

"Yeah. And since one of the guards saw you two leave together last night, the place is filled with speculation."

Storm had thought it might be. She gave up the pretense of working and leaned back in her chair. "So you're in charge of officially verifying the facts?" she asked politely.

Morgan chuckled warmly. "Not at all. I'm just incurably nosy. I'm also very impressed—if, that is, you *are* responsible for Wolfe's lousy mood."

"Oh? Why is that?"

"Because, from what I've seen these last months, Wolfe hasn't let any lady get close enough to even barely annoy him, much less get under his skin to the point that he's snapping everybody's head off."

"As I understand it," Storm commented dryly, "he's let plenty of ladies get close."

"Oh, physically, sure. But not emotionally. Even Nyssa Armstrong couldn't make a dent—and she's been enslaving men since she hit her teens."

Storm pursed her lips thoughtfully. "I somehow doubt Wolfe could be enslaved by any woman." She kept to herself the thought that it was likely to be the other way around.

Morgan half nodded in agreement. "He'd have to be willing, that's for sure. The right woman could do it. Is that you, by any chance?"

"I'm not his type," Storm replied placidly. "Hardly five-foot-nine and sleek. And nowhere near a Barbie doll."

It was obvious by then that Morgan wasn't going to get the answers she'd been probing for, and her chuckle this time held graceful acceptance. "Okay, okay, I know when I'm being warned off. But, just for the record, I think the reason Wolfe's snapping at everybody is because you *are* his type—and he's getting real nervous about it."

Storm smiled slightly, but all she said was, "I'll note down your opinion. For the record."

Morgan's smile grew wider. "You know, both

you and Wolfe are so closemouthed you'll drive each other nuts. Oh, boy, is this going to be good. I'll get myself a front-row seat and just watch from the sidelines, shall I?"

"Suit yourself."

Laughing, Morgan removed herself from the desk. "Listen, if you don't get a better offer, I know a great café just around the corner where we could have lunch. Interested?"

"Sure," Storm said, adding blandly, "if I don't get a better offer."

"Well, give me a call if you do; I'll be in my office the rest of the morning."

"Gotcha."

For a few minutes after Morgan had gone, Storm remained at her desk looking somewhat blindly down at the blueprints. Morgan, she thought, would make a first-class friend. She was talkative, yes, but honest and without an ounce of malice.

But she was also unusually perceptive, highly observant, and very, very smart—and that was why Storm couldn't drop her guard with the other woman. Not now, at least. And, depending on how things turned out, maybe not ever.

That thought was a reminder of her responsibilities, and a glance at her watch confirmed the time. Storm rose from the desk and went to shut the door firmly. She had already discovered that this room, like most meant to house sensitive electronic equipment, was specially insulated and virtually soundproofed, so she had no qualms about using the phone. Especially since she had done some quick rewiring yesterday and used a couple of state-of-the-art devices to ensure that no one could pick up another phone in the building and eavesdrop on the line she was using.

She made herself comfortable in her chair, mentally organized her thoughts, and picked up the receiver. She punched a number from memory, and her call was answered on the first ring.

"Yeah?"

"It's me. I've spent the morning going over the blueprints. For a big building with too many doors, this place is pretty tight."

"Can you handle the security system?" he asked.

"Of course I can. I already told you that."

"All right, don't get your Irish up; I had to ask."

"Ireland was a few generations back," she said dryly. "And only on one side. These days, my temper's pure Cajun."

He sighed, about halfway amused. "I'll keep that in mind." Then his rather cool voice turned businesslike again. Businesslike and definitely critical. "I'm not so sure you should have told Wolfe Nickerson about the phone patch. Not this early, anyway. He was already suspicious of Ace Security; this is not going to help."

Storm kept her voice calm. "I believe I was able

to use something else to deflect his suspicions away from security precautions."

"What did you use?"

"I pointed him at Nyssa Armstrong."

There was a long silence, and then his voice came over the line very softly. "You did what?"

"You heard me."

"Why the hell didn't you tell me this last night?"

Gently, she said, "Because I didn't see the need to. And since I'm the one in the hot seat—it's my call."

Another long silence, and when he spoke it was obvious he was holding on to a formidable temper. "I see. Then do you mind telling me—"

A firm knock on the door, loud enough for him to hear, interrupted him. Quickly, he said, "Call me again later—"

"Wait," she said. Raising her voice, she invited the visitor to enter. Since the knock had been so emphatic, she wasn't at all surprised when Wolfe came in. "Be with you in a minute," she told him calmly, and then, into the phone, said, "You were saying?"

"It's him, isn't it? He's right there in the room?"

"Yes, you're right." She watched Wolfe close the door behind him.

The silence this time was brief, and the voice on the phone was unwillingly amused. "You'd play with dynamite in a forest fire, wouldn't you, Storm?"

"Sure. It's on my résumé."

He sighed. "Well, never mind. Just call me when you're free and we'll set up the next meeting. We have to discuss this before it goes all to hell."

"I'll do that. Thank you very much, sir."

He made a rude noise—obviously because he knew her courtesy was for Wolfe's benefit—and hung up.

Storm cradled the phone and looked at the visitor towering over her desk. Judging by his impassive face, he wasn't going to mention last night. In a voice of drawling politeness, she asked, "Is there something I can do for you?"

Instead of answering that, Wolfe said, "You mentioned your résumé; planning to change jobs?"

"It's crossed my mind once or twice. Besides, it never hurts to keep your options open."

"I suppose." He looked as if he could have said more on the subject, but it was clear he wasn't suspicious of the call.

Before he could tell her why he'd come in, Storm, characteristically, strolled in where angels would have been hesitant to go. "I hear you've been a mite testy this morning," she offered solemnly.

His impassive mask cracked a bit as his mouth tightened. "Morgan talks too much."

Storm chuckled. "I doubt even Morgan would argue with that assessment. Comfort yourself with the knowledge that she has your best interests at heart."

"I don't need her help," Wolfe snapped. "And I want her to mind her own damned business."

Storm leaned an elbow on the blueprints, propped her chin in her hand, and gently drawled, "People in hell want ice water; that don't mean they get it."

Wolfe stared at her. For the life of him, he couldn't think of a thing to say.

She smiled slightly. "Something my mama used to tell her kids. And we've both lived long enough to learn the truth of it. What we want doesn't count for a whole hell of a lot. You won't shut Morgan up without a gag, and even if you did, someone else would be happy to spread the news that you were something less than your usual calm self."

He couldn't deny the truth of that. And, even more, he knew he was only making matters worse by his attitude now. It wasn't as if he was hiding anything. He was in a rotten mood, and everyone knew it.

Part of him wanted to hang on to that mood, because it provided a sort of insulation between his turbulent feelings and the cause of all that chaos— her. But, as usual, her lazy voice and vivid face had the trick of both fascinating and irritating him until he found himself answering her taunts and jabs instead of letting them roll off his back.

Like now, for instance.

"Little bit under the weather, Wolfe? Get up on the wrong side of the bed? Or maybe you just had a hard time sleeping last night?"

"None of the above," he retorted. "And if that last was a passing reference to the haunting effect of your charms—"

"It was."

Distracted, he said severely, "Don't you have an ounce of feminine guile?"

"Not even a spoonful," Storm said with a faintly wistful expression that was disarming.

He tried not to let himself be disarmed. "Well, cultivate it, why don't you? It's not exactly subtle to ask a man if you gave him a sleepless night."

"Maybe not, but I'm curious. Did I?"

Somewhat grimly, Wolfe said, "I wouldn't answer that if it was my ticket into heaven."

Storm smiled at him. "You just did. Why, Wolfe, I had no idea my—charms, didn't you say?—were so potent."

He drew a deep breath and tried to hold on to his temper, his resolve, and his wits—in pretty much that order. "Look, I didn't come in here to discuss anything except business."

"Chicken," she murmured.

Wolfe gritted his teeth. He was *not* going to let her get to him again. No way. He was completely in control. "I came in to take a look at that phone patch."

Storm didn't respond for a moment, since the

computer's beep announced the need for a new CD. She got the machine busily working again, then returned her gaze to Wolfe. Between his refusal to admit anything unusual had happened between them and the fact that she'd had way too much coffee, it probably shouldn't have surprised Storm to feel a rush of dangerous recklessness. In fact, it didn't surprise her, because she was completely caught up in the impulse.

She didn't get up from her chair. Instead, she pushed it back a foot or so and slightly to one side, leaving enough room—just barely enough room—for Wolfe to get underneath the desk. She produced a flashlight from a bottom drawer of the desk, set it on top, and then sat back in her chair and said, "Be my guest."

CHAPTER
NINE

If Wolfe hesitated, it was only for a second. He came around the desk, picked up the flashlight, and went down on one knee. "Where is it?" he asked somewhat tautly.

"Right side, toward the front of the desk," she answered. "Where the phone lines are run up through the floor."

Storm was pushing it, and she knew it. She had no business acting this way. Especially when she had to acknowledge that it was entirely possible that he felt nothing for her except a male's virtually automatic temptation for an attractive and available female.

And, anyway, she had a job to do, dammit.

A job that included lying to him.

He came out from under the desk and sat back

on his heels. Turning off the flashlight, he set it on the desk and said, "You were right; it does look like it was done in a hurry." He didn't meet her eyes.

They were so close to each other that Storm's knee was touching the black leather covering his arm. She didn't want to talk about phone patches but had no choice.

No choice.

"It wouldn't have taken long. Five, ten minutes if they knew what they were doing." She watched a muscle bunch underneath the tan skin of his jaw and wondered if it was due to anger or something else.

He started to get up, but he turned toward her as he went onto one knee, until they were almost facing each other—and he froze when, without thinking, she reached out to him. Her fingertips touched his dark shirt.

Wolfe turned slowly the rest of the way until they faced each other completely. His hands lifted to her denim-covered knees, the weight of them warm and hard. She didn't resist when he eased her legs apart, or when his hands slid up the outsides of her thighs to her hips and pulled her toward him.

It was a starkly erotic position, and everything female in Storm responded wildly. Her inner thighs pressed against his sides just at his waist, and her hands lifted to his shoulders. They were almost eye to eye.

"Did I give you a sleepless night, Wolfe?"

"Yes, dammit," he said, his voice as rough as the surface of granite but not hard at all.

"But I'm not your type. How could I disturb your sleep?"

"You're going to make me admit it, aren't you?"

"I'm just asking a simple question."

"Then I'll answer it." His head bent toward her, his eyes focused on her lips, and his voice roughened even more. "I'm taking your advice—broadening my horizons."

"It's about time," she whispered, just before his mouth covered hers. She had forgotten all about the unlocked door and wouldn't have cared very much if someone had reminded her.

Wolfe had forgotten their lack of privacy himself. The way she was moving against him sent his already burning desire soaring until he was on the verge of completely losing control.

He probably would have given up the struggle, but the clear tone of the computer's beep, so alien as it intruded on flesh-and-blood passions, recalled him at least partially to his senses. The machine was indicating its need for more information—and to Wolfe it was a glaring reminder of where they were.

With an effort that nearly killed him, Wolfe put his hands on her shoulders and eased her back away from him. Trying to control his voice so it didn't sound so rough, he said, "Storm, we can't. Not here."

"No," she said huskily, "I suppose not." Very

slowly, she drew her arms from around his neck, letting her hands drop to her thighs.

"We can go somewhere," he said, making it a question, his voice low. "My place is closest."

Storm looked at him for a long moment in silence, her eyes clear now, as direct and honest as usual, and the faintly ironic drawl was back when she sighed and said, "You aren't going to like this, I'm afraid."

"I'm not going to like what?"

"What I have to say."

Wolfe released her shoulders and slowly sat back on his heels. A number of possibilities flitted through his mind, but what they all boiled down to was simple: She wasn't going with him back to his place. "And that is?"

Storm didn't flinch at the hardness of his voice, and she didn't look away from his suddenly stony face. "We both know I'm only going to be here a few weeks at most, then I'm gone to my next assignment—probably out of the country."

He nodded slightly, waiting.

She drew a quick breath, the only sign yet that this was more difficult for her than she was letting on. "Maybe to you, the situation seems to be tailor-made for an affair. And maybe it is. I can't say I'd be . . . entirely unwilling. We both know that. But I know something else, Wolfe. I know myself. And I know there's a line I won't cross. An affair is one thing, but what I refuse to be is a one-night stand—

or even a three-day fling. I won't be a toy you play with for a while until you see the next one in a store window somewhere. I'm no Barbie doll."

"I know that," he said evenly.

"Do you?"

"Yes." He wanted to reach out for her again but wouldn't let himself. "So what do you want from me? A promise?"

"No. I just have to know this means something to you, something other than having one more bedmate to add to the list. Once we settle that, I'll never bring up the subject again, no matter what happens between us. But I have to be sure of that much before this goes any further. I have to."

Looking into her grave eyes, he knew she wouldn't back down. If she said there was one answer she needed from him before she was prepared to go any further, then that was precisely what she meant.

He also knew that if he hadn't stopped, she wouldn't have asked for that answer, and the knowledge was maddening to him.

She wasn't asking for very much, but it was more than he was prepared to give. He wasn't ready to examine his own feelings about her, and he sure as hell wasn't ready to make any kind of a commitment. Even one lasting only a few weeks.

Wolfe got to his feet slowly and moved away from her, around the desk. He wished he could have said something flippant or careless, but that was beyond him. Instead, because he couldn't think of anything else, he simply ignored everything except business.

"I haven't made up my mind about using that tapped phone line as a trap. Am I wrong in assuming it doesn't become any kind of threat to the museum or the new exhibit until the program is completely written and loaded?"

"No, you aren't wrong." Her voice was as calm as his had been. "Anyone with enough expertise to tap into the line would know better than to try and find a hole in an incomplete security system. The holes don't become visible until the entire plan can be studied. There's really no possibility of a threat to the Bannister collection until the new system is complete and on line."

"Then leave the patch in place and I'll let you know," he said briefly. Without looking at her, he left the room.

He had closed the door behind him, and Storm gazed at it somewhat blindly as she sat back in her chair. She didn't want to think about much of anything, least of all why she had issued an ultimatum to Wolfe, but it was impossible not to. She had done it out of a sense of honesty, knowing herself too well not to believe that a brief fling with Wolfe would have been hideously destructive to her—and she would have struck out at him in her pain. So she asked for more than a fling.

That was simple enough, clear and the truth.

What was more complicated, and less clear, was her other reason for trying to stop the headlong rush toward consummated passion. It also had to do with honesty. Or, rather, the lack thereof.

It had to do with duplicity.

She had also asked because she knew it was too soon, that he would draw away—perhaps for good. She had deliberately used his reluctance to stop something over which she seemed to have very little control.

Not very honest, perhaps, but Storm was only trying—rather desperately—to avoid a much greater deceit. If they became lovers, the question of trust became increasingly important. Once intimate, it was likely Wolfe would trust her more and more. And that was what she was afraid of. As long as he was even mildly suspicious of her, or at least a bit wary, she couldn't really hurt him with her lies.

But what would happen if they were lovers when he discovered the truth?

Looking at her silent, watchful cat—who had more or less turned himself into a tactful statue while Wolfe was in the room—Storm heard herself murmur, "I should tell him the truth, shouldn't I?"

Bear sneezed, which was his way of expressing a negative opinion, and Storm sighed tiredly. He was right. She couldn't do that. But it would have been so easy. All she really had to do was to tell Wolfe calmly not to worry about the phone patch; the tap only looked as if it went into a phone line. That was how it was supposed to look.

She should know, after all.

It was her handiwork.

Shortly before noon Morgan received a phone call that shook her very much. It was from Inspector Keane Tyler, and it was brief and to the point.

"Morgan, this morning we discovered the body of an Ace Security employee, shot to death in her car. Looks like it happened yesterday just after she left work."

For a moment, Morgan was too shocked to think. But then she forced her mind to begin working again. "I gather you guys don't think it was a robbery or just a random shooting?"

"No way. She had quite a bit of money in her purse, as well as her few good pieces of gold jewelry. As a matter of fact, it looks like she had slowly emptied her bank account over the last couple of weeks, and kept the money with her in cash."

"You think she was ... paying blackmail?"

"We think she was being blackmailed, yes, but not for money. Carla Reeves had a prison record. God knows how she managed to get a job with Ace, since she was convicted of stealing information—on security systems—for her boyfriend about eight years ago at her last job. But that's Ace's black eye, and their worry."

"Not to mention ours," Morgan muttered.

"Yeah."

"So you believe somebody was using her prison record to force her to get information from Ace?"

"That's the current theory."

"And she was killed—why?"

"She was no longer useful to the blackmailer because she'd given him all she could, or else he was afraid she could I.D. him to the police. We think she was planning to run—and didn't run fast enough."

"Jesus."

Keane sighed. "We're alerting all of Ace's clients, especially those with security systems that could be vulnerable. Wolfe says you guys are getting a brand-new system that won't be in Ace's database, so that's all to the good. But I thought I'd let you know what's going on anyway. It never hurts to be aware that there's a pretty ruthless player in the game."

"I'll say." Morgan paused. "So you've talked to Wolfe?"

"Yeah. Caught him on his cell phone. He said he'd be heading your way to talk about this."

"Thanks, Keane."

"No problem. Watch your back, huh? I know you haven't done anything somebody could use to blackmail you, but I also know this guy is capable of anything. And you're the director of the *Mysteries Past* exhibit. So be careful."

"I will." She cradled the receiver slowly and sat there thinking, not liking any of her thoughts.

Wolfe came into her office about five minutes later, but their discussion was brief.

"It doesn't really affect us, at least not directly," he said. "Makes me even less inclined to trust Ace, but even I have to admit they're doing every blessed thing they can to ensure the safety of the exhibit and keep Max happy."

"The new security system will make us less vulnerable all the way around, right?"

"In theory. We're no longer dealing with anyone from the local office of Ace, and if the blackmailer got his hands on our original security system specs— the company troubleshooters are still trying to figure out just what got taken or copied—they won't help him now."

"He killed her, Wolfe. She wasn't useful anymore, so he just . . . killed her."

Wolfe drew a breath and let it out slowly. "I know you've understood the pricelessness of the Bannister collection before now, but only intellectually. Think about that life snuffed out without hesitation. That was just one would-be thief, one man who wanted to possess priceless things. Multiply that by a hundred or so, and you begin to see the real stakes. People have been killed for the collection before, Morgan. Right now, here in the city, there are probably at least a dozen other thieves prepared to kill in order to get their hands on it. Hell, on any part of it."

It was Morgan's turn to draw a breath. "Welcome to our nightmare."

"Exactly."

"Do we tell Storm?"

"I will, if she doesn't already know."

"Okay." Morgan thought about it. "Do you think Max would consider giving me a raise?"

Wolfe smiled. "I wouldn't be a bit surprised."

Morgan sighed, not really cheered by that likelihood; she already made a very healthy salary. She hesitated, then said with a stab at mild interest, "Nobody thinks the thief blackmailing the Ace employee is Quinn, do they?"

"Not his style," Wolfe said flatly. "For all his sins—and there are plenty—he's never injured, blackmailed, or terrorized anyone to get what he wanted. No, he isn't even on the suspect list for this."

"Good," Morgan said, and when Wolfe frowned at her, added casually, "I mean, it's good that we can narrow the list even a little. Right?"

"Yeah. Yeah, I guess it is."

By the time Morgan stopped by the computer room to collect her for lunch, Storm had herself well in hand. Years of practice had taught her how to present a certain face and attitude to the world no matter how she was feeling; it was an ability she needed very much at the moment. Whatever her private concerns or hurts, she preferred to deal with them alone.

She enjoyed the lunch, encouraging Morgan's talkative disposition during the meal so that she found out a great deal about the museum and its inhabitants—and didn't have to say very much about herself. Storm wasn't a secretive person by nature, but since she did tend to listen more than she talked, it was never difficult to keep her thoughts to herself.

When they returned to the museum, Morgan said, "If now's a good time to go over the security gadgets installed for the exhibit, let's do it. Unless I discover another problem, all the hardware's in place and all the display cases are pretty much finished. Since there aren't any workmen cluttering up the wing today—how about it?"

"Sounds good to me." Storm bent to remove a clipboard from one of her desk drawers, which held a sheaf of papers all dealing specifically with the *Mysteries Past* exhibit as well as the museum in general; there were several scaled-down floor plans of the various wings, enlargements of specific areas that would likely prove troublesome to security, and detailed diagrams of the all-important display cases—especially those newly built cases that would soon house the priceless Bannister collection of gold, gems, and artwork.

"Is he going?" Morgan asked in amusement, gesturing to Storm's shoulder, where Bear rode comfortably.

"Afraid so," Storm answered. "He wasn't happy about being left here alone while we had lunch, so he's sticking close. Don't worry—he'll stay on my shoulder until I lift him off."

Morgan accepted that amicably, and the two women made their way through the museum to the second-floor wing, still closed to the public. They passed through the thick velvet rope at the base of the marble stairs, ignoring the signs forbidding the public to enter. Once they reached the top of the stairs, Morgan led the way, briskly and efficiently detailing the layout of the forthcoming exhibit.

Both women were completely businesslike and worked well together. Storm asked very specific questions, first about the location and placement of all the general security hardware—pressure plates, laser and infrared motion detectors, heat detectors, and so on—and second about the specific security designed to guard the individual pieces of the collection in their various display cases.

Morgan answered promptly and concisely, having to refer to her clipboard of notes only occasionally. Her own curiosity showed when she said, "Clue me in, will you? I know all this security hardware is already hooked up and that it can be turned on with the flick of a few switches. I also know that everything is connected to the equipment in the computer room and the security room. So—your job is to put together a program to run everything?"

Storm nodded. "Right. For instance, a motion-detector alarm is great, but since there are dozens of them, security could waste valuable time—without a monitoring system—while they tried to determine which one had been tripped. And if we don't know, very specifically, which security key card is used to turn off corridor alarms, then one could probably be counterfeited to give an outsider access without alerting security. What I have to do is set up the system so that every piece of hardware works in conjunction with all the other parts *and* allows security personnel to monitor exactly what's going on.

"I also have to make every alarm location-specific, which means assigning every individual piece of security a number to mark its position. The system has to be set up so that it's so tightly interconnected there'll be no way a thief can disable *one* part without disturbing two or three other parts and setting off alarms; it also has to be virtually impossible for anyone to disable the whole system. And the closer he gets to anything of value, the tougher the system has to be."

Morgan whistled softly. "That's a lot of variables to take into account."

"Tell me about it. About three years ago, I really screwed up a system. Believe it or not, I forgot to take into account the cleaning crew. They had their own security cards, just like the guards, but they naturally had to dust and polish the display cases, which were highly touch-sensitive. This was in a huge jewelry store, by the way. The system went on line just perfectly—and a bare hour after closing, alarms were going off like you wouldn't believe. It took me two days to calm everyone down and another two to incorporate that variable into the system."

Morgan grinned. "Our crew does the floors during hours, a section at a time, and comes in twice a week after closing for the rest. You *are* aware of that, I hope?"

"Definitely aware. And it's a pain to deal with. Actually, to limit risk, I'll have to set up the system so that the observing guard—who will have to be present in the room at all times—punches in a coded request at the control panel." She nodded toward the doorway of the room they were currently in, where what looked like a simple keypad was designed to be hidden inconspicuously behind a bit of molding. It was visible now, like all the control panels in the wing.

Fascinated, Morgan asked, "Then what?"

"Then the computer program will make several changes. Pressure plates, as well as the pressure-sensitivity of the glass in the display cases, will be temporarily deactivated; laser and infrared motion detectors will switch to just monitor all activity rather than sound alarms—and that monitoring will be so precise, we'll have a computer printout of every movement anyone in that room makes; and the internal alarms of the cases will be intensified so that the slightest touch of the contents will trigger the alarms. And, of course, all that will be observed visually by security personnel watching monitors in the security room."

Morgan frowned slightly. "For the *Mysteries Past* exhibit, we have brand-new, state-of-the-art alarm systems installed in this wing, but the rest of the museum isn't so up-to-date. Since your security system is for the entire building, you'll have to make this thing come together even with a jigsaw puzzle of different parts?"

"Yep."

"In less than two weeks?"

Solemnly, Storm said, "That's why they pay me the big bucks."

"It sounds like you earn every penny." Morgan shook her head slightly.

"I do—but don't run away with the idea that what I do is impossible. I've had tougher assignments, believe me."

"If you say so." Glancing at her watch, the brunette added, "Damn, I've got to get on the phone and track down a decent gemologist."

"I thought the collection would stay in the

vaults until just before the exhibit opens," Storm said in an idle voice.

Morgan nodded. "That's the plan, but I still need a gemologist fairly soon. Since the collection's been in storage for thirty years, it's going to need to be examined, all the pieces cleaned and readied for display. Plus, Wolfe says that Lloyd's wants a new appraisal prior to the exhibit opening. Which means I either have to find an extremely talented gemologist able to provide an appraisal *and* get the collection ready for display, or else find two different people with specialties."

"That makes sense. Well, good luck."

"Thanks. If you need any more information about the exhibit or whatever, I'll be in my office." Morgan hesitated, then said in an innocent tone, "The best person to take you over the rest of the museum's security is, of course, Wolfe. Even though it isn't really his responsibility, he made it his business to know everything about the current system. So he knows more than anyone else here, I expect."

Storm was well aware of that. Maintaining her calm, she said, "So I've heard. If you see him on the way back to your office, do you mind telling him I could use his help? I'll be on this level, North wing—with the paintings."

"My pleasure. Oh, and be sure to check out that big painting in the smaller gallery, will you? It's near the door."

"Check it out? Why?"

"You'll understand when you see it."

Storm was left somewhat puzzled, but when she made her way through the second floor into the North wing (the *Mysteries Past* exhibit was to be housed in the West wing), it didn't take her long to find the painting in question. And it was immediately apparent to her that Morgan's sense of humor was showing.

For something that had been painted hundreds of years earlier, it was curiously apt. Beneath violently stormy skies, dark clouds split open by a bolt of lightning, a lean gray wolf hunted on the edge of a forest. The animal had his back to the lightning and so couldn't have known he was about to be struck.

Storm was standing in one of the galleries marking the placement of video cameras on the corresponding floor plan she had on her clipboard when she sensed more than heard someone come up behind her. Despite the fact that several visitors to the museum had wandered by her in the last minutes, she knew it was Wolfe and spoke to him without turning around.

"I hear Ace lost an employee yesterday."

"Yeah. Security can be dangerous work. Especially if you're vulnerable to blackmail."

"Good thing I'm not," Storm said, then went on

calmly, "With the new software in place, the gaps in all this old hardware are really going to show. They need more than video cameras and a few laser grids."

"I know," he said without expression. "But it would cost a fortune for the museum to upgrade and remodel, and it'd take at least a year to do it. They can't afford it, at least not now. Maybe if *Mysteries Past* brings in enough revenue, they'll be able to swing it in the next year or two. In the meantime, if Max hadn't donated the new computer system, you'd be working with ten-year-old machines, so be grateful for small favors."

Despite his calm voice, she was completely aware that he was more than a little tense; she could feel it. That was encouraging to the reckless part of her but a warning sign to her sensible and cautious side.

Storm studied the wall nearest her, ignoring the paintings because she was looking for something else. To Wolfe, she said, "The grids are activated after hours, true?"

"Yeah."

"So whenever the guards have to traverse a corridor, they use key cards to shut the grid off until they pass through."

"Right."

She made several notations on the floor plan for the room, then turned and went back to the doorway, where she stood eyeing the gallery thoughtfully. She still didn't look at Wolfe, even though she could feel his gaze on her, and she kept her voice tranquil when she spoke. "Every laser port is so visible they might as well have hung up signs."

"I know that."

Storm's keen ears caught the slight change in his deep voice. Good—she was beginning to annoy him with her businesslike attitude. Fixing him with a bland stare, she said, "If I'm going to get the new system written and on line as quickly as possible, I need to go over the security hardware throughout the building. Morgan took me through the West wing; you seem to be the accepted expert on the rest. If you have the time, I'd like to get it done today."

He could hardly refuse, and they both knew it. So he merely nodded, said, "Tell me what you need to know," and followed her from the gallery.

For the next three hours, Storm kept their pace brisk enough to try the stamina of a marathon runner. It was a very big building, and if she didn't examine every inch she certainly went over it foot by foot. She wasted no words, asking brief questions and not encouraging anything but terse replies in return.

Her cool, businesslike attitude was steadily feeding Wolfe's temper, and nobody had to tell him how irrational that was.

Dammit, he couldn't even yell at her to relieve

some of the pressure. She wasn't goading him, for one thing, and besides, how could a man yell at a little blonde woman with a little blond cat on her shoulder?

It was nearly five o'clock, and since most of the visitors seemed to have left the museum, they were alone by the time they had reached the final area to be covered. It was the South wing, first floor, where the museum's existing gem collection was housed, and no one else was anywhere to be seen. This area was only a bit better protected than the rest, boasting display cases that were, Storm said briefly, "Slightly younger than God."

It wasn't the first disparaging comment she'd made during the afternoon, but it was the first in more than an hour, and it gave Wolfe an opportunity to vent some of the pressure building up inside him.

"Don't be so condescending," he snapped, relieved to have something to get mad about.

Storm rounded on him as if she'd been waiting for the same opportunity herself. They were no more than a couple of feet apart, so she had to tilt her head back a little to meet his angry gaze. Despite that, it was obvious she didn't feel the slightest bit dismayed by his greater size or by his anger.

"Who, me?" Her drawl was, in some manner Wolfe couldn't define, peculiarly cutting.

"Yes, you. You haven't missed a chance to ridicule the security in this building."

"That's probably because there isn't any. You want to tell me how the hell I'm supposed to design a system to protect this building when ten-year-old laser grids are expected to function side by side with pressure alarms older than I am? Older than you are, for that matter."

That last mocking remark nearly surprised a laugh out of him, which was about par for the course where his conflicting reactions to her were concerned, but he managed to bite it back. Using a bit of sarcasm himself, he said, "Hey, you're the one who seemed to think this would be a piece of cake, genius. I haven't heard anybody else call it easy, so I doubt you were lured here with false promises."

"I wasn't lured anywhere," she said, the clipboard tucked under one arm and both hands planted on her hips. "I was sent here to do a job, which I will do. Nobody promised me a thing, false or otherwise, except my usual pay. And a bonus if I could get along with you."

For at least a moment, Wolfe thought she was serious. Given his past communications with Ace Security, which could best be termed acrimonious, it wouldn't have been all that surprising. But then he saw the gleam of amusement in her green eyes, and he realized she was pulling his leg. A split second later, he realized something else.

"You've been goading me all afternoon, haven't you?" he demanded. "Ridiculing the security here because you knew it'd make me mad."

"Something like that," she murmured.

"Why?"

Storm was smiling slightly. "You've been very tense. I thought it might help if you could let off a little steam."

Wolfe drew a breath. "I see." Dammit, she was still pushing buttons—and all the right ones too. Worse, she was reading him like a book written in that easy-on-the-eyes crystal-clear type. And worse yet, she was so nonchalant about his temper that she was perfectly willing to deliberately incite him to lose it.

"What are you—three parts witch?" he demanded.

"Only one part. The other two parts are Irish and Cajun."

Wolfe all but winced. "If that isn't a combustible mixture, I don't know what is."

"Yeah. And you don't want to get your fingers burned."

It shouldn't have surprised him, Wolfe reflected wryly, that she would ruthlessly return them to the point where he had earlier walked out of the computer room. If he had learned nothing else about Storm Tremaine, he had learned she was utterly fearless in confronting whatever obstacle stood in her way. Even if it was him.

Carefully, he said, "We ended this discussion a few hours ago."

"No, the discussion didn't end. It just stopped. Rather abruptly, as I recall."

Wolfe jammed his hands into the pockets of his jacket and settled his shoulders. It was probably better to clear the decks here, he thought, where the possibility of being interrupted at least kept him from following his instincts.

"All right, then," he said grimly. "We'll finish it. I'm not about to lie and say I don't want you; we both know better. But I'm also old enough to have learned that it isn't going to kill me if I don't get what I want. You pointed out something along those lines yourself."

Storm regarded him thoughtfully. She was getting herself into more trouble than she needed, and she knew it, but she couldn't seem to stop herself. So it didn't really surprise her when she heard herself say, "Let me get this straight. You want me—and heaven knows I've offered—but it isn't going to happen because I asked for one small assurance you can't—or won't—give?"

He nodded, silent.

Very softly, she said, "Some women need promises, Wolfe. Even if they're only lies."

C H A P T E R
TEN

I'm not going to lie to you." He kept his voice even.

At least, she thought, not about this. And she wondered if that should be her guideline as well; even if part of her life was filled with lies, she could keep this part honest. Couldn't she? Or would Wolfe hate her even more when he discovered the truth about her?

For an instant, Storm wavered. But looking at him, overwhelmingly conscious of the unexpected strength of her own longing, she silently gave up the struggle. There would be time later to count the cost; for now, she felt an enormous relief in having made the decision.

With a faint smile, she said, "We all pay prices for what we want, don't we? I'm willing to set aside all those quaint, old-fashioned ideas drummed into me since childhood, throw myself into a brief affair knowing it won't lead to the altar—and I'll pay a price for that. But I'm not asking anything of you except one small assurance that I'll be a little more than another notch on your bedpost."

"I don't do that," he said tightly.

"Oh, sure you do, Wolfe. Not literally—at least, I suppose not—but you must be keeping count. There wouldn't have been so many if the number didn't matter."

That gave him a very sobering shock—because she just might be right. Before he could react, she was going on in the same quiet drawl, the tone matter-of-fact.

"Anyway, my point is that I can only meet you halfway. No matter which way you look at it, I'm giving up a lot more than you are, so I'll be damned if I give up my pride as well."

"You make it sound like a battle," he said.

Her smile turned a bit rueful. "It probably will be, considering the sparks we strike off each other. But I'd prefer to look on it as a kind of grand adventure." She hesitated, then added, "One I've never had before."

Wolfe forced himself to wait a moment so that he wouldn't blurt out the question. Slowly, he said, "Are you saying what I think you're saying?"

Characteristically, Storm answered bluntly and with a total lack of self-consciousness. "That you'd be the first man in my bed? Yes, that's what I'm saying."

"How old are you?" he demanded.

"Pushing thirty," she said promptly, then chuckled. "Well, twenty-eight, anyway. Naturally, being a proud woman, I have to assure you that there *have* been offers in the past."

"I don't doubt it."

Storm eyed him, decided that he was still somewhat stunned by her revelation, and kept talking to give him time to pull himself together.

"Of course, I had boyfriends in high school and college, and the pressure got a bit intense from time to time, but I was never really tempted to experiment. I suppose I just wasn't ready. And with six older brothers, all a bit fierce about their baby sister, nobody pushed me too hard." She shrugged. "Then, after school, my career was—is—pretty demanding. Till you stalked into my life yesterday, I still wasn't tempted."

Wolfe cleared his throat and forced a note of mockery. "Then you took one look and tumbled, huh?"

Storm laughed. "Something like that."

Fighting a silent battle with himself, Wolfe said, "If you've waited this long, why settle for an affair?"

Storm looked faintly surprised. "I haven't been *waiting,* not the way you seem to mean. Despite my upbringing, it wasn't fixed in my head that it had to be marriage or nothing; I'm a bit too independent by nature to think that way. In fact, I like my life just fine as is, without the encumbrance of a husband—or lover." She shrugged. "Maybe that's why the timing's right now; because I want a man who doesn't want ties. Looks to me like it suits us both. In a few weeks, I'll be on my way again, free as when I got here."

"And me?"

"You too. No demands, no complications, no hurts—no problems. Just what I trust will be a pleasant memory for both of us."

Wolfe knew he'd be a fool to turn her down. There had been a few similar offers in the past, which he had promptly accepted and for which he felt no regrets. But Storm . . . Every instinct warned him that, with Storm, there could never be anything simple and uncomplicated, least of all an affair.

"No," he said harshly.

She didn't flinch at his tone or appear the slightest bit ruffled by the rejection. In fact, she smiled at him, and her drawling voice remained casual and matter-of-fact.

"Maybe I should have warned you about the Tremaines. We don't give up so easily."

Wolfe didn't say a word when she turned and headed briskly for the computer room. And he didn't move. He just stood there, surrounded by lighted display cases of gems in a virtually silent museum, and he would have sworn he could see the gauntlet flung down on the marble floor in front of him.

As she neared the computer room, Storm's steps slowed and she drew a deep breath.

"Yaaa," Bear murmured in her ear.

She released the breath. "Shut up. I've burned my bridges."

Refusing to think about anything, she called for a cab as soon as she got to her desk, then gathered up what she needed to take back to her hotel and left, locking the door behind her. It wasn't yet six o'clock, but since she planned to work in her suite, she didn't feel guilty about leaving early.

No one could have said Storm bolted from the museum, but she didn't waste any time in leaving. Making a mental note to rent that Jeep she'd mentioned to Wolfe, she paid the cab in front of her hotel and went up to the suite. She dumped everything she was carrying onto the couch—including Bear—and immediately sat down to wrestle her boots off.

Half an hour later, she was comfortably dressed in an old, frayed sweater and leggings and was curled up on the couch. She had a meeting later—not here as before, because he was wary of being seen here too many times—and her supper was on its way up from room service. She turned on the television, more to provide background noise than anything else, and began sorting through her notes and diagrams.

She tried not to think about Wolfe, but his face kept intruding on her thoughts. Those eyes of his, so fiercely blue, seemed burned in her memory, like the sharp angle of his jaw and the curve of his sensual lips.

Burned, like her bridges. There was no going back now, she knew. Impossible to turn around, even if she'd wanted to. She was following her heart, allowing it to lead her even though her head told her she was likely to regret it. But Storm could only do her best. With all the lies in her life, her only choice was to pick a dividing line and stick to it. It was a chancy decision, and she knew it, but she didn't really have a choice.

Because of a promise given, she couldn't tell Wolfe the whole truth, and because of what she had come here to do, he was the last man on earth she should have gotten involved with on any personal level—least of all an intimate one.

It wasn't until much later that evening, when she was on her way to the meeting, that the real crux of the matter became clear in Storm's mind. The simple truth was, she was caught between two very strong-willed men, bound to obey one—and seemingly fated to fall in love with the other.

* * *

Wolfe caught himself pacing his comfortable sublet for at least the third time since he'd arrived home at eleven.

He was being an idiot. He should take what Storm offered, put another notch on his goddamned bedpost, and then cheerfully wave goodbye to her when she left in a few weeks.

That was what he should do.

So why was he even hesitating?

It was nearly midnight when he sat down to make a call, forcing himself to concentrate on business. The number he called was a familiar one, a special private line to an office in Paris. He waited for the connection to be made, slightly impatient because it took longer than usual. When the receiver was finally picked up, the deep voice sounded very harassed—and very French, even though it snapped only a one-word name.

"Chavalier."

"If your mood's that rotten," Wolfe said, "I'll call back some other time."

"Nothing's wrong with my mood," Jared Chavalier said, now sounding no more French than Wolfe did. "It's the rest of the world causing problems."

Wolfe grunted. "Know what you mean. Listen, can you do me a favor?"

"I suppose you want me to check Interpol's files for information of some kind, as usual?"

"Yeah. Max's exhibit is due to open in just a few weeks now, and I'm trying to anticipate problems."

"Also as usual," Jared said. "Okay, what do you need from me?"

"Two things. I have a few questions about one of our local collectors, and I'd appreciate any information you can dig up. Her name's Nyssa Armstrong." He spelled the name briskly, adding her address.

"Got it. And the second thing?"

Wolfe hesitated, then said, "I'm more than a little worried about the security company we're using. Max still has faith in them, but after the first technician they sent us screwed up, I started to wonder. Then they lost an employee, who had apparently been blackmailed before she was murdered. And since I've seen Nyssa coming out of their offices here in the city—when I happen to know she uses a different security company herself—I can't help but be concerned. At the very least, the company seems too damned prone to leaking information. Their reputation is excellent, but I'd like to know more than what I've found in the public record." He named Ace Security, provided the address and other necessary information, and said, "See what you can find out about the outfit. All right?"

"No problem. It may take a few days, though. I have to use the computer on a time-sharing basis, remember, and this isn't exactly official business."

"Yeah, I know. The collection isn't threatened until we take it out of the vaults, so I have some time before the information's critical. Just let me know."

"All right."

When he cradled the receiver a few minutes later, Wolfe rose to his feet and went to the living-room window. The apartment boasted a fairly spectacular view of the San Francisco Bay, and in the daylight it was possible to see either a fog bank or the Golden Gate Bridge—whichever happened to be visible. But right now what Wolfe saw were the multicolored lights of the city, some of them hazy because a light fog was rolling in.

He wanted to continue thinking of business, but as he idly watched the lights and the fog, his thoughts returned to Storm. Her hotel wasn't very far away. In fact, if he went and looked out his bedroom window, he could see it.

He was almost overwhelmingly tempted to pick up the phone again and call her, just to hear the lazy drawl of her voice, but he resisted the urge. She had the trick of throwing him off balance, of maneuvering him, and it was that more than anything else that he was wary of; no matter what happened next in their relationship, he wanted to make damned sure he had at least some control over his own choices.

* * *

For a long time after he hung up the phone, Jared Chavalier stared down at the notes he'd made while talking to Wolfe. Then he sighed, tore off the top page of the pad, crumpled it up, and threw it somewhat viciously toward a nearby trash can. It missed, which didn't improve his mood.

He got up and went to a window, gazing out without paying much attention to what he saw. His eyes moved restlessly, though, scanning the horizon even while his mind was occupied with methodical thoughts.

"Shit," he murmured finally, English expressing his feelings far better than French would have. He took a good look at the view then, noting that the fog was thickening, blotting out the lights of the bridge. It looked miserable out there, and for a moment he wished he were back in Paris. He muttered another curse, then returned to the spindly desk his hotel provided. He didn't pick up the special phone, the one that would accept only calls routed through his Paris office. Instead, he picked up his cell phone.

When his call was answered, he didn't offer a greeting, but simply said, "We've got a problem."

For the next two days, Storm barely saw Wolfe. She didn't go out of her way to see him, biding her time patiently and allowing her work to occupy her. In truth, because she was on such a short schedule, the project filled more than her usual working hours, and she always spent at least several hours in her hotel suite each evening going over plans, diagrams, operation manuals (dealing with the security hardware), and her notes as she planned a rather involved computer program.

By Friday afternoon she had begun writing the program, filling the first sheet of a brand-new legal pad with line after line of precise mathematical formulas. She expected it to take her another three or four days to finish writing the program and to go over it for possible problems—though there would likely be a few bugs showing up only after the program was installed and running. There usually were.

The work occupied her thoughts and attention, for which she was grateful, but it didn't do much to help her sleep. She was acclimated by now, the jet lag past, but dreaming about Wolfe had become a habit that left her nights somewhat disturbed. Even Bear had taken to napping often during the day—a feline habit but not one of his—because she kept him awake tossing and turning half the night.

The situation might have continued indefinitely—since Wolfe was a stubborn man and since Storm was still worried about gaining his trust under false pretenses—but the status quo was disturbed late Friday afternoon when a visitor came into the museum.

"Hi, there."

Startled, Storm looked up to see Nyssa Armstrong standing just inside the doorway of the computer room. The older woman, polished and sophisticated in a silk dress with her pale gold hair bound up in a refined chignon, makeup perfect and a bland social smile on her precisely painted lips, made Storm feel instantly threatened—and that reaction had nothing at all to do with business.

In a contest of elegance, Nyssa won hands-down. Storm was dressed with her usual casual indifference in faded jeans, boots, and a thick green sweater about two sizes too big for her. In addition, her hair was full of static electricity today, there was a smudge of ink on her nose and a pencil tucked behind each ear, and she had chewed one thumbnail down to a nub.

For one awful moment, Storm couldn't help wondering what on earth made her even imagine that Wolfe could possibly prefer her to someone like this sleek creature. And if the memory of his desire was reassuring, the fact that he'd avoided her for the past two days wasn't.

Highly conscious of her own disheveled state, Storm was nonetheless concerned first with security. She rose to her feet, smoothly turning the legal pad on which she'd been working facedown, and went around the desk to face the other woman.

"Ms. Armstrong, you shouldn't be back here," she said mildly. "Didn't one of the guards stop you?" Wolfe had posted a guard at the end of the hallway of offices the day after Storm told him about the phone patch.

Nyssa widened her blue eyes innocently. "Oh, he let me pass. I've been here several times to visit Max—and Wolfe, of course. The guards know me."

Storm made a rather grim mental note to do something about *that*. "I see. Well, since you're here—what can I do for you?" She stood in such a way as to prevent Nyssa from coming farther into the room.

"Actually, I came to see Wolfe. You don't mind, do you, dear?"

For a moment, Storm didn't trust herself to speak. First of all, she disliked being called "dear," especially by another woman and most especially by a woman she'd encountered only once before in her life—and then in the ladies' room of a restaurant. She also had no trouble whatsoever in deducing the fact that Nyssa was bent on making trouble.

Pleasantly, Storm said, "Why ask me? Whatever's between you and Wolfe is entirely your own business. But his office is down the hall, you know."

In a voice every bit as spuriously polite as Storm's, Nyssa said, "No, I didn't know that. I've never actually been in his office, you see."

"Then I'd be happy to show you," Storm said,

all but nudging the other woman back out into the hall so she could close the door to the computer room. "This way."

"You have such a lovely accent," Nyssa said, following. "Georgia? Alabama?"

"Louisiana." Storm happened to know Wolfe was presently in his office, because she'd seen him go past her door nearly an hour before. So she rapped sharply on the door, opened it, said, "You have a visitor," and motioned Nyssa inside before Wolfe could even begin to rise from his chair.

She didn't wait to see what reaction Nyssa would be greeted with but closed the door and turned to go back to her own bailiwick. It didn't much surprise her to find Morgan waiting at the door of her own office—a door that had been closed when Storm led Nyssa past it.

Leaning against her doorjamb, Morgan said gravely, "I see she's hunting again."

Storm paused and considered the matter. "Looks that way," she allowed.

"And that doesn't bother you?"

"Why should it? Except for the fact that she has the eyes of a serial killer, I'd say she's perfect for him."

Morgan lost her solemnity as she grinned. "Meow."

Storm felt a smile tugging at her own lips. "Okay, so the woman gets on my nerves."

"I'm glad to hear you've got nerves. I was beginning to wonder. And I certainly hope you mean to
do something about Nyssa's blatant attempt to get
her claws into Wolfe."

"He's a big boy. He can take care of himself."

"Yes, but that's hardly the point, is it?" Morgan's
amber eyes were gleaming.

Storm shook her head. "Her primary interest is
the exhibit, and we both know it. Taking Wolfe
away from me—if that's what she imagines she's
doing—is nothing more than a pleasant diversion
for her."

Morgan nodded, grave again. "True, very true.
So it doesn't bother you a bit, huh?"

"Not a bit."

"Uh-huh. So why're your hands clenched into
fists?"

Storm looked down and made a conscious effort
to relax her hands. It was surprisingly difficult. She
flexed her fingers and cleared her throat. "I'm a little tense. Big deal." She squared her shoulders de-
terminedly. "It's been a long day. I think I'll pick up
all my toys and go home now."

"And if Wolfe should ask?"

"What makes you think he would?"

Reflectively, Morgan said, "Probably because
he's been getting more than a little edgy lately
when he doesn't know where you are. He usually
asks me or one of the guards. When you vanished

at lunchtime yesterday, I thought he was going to drive us all crazy prowling around until you came back."

A little blankly, Storm said, "I didn't see him when I came in."

"No, I imagine he made sure you didn't."

This was very interesting, but Storm mentally allowed a bit of room for exaggeration; Morgan wouldn't do it consciously, but since she was clearly rooting for a relationship between Wolfe and Storm, she could have allowed wishful thinking to cloud her otherwise clear perceptions.

"He won't ask," Storm said.

"Oh, I think he will."

She didn't think he would, but Storm felt a burst of recklessness seize her. "*If* he should ask, you can tell him I said he'd better watch the pillow talk with Nyssa—I'd hate to have to change the computer access codes."

Morgan's eyes grew huge. "Are you sure you want me to tell him that? In those exact words, I mean?"

"Why not?"

"Oh, no reason. I suppose you know what you're doing."

Privately, Storm doubted it, but she wasn't about to back down. "Certainly I do. See you Monday."

"I hope so."

Storm's vast irritation carried her through the

next hour in fine style. She gathered up the work she meant to do over the weekend, picked up Bear, and went out to the parking lot where her rented Jeep waited. When she got to her hotel suite, she dumped everything and immediately went to take a shower, trusting lots of hot water to ease the tension she felt.

It only half worked, but that was enough to make her laugh ruefully at herself as she was drying her hair a few minutes later. Since he'd avoided her for the past two days, she figured Wolfe wouldn't be interested enough in her whereabouts to ask Morgan—no matter what the brunette thought—so the really nasty message calculated to enrage him had been wasted. And her anger at Nyssa was fairly useless; she'd encountered enough women like the older blonde to have learned that the sleek, polished surface of them was like armor.

The realizations left Storm feeling slightly drained and more than a little depressed. She changed into one of her comfortable working ensembles, this one made up of a flannel-lined but silky-looking black top and leggings that resembled pajamas and a pair of thin black socks because her feet were cold.

She turned the television on to a news program and was just about to find the room-service menu when a sudden pounding on the door made her jump. It didn't take a lot of imagination to figure out who the visitor was, and Storm wasn't sure how she felt about it as she went to open the door.

It was Wolfe, and she'd never seen him so mad.

"May I come in?" he asked with exquisite politeness.

She stepped back and allowed him to pass, then shut the door and followed him into the living area. In her best damn-the-torpedoes tone of voice she said, "You must have gotten my message."

Wolfe had shrugged out of his black jacket in the gesture of a man who wanted to be prepared for anything and tossed it over the back of the couch—narrowly missing Bear, who hunkered down and watched silently.

"Yes, I did, and what the *hell* did you mean by it?" Wolfe snapped, glaring at her.

Since she was wearing only socks, he towered over her by more than a foot, and rage came off him in waves so strong they were practically visible, but Storm didn't back down or back away; it simply wasn't in her. Taking up for herself as a child with six older brothers to torment her—all of whom were considerably larger than her— had taught her not to give an inch of ground willingly.

She planted her hands on her hips, raised her chin so her eyes met his dangerous ones, and snapped right back at him.

"I thought my meaning was perfectly clear. But

if you want words of one syllable, I'll give them to you."

"What I want is a goddamned apology. You had no business saying that—and to Morgan, for God's sake; it'll be all over the city by Monday—"

"Like it isn't already? Listen, if you think for one minute that Nyssa's plans for you are secret—think again. You're already party gossip in this city, hero. She's got you on her hook. And from what I hear, Nyssa hasn't lost one yet."

"I am not on her hook!" he bellowed. "Goddammit, I *told* you she didn't get what she wanted from me. I wouldn't give her first look at the collection no matter what she offered, and if you can possibly believe anything else—"

"Yeah, what?"

Wolfe made a visible effort to calm down, and when he spoke again his voice was more controlled. "You honestly think I'd give in to her? Even worse—you think I'd give away security secrets or even useless information as payback for a good time in bed? That's what you think of me?"

"What I think? I think you could give stubborn lessons to a jackass," she snapped.

He stared at her. "Is this the same fight we started a minute ago?"

"No, it's a different one."

She was trying to knock him off balance again, he decided, and it made him even madder. "I don't want to start a new fight until the old one's finished. Are you going to apologize for what you said, or not?"

"Not." She lifted her chin an inch higher. "So that finishes the first fight."

CHAPTER
ELEVEN

On some level of his mind, it occurred to Wolfe that absurdity went a long way toward defusing anger, but he was still mad enough not to recognize that their fight was beginning to lean in a comical direction.

He was so mad he was almost shaking; he wanted to yell and destroy things. Unfortunately, the focus of his rage was a tiny blonde—even smaller than he was accustomed to without her boots—who could give a few lessons in stubbornness to donkeys herself, and whom he couldn't have lifted a hand against no matter how furious he was.

She stood there glaring at him, her small, expressive face angry and her green eyes bright with temper, and he knew that no matter how much he raged, she wasn't going to back down so much as an inch. It was maddening.

"Ahhhh, *hell*," he muttered. "What's the second fight about?" The question didn't strike him as at all ridiculous at the time, though it would later.

"Your stubbornness."

"Look who's talking."

"Me, stubborn? I'm not stubborn. I'm just right."

Wolfe felt them drifting off track again, but he couldn't seem to stop it. "Right about what?"

"Your stubbornness."

"This is a ridiculous conversation," he suddenly realized.

"I'm serious," she snapped.

He stared at her. "If you expect to be taken seriously, never wear pajamas with feet in them."

Storm returned his stare for a moment, then looked down at her feet bemusedly. She looked back at Wolfe and burst out laughing. He found himself laughing as well, the anger gone as though it had never existed.

When she could, Storm said, "I'm not wearing pajamas with feet in them, I'm just wearing socks that happen to match my leggings." She was leaning a hip against the back of the couch, relaxed now that the confrontation was over.

"Oh. Well, they look like pajamas with feet in them."

She swallowed a last chuckle as she looked at

him. He was smiling at her, that utterly charming smile she hadn't seen from him in days, and she hoped it would be a long time—if ever—before he found out that he could win any argument with her by using his softer side.

Dryly, she said, "Okay, I was out of line with what I said about you and Nyssa."

"Thank you," he said promptly, accepting the apology without crowing about it. "And just so you don't think I take your opinion lightly, I am checking her out."

"I thought you'd already done that," Storm murmured, unable to bite back the mild sarcasm.

"Don't start again," Wolfe warned her severely. "What I should have said is that I am *having* Nyssa Armstrong's background checked out."

"Oh." Storm looked at him thoughtfully. "By who?"

He shrugged. "I have a contact with the police. It's useful in my line of work."

"I guess it would be. So—you think she could be a threat to the collection after all?"

Wolfe hesitated, then shrugged again. "It's a possibility. She's certainly not hiding her interest. That's why she came to the museum today, by the way."

Storm smiled slightly. "You mean it was business, not personal? Think again. She came by the computer room first, remember, so I know what was on her mind. The collection, sure, but you too. She enjoys being a vamp."

"I haven't heard that word in years," Wolfe said, shaking his head.

Storm barely hesitated. "Maybe I should take a lesson from her. Much as it galls me to admit it, I seem to be a total failure as a seductress."

Wolfe hesitated, but only for an instant. "No, you aren't a failure."

"More sleepless nights?" She was smiling a little, her green eyes softened.

"They're getting to be a habit. What have you done to me, Storm?"

She was silent for a moment, just looking up at him, and then she straightened away from the couch and took two small steps, exactly halving the distance between them.

Meeting him halfway.

Wolfe was never sure afterward if he made a conscious decision or an instinctive one. In any case, he closed the remaining distance between them with one step and pulled her into his arms as if something had snapped.

Her green eyes gleamed up at him. "I want you," she said huskily. "You aren't going to say no this time, are you? Don't say no again, Wolfe."

"No," he said, pulling her hard against him and covering her mouth with his.

At some point he carried her to the bedroom, although Storm could never remember afterward just when. She didn't remember who did what, but clothing fell away and they were somehow on the bed, and she didn't care what might happen tomorrow.

Ed wasn't exactly spineless, but he had a well-cultivated sense of self-preservation and that usually told him when to keep his mouth shut. This time, he ignored the instincts screaming a warning.

"Are you out of your mind? Pulling another job so soon after the last one? We need to lay low, that's what we need to do, and wait until people relax a little bit."

"You're the one who's out of his mind. Security in this town is just going to get harder—not easier. Give people time to shore up their defenses, and that's what they'll do. We strike now, while there are still vulnerabilities to be exploited."

"Jesus Christ, you—" He broke off, blinking, when he saw the gun. "Hey, now—"

"How many times are we going to have this conversation, Ed? Because I'm getting a little tired of it. Either you do what I tell you to do, or I'll find someone who will."

Ed didn't have to be told that retirement from this particular gang would most likely be permanent. He took a deep breath, and nodded. "Okay. You're the boss. When do we hit the museum?"

"Tomorrow night."

Keeping his voice neutral, Ed said, "There aren't too many pieces we'll be able to carry out of there."

"There are enough." The gun was put away, but obviously remained within reach.

Ed took due note. He wasn't ready to retire just yet.

Wolfe didn't remember much of the next minutes. He thought they both dozed for a little while, still lying close together on the tumbled bed.

It occurred to him vaguely that it was still early, though it took a moment for him to verify that fact; he didn't want to move, and since his arm was covered by the warm weight of her hair he couldn't see his watch. But he turned his head far enough to see the clock on the nightstand, which told him it wasn't yet eight o'clock in the evening.

Storm lifted her head from his shoulder then, startling him; he hadn't realized she was awake. And if he'd tried to predict her first words after having taken a man to her bed for the first time, he would have missed by a mile. As usual, her reaction was completely unexpected.

Her green eyes were grave and her lazy voice unutterably sweet when she said, "Thank you."

Wolfe felt something inside him turn over with a peculiar, almost painful lurch. "For what?" he murmured, lifting one hand to brush back baby-fine strands of her golden hair. His fingers lingered to stroke her warm, silky skin.

She smiled. "For being my first lover. You made it wonderful for me."

"I hurt you," he said.

Storm was matter-of-fact. "I expected that. But it wasn't bad at all, because you made me want you so much I barely felt the pain. I know it could have been a lot worse. I don't think it was easy for you, having to be so patient with me, and I just want you to know I'm grateful."

There was nothing in her green eyes except honesty, and Wolfe felt another of those odd little lurches inside him. He'd never before been thanked for making love to a woman and didn't really know how to respond. Especially since he thought it would have taken an absolute monster to *not* be careful with her, given her delicacy and her inexperience. He didn't know whether to point out that fact to her or simply accept her thanks with what grace he could muster.

Finally, opting for the latter because he needed to at least try to keep things casual between them, he said a bit dryly, "Don't mention it."

Storm smiled at him and kissed his chin, then pushed herself up onto an elbow. "I'm probably being hideously unromantic in thinking of food at a time like this," she said, "but it's nearly eight and lunch was a long time ago. Why don't we order something from room service?"

"We can go out if you'd rather," he told her.

"I'd rather stay here with you." Then she hesitated, and there was a flash of vulnerability in her eyes, gone so quickly he almost didn't recognize it. Her voice remained casual and matter-of-fact when she asked, "You are planning to stay the night, aren't you?"

His hand had fallen to her shoulder when she moved, and his long fingers probed the fineness of small bones under silky skin. "If I'm invited, I plan to stay here all weekend. We'll discuss next week later."

Storm said merely, "You're invited," and tilted her head briefly to rub her cheek against his hand. Then she pulled gently away from him and slid from the bed.

He couldn't take his eyes off her. But he saw her wince slightly as she got to her feet, and concern for her tempered his renewing desire. "If you take a warm bath now, your muscles will appreciate it later," he said lightly.

She stretched cautiously, entirely unself-conscious, and made a slight face. "I think you may be right. I'm not used to doing anything in bed except sleeping or reading a book."

Telling himself there would be plenty of time to satisfy this hunger he felt for her, Wolfe sat up and swung his feet to the floor. Light. He needed to keep things light and casual. "I'll get the menu and place the order. By the time you finish your bath, the food should be here."

"Sounds like a plan." She smiled at him and went into the bathroom, and a moment later he heard the tub beginning to fill.

He got out of bed and found his briefs and pants but didn't bother with his shirt except to pick it and Storm's things up off the floor and toss the clothing over a chair. He went into the living room of the suite to find the room-service menu, and it wasn't until he got the folder from the top of the desk that he remembered the third occupant of the suite.

Bear was exactly where he had been all along, on the back of the couch near Wolfe's black leather jacket, sort of crouched in that odd position cats seemed to find comfortable, with his paws folded under him and his long tail tucked alongside him. He regarded Wolfe enigmatically through green eyes eerily like Storm's.

"Hello," Wolfe said experimentally. He was unaccustomed to cats but had the feeling he should speak to this one.

Either Bear was feeling unsocial or else he simply hadn't decided whether to accept a man's—or this man's—presence in Storm's life, because he remained silent. And that vivid little face with its clear green eyes remained enigmatic.

"So much for that," Wolfe muttered, and carried the room-service menu back into the bedroom.

He glanced at the menu, realized he didn't have the faintest idea what Storm might like for her supper, and went to the bathroom door. It was open a few inches, and the water was still running in the tub. He knocked lightly on the door and asked if she was decent.

Storm sounded amused. "No, but come in anyway." And when he obeyed, she said, "Could you turn the water off, please? I don't want to move."

He did as she asked, his attention once more completely taken up by her. She was lying back in the large oval tub, up to her neck in bubbles. Her hair was piled somewhat carelessly atop her head, which made her appear even more delicate and, to Wolfe, wildly sexy in yet another way. He couldn't stop staring at her.

"Thank you," she murmured, her head resting back on the lip of the tub. She looked up at him with slumberous eyes, and a contented smile curved her lips. "You ought to get a medal for suggesting this."

"I'll think up a reward for later," he said, going down on one knee on the mat beside the tub. He forced himself to concentrate on practicalities. "In the meantime, what do you want from room service?" He opened the menu and held it above the bubbles so she could see it.

Storm sighed luxuriously. "I could get used to this."

Before Wolfe could frame a retort, the phone in

the bedroom shrilled a summons. Storm shook the bubbles off her hands and took the menu away from him, saying she still wasn't ready to move, so he went out to answer the phone.

Whoever it was obviously didn't want to talk to him, hanging up after an instant of silence. When he returned to the bathroom, Wolfe said ominously, "If a man answers..."

Undisturbed, she said promptly, "Yeah, except you're on the wrong end of that equation. I'd only tell a lover to hang up if I was married and afraid my husband would answer. It was obviously just a wrong number. Does chicken sound good to you? Or are you a steak-and-potatoes man?"

"I'm a food man, not at all picky."

"Glad to hear it." Storm handed the menu back to him and pointed out exactly what she wanted, then told him to order whatever he liked for himself. "I'm on an expense account, and Ace is paying," she said.

Wolfe lifted an eyebrow at her. "Is that usual?"

"For me, it is. One of the perks for being willing to go wherever they send me." She eyed him with amusement. "And even if they found out they were feeding you this weekend, they wouldn't object. As I understand it, when you threw your weight around, and added Max Bannister's in for good measure, my boss was willing to do just about anything to please you. In case you're interested, it cost them big bucks to pull me off the job in Paris and get me here fast enough to suit you."

Wolfe smiled wryly. "Shows you what can be accomplished by a bit of fire and brimstone and a dash or two of blackmail."

She chuckled and then closed her eyes. "I have a feeling you're pretty good at that sort of thing. I certainly *know* about your ability to conjure the fire and brimstone."

"Look who's talking. Do you want coffee, tea, or a soft drink?"

"No—milk. I'll need my strength."

"You think so?"

She grinned at him. "Don't you?"

Wolfe looked at her in the bubble bath, then nodded. "As a matter of fact, I do." He went to place the order.

Morgan had spent far too many of her evening hours recently standing watch outside various museums and jewelry stores; by Friday night, she was determined to stop wasting her time.

He'd been right, damn him. When he didn't want to be found, he wouldn't be found, period. Whatever extra sense or awareness had led her to him that once had remained maddeningly silent ever since.

She'd missed her chance to put his ass behind bars, and it served her right.

It did no good to console herself with the knowledge that Quinn was the most infamous cat burglar in the world, for God's sake, and most of the police forces in existence had been after him for at least ten years. There was just no way her amateur efforts were going to locate him—even if she *could* feel when he was near.

When he let her feel it.

Dammit.

At any rate, since she had no other plans for the evening and was feeling too restless to sit at home and read or watch television, Morgan decided around eight that night to go to the museum and pick up some paperwork she could deal with over the weekend. It wasn't unusual for her to go to the museum after hours, and one of the guards let her in as soon as he saw her from inside the lobby.

"Hi, Steve," she said cheerfully as she came in. "Anything happening today?"

The middle-aged guard shook his head. "Nah, not much. Mr. Dugan was here until after closing. Oh—and Mr. Bannister's back in the city. He dropped by a few minutes ago to take a look at the *Mysteries Past* wing. Had somebody with him. A cop, I think."

Morgan frowned at him. "A cop? Are you sure?"

"Well, he was wearing a gun in a shoulder holster, that much I'm sure of. I guess he could have been some kind of bodyguard for Mr. Bannister, but he didn't act that way. Hold on a second." The guard went to the desk in one corner of the lobby, spoke briefly with a second guard seated there, and studied the logbook. Then he returned to Morgan. "Mr. Bannister signed them in—himself and a guest, unnamed. They're still here, according to Brian. Upstairs at the exhibit, most likely. I'll sign you in, Morgan."

She nodded her thanks a bit absently and, rather than moving toward the hallway of offices on the first floor, chose instead to head for the stairs and the West wing of the second floor. She was surprised that Max was back from his honeymoon at least a week earlier than expected but, even more, she was curious to see who he had brought to inspect the exhibit wing.

She was casually dressed in jeans and a sweater, her long hair in a ponytail, and her Reeboks made no sound on the marble floor as Morgan moved swiftly up the stairs. She didn't have to worry about using her key card to deactivate corridor alarms or other security devices, since those in this wing were currently inactive; nothing of value was in place yet, so there was nothing to protect.

Morgan wasn't sneaky about it, but as she began making her way through the wing she found herself walking with lighter steps and being cautious. After all, she told herself, since Max had brought this man here after hours and hadn't recorded his name in the security logbook, perhaps no one was meant to know—officially, anyway—about his presence.

Of course, that didn't in any way deter Morgan. She was nothing if not curious.

Moving as silently as a whisper, she paused finally in the shadow of a darkened display case quite a bit larger than she was, where she had a perfect view of the two men. They were standing some yards away, in the main room of the exhibit, where other display cases were lighted as if for inspection. But neither man was looking at the cases.

In fact, Max was leaning back against one of them carelessly, and the other man was drumming his long fingers against glass that would, when the collection was in place, bristle at this hour with touch-sensitive alarms.

The two men were a striking pair. Both wore dark raincoats, and there was a curious similarity in them that had little to do with physical appearance and much more to do with stance and a kind of inner toughness that was visible in both.

The man who was a stranger to Morgan was probably in his mid-thirties, slightly over six feet tall and built athletically, with gleaming sable hair and odd, pale eyes that looked even at a distance sharp enough to cut; he was handsome in a strikingly elegant way, almost aristocratic and curiously foreign.

Max was a bit older, two or three inches taller, broader through the shoulders and visibly more powerful in terms of physical strength; his black hair, steel-gray eyes, and rugged good looks would have tagged him as an American in any city of the world.

Morgan didn't move and hardly breathed, watching them intently and listening as they talked; she only wished she'd been privy to the beginning of the conversation.

"Second thoughts?" the stranger asked Max, his voice unaccented in the way that was common to people who had lived all over the world.

"You know better than that, Jared. I gave my word, and I mean to keep it. The collection will be displayed here, as planned." As usual, Max's voice was low and calm, and unexpectedly soft for a man who looked as if he'd been hewn from granite.

"No matter what?" Jared's handsome face held a somewhat wry expression as he looked at the other man.

"Nothing's changed. Your people at Interpol have tried for years, like police all over the world, but nobody's even gotten close. You have to have bait for a trap, and the only bait with any chance of catching him is the Bannister collection."

Jared sighed. "That sounds so simple, dammit. Why am I having nightmares?"

"Because you're a sensitive soul?" Max murmured.

Jared said something rude, then sighed again. "Look, I'm sorry I called you back early, but we

have a number of problems. The biggest one looming right in front of us is your security expert."

Max cleared his throat. "Well, it's not as if we
didn't expect as much."

"That doesn't alter the fact that he's going to
raise hell and breathe fire when he finds out what
we're planning to do. Tell me something. Did we
ever have a plan for that eventuality?"

Rubbing the back of his neck with one hand,
Max said ruefully, "As I recall, we decided to jump
off that bridge when we came to it."

"That's how I remembered it. Damn."

"Well, we can always—" Max broke off
abruptly, turning his head to look toward the
doorway. Morgan froze, but she had the weird
feeling he saw her.

"What?" Jared asked, tensing visibly.

Max looked back at him, calm as always.
"Nothing. But maybe we'd better finish this discussion somewhere else."

Morgan didn't wait to hear any more. Moving
as swiftly and silently as she could, she slipped
away and hurried down the stairs to the first-floor
lobby. She went to her office and picked up the papers she'd wanted, hoping that if Max came down
before she got out he'd see her homework and not
ask questions.

But he wasn't in the lobby when she signed out
at the desk or when Steve reappeared to see her out
of the museum. Morgan thought she was probably

as casual and cheerful with the guard as always, but since her thoughts were in a whirl she couldn't be sure of anything.

She got into her small car and immediately pulled away from the curb in front of the museum, but she drove only a couple of blocks before she pulled over and turned off the engine. She was halfway home, only two blocks from her apartment building, but she had no interest in going home.

Her first coherent thought was, characteristically, a spurt of annoyance at Max. He might have told her, she fumed silently.

Because there was only one thing Morgan could think of to explain the conversation she had just overheard. Max was working with a man from Interpol, allowing his priceless collection to be bait for a trap set to catch Quinn.

Morgan didn't know quite how she felt about that, and the not knowing unnerved her. She should have been cheering, she told herself grimly. One less thief in the world was, after all, a thing to cheer for. And even though Quinn's reputation described him as two parts ghost and one part shadow, Morgan had felt the reality of him; he was a man, and any man could be caught if the trap was good enough.

After a few moments, she started her car again and pulled away from the curb. But she didn't go to her apartment. Instead, she went across town to the museum that was next on her mental list of places Quinn might find inviting. She cussed at herself for doing it, but even her own scornful words failed to have much effect on her. Sighing, she stopped for coffee in a paper cup and parked on a street with a view of the rear of the museum, locked her car doors, and settled down to wait.

Sipping her coffee and watching the big building that was shrouded by an incoming fog, Morgan slumped down in her seat and brooded about Quinn. Would the trap being set by Max and the man from Interpol catch Quinn? Could it? Quinn had built a reputation for being daring, nerveless— and utterly scornful of so-called security. In fact, he seemed to delight in flaunting his seeming wizardry in slipping undetected through the electronic mazes of state-of-the-art technology.

Keane Tyler had said as much, that Quinn was undoubtedly brilliant and undoubtedly looked for challenges that required him to test his own limits. But even he *had* limits, that was the point. Would he reach them this time?

Would the security system Storm was busy creating pose any more of a problem for Quinn than all those he had so effortlessly flaunted? There was probably at least a fifty-fifty chance that Quinn could beat Storm's system just as he had beaten so many other crackerjack security experts. Unless . . .

If a *trap* was being set, then there had to be a deliberate weakness somewhere, a hole—or, at least, a soft spot—where a thief could see it and believe it was there by accident. He would have to be guided into place, lured into a position where he could be caught.

Trapped, like an animal in a cage.

Morgan chewed on her bottom lip as she stared at the museum, trying—and failing—to sense him.

"Where are you?" she murmured. "Dammit, Quinn . . . where the hell are you?"

CHAPTER TWELVE

The room-service waiter had just left when Storm came into the living room. Though Wolfe wanted to keep things casual, he couldn't resist touching her. So when she reached him, he did, one hand at her waist and the other surrounding most of her face as he pushed her chin up gently and kissed her.

Storm responded instantly and sweetly, and when he at last raised his head she smiled up at him with unshadowed pleasure. "You do that very well," she murmured. "But I suppose you know that. With all your experience, I mean."

Since he was beginning to anticipate her singular honesty, the comment didn't unnerve him—but he could feel a wry smile tugging at his lips. "Has it occurred to you that it could have absolutely nothing to do with experience, and everything to do with a certain...chemical reaction between two people?"

Still smiling, Storm moved away from him toward the dining table where the waiter had placed their food. "Chemical reaction?"

He thought that, despite her smile, his question bothered her, but he wasn't sure. Still, Wolfe wished he could have taken back the words. He had only intended to steer the conversation away from any discussion about his past sexual experience, but he hadn't meant to sound so dispassionate about it. Before he could try to clarify what he'd meant, Storm spoke again.

"Is that a common thing? Chemical reactions?" She sat down at the table and began unfolding her napkin, looking across at him with simple curiosity. "I mean, if you watch TV or go to the movies you see some pretty intense passion that rarely lasts for long. Do the chemicals lose their potency, or what?"

"Why ask me?" He went to his own place at the table and sat down.

"I thought you'd know if anybody would."

He looked for signs of sarcasm or mockery in her expressive face and honest eyes and found none. Her seriousness disturbed him, because he was torn between the urge to assure her that she was—that *they* were—special and the wariness he still felt about committing himself.

Finally, he said, "I believe you once pointed out

to me that I must be satisfied with brief, surface relationships—given my track record. So I'm probably the wrong person to ask about lasting passions." He didn't like that response any more than he had his earlier one, but he was finding it impossible to talk to her about this.

Storm nodded gravely. "I hadn't thought about it that way, but I suppose you're right." With a slight shrug, she abandoned the subject. "Listen, I've always wanted to see a ball game in San Francisco, and the Giants are home this weekend. How does that sound for tomorrow night?"

Wolfe agreed that it sounded like fun, relieved by the change of subject, and during the next few minutes he found himself engaged in a spirited debate with Storm about the pennant chances of various baseball teams. It didn't really surprise him that she was as knowledgeable about the sport as she seemed to be about everything else that interested her, especially when she ruefully pointed out that as one of only two females in a family containing seven males, learning to appreciate sports had been a simple matter of self-preservation.

By the time their meal was finished, Wolfe discovered that she was not only a baseball fan but also enjoyed football and hockey, despised basketball and boxing, was bored by tennis except as a player, and became unashamedly sentimental and patriotic during Olympic competition.

She had strong and definite views about politics

and world affairs but was nonetheless able to discuss both without losing her temper, and it didn't appear to disturb her in the slightest whenever Wolfe disagreed with her.

By the time room service had cleared away the clutter left from their meal and they were sitting together on the couch, he realized without much surprise that he didn't feel his usual restless urge to retreat after sex. He didn't want to return to his own place. He wanted to remain here with her.

Even though it wasn't a surprise, it was still a disconcerting realization.

If she was aware of the effect she had on him, Storm didn't show it, and she was so relaxed and comfortable with him that it seemed obvious she considered this new stage in their relationship what she had professed she could "handle"—a casual affair that would last no more than a few weeks.

But, true to her word, she didn't bring up their relationship in any way. It was clear that, as far as she was concerned, Wolfe had tacitly accepted her terms when he had taken the step to meet her halfway, and that was all the assurance she needed.

"You've gone all quiet."

Wolfe turned his head and looked at her. She was on her knees beside him on the couch, turned toward him. She had been petting Bear, but the little cat had gotten down off the couch and gone to curl up on a chair by the window—which sort of relieved Wolfe; he didn't think that cat liked him very much.

"Have I?" He smiled at her. "I'm sorry."

Storm shook her head slightly. "No reason to be sorry. But if there's something you want to talk about...?"

He hesitated, but finally shook his head. His feelings were too new and too unfamiliar for him to be ready to examine them closely. "No, not really." He gestured slightly toward the coffee table, where Storm's notes, diagrams, and other paperwork were piled high. "You brought a lot of work home."

Gravely, Storm said, "Well, having bragged I could get the new system written and on line in ten days or less, I've had to work pretty hard. It's my own fault, though."

Wolfe didn't disagree with that, but he did frown. "I won't hold you to that estimate. If you can get the system on line anytime in the next two or three weeks we'll still be ahead of our original schedule."

"Good, then I'll take the weekend off," she said promptly. "If I get a better offer, that is."

"What would you consider a better offer?" he murmured, slowly drawing her toward him.

Just before her lips met his, Storm whispered, "Whatever you've got in mind."

* * *

It was long after midnight when the lamplit room became peaceful again and Storm fell asleep in his arms. As before, Wolfe thought he might have dozed, but not for long. He found himself awake, listening to her breathing and feeling it warm against his skin. Careful not to wake her, he stroked her wonderful hair, her back, shaped the curve of her hip as she lay against him.

He couldn't resist touching her, and he'd more or less stopped trying. He had also stopped trying to convince himself that his obsession with her was something that would burn white-hot for only a while before dying down to ashes. The truth was, this slight, drawling, green-eyed woman with her erotic mouth and fearless temper had touched something in him that had never been touched before. He hadn't meant to let her get under his skin, but she'd gotten there somehow.

Under his skin.

Storm stirred when she felt the bed move and the warmth of his body leave her. She opened one eye, saw the sun shining through the drapes, and immediately closed it again. "Oh, God, it's the crack of dawn," she murmured.

Wolfe bent back over the bed and kissed her cheek, then her mouth when she turned her head toward him. "It's not that early," he told her. "Almost eight. I'm going to take a shower."

She turned over onto her stomach and half buried her face in the pillow, then let out a muffled groan. "I need more sleep." She heard him chuckle and kept her eyes closed until she heard the shower begin running.

It was difficult for her to think so early in the morning, and there was a large part of her that simply wanted to enjoy what she had found with Wolfe, but, as always, her sense of responsibility nagged at her. She raised herself up on her elbows and looked toward the bathroom door, where steam wafted out from his shower, and her sigh was a bit ragged.

After a moment she pulled herself to the edge of the bed and sat up. She reached for the phone, called a familiar number and, when he answered, said, "Don't call here again; he'd notice another wrong number. I'll have to keep in touch with you."

A bit grimly, he said, "Do you know what you're doing?"

Storm let out the ghost of a laugh. "I've been asking myself that for days. But . . . it's a little late to turn back now."

He was silent for a moment, and when he spoke again his cool voice held a note of genuine concern. "What are you going to do when he finds out the truth? I know him, Storm, and I can tell you that, to him, a betrayal of trust is worse than anything else could be. He won't forgive easily. Maybe not at all. I can run that risk. Can you?"

She continued to gaze blindly toward the bathroom door. "Like I said... it's a little late to turn back. You said once that I didn't have a choice. I still don't." She drew a quick breath. "I'll probably be with him most of the day, and maybe tomorrow too, so it's best if I call you from the museum on Monday."

"Take care," he said quietly.

Storm cradled the receiver and sat there on the edge of the bed for a moment. It had taken all her resolution not to tell Wolfe that she loved him; only the knowledge that she couldn't tell him that when so much else was lies had kept her silent.

The worst lie was the one he would see when he finally discovered the truth. He would realize that part of her job had been to distract him, to keep his attention away from the installation of the new computer program and his suspicions away from Ace Security for as long as possible. He would see that very clearly. And he would very likely believe that her determined pursuit of him had been a means to that end.

Storm didn't know if he would ever believe her when she denied that, but she didn't have very much hope. If he knew her well enough... perhaps. If he cared about her enough to forgive the betrayal of trust... perhaps. If he understood her reasons... perhaps.

Storm rose from the bed and went to the bathroom. She could see him moving behind the frosted-glass shower door. She paused for only a moment, enjoying watching him, then slipped into the stall with him.

"Hi."

"Hi, yourself."

"I'll wash your back if you'll wash mine," she offered.

"Deal," Wolfe said, and pulled her into his arms.

After spending most of Friday night parked outside one museum and two jewelry stores, Morgan was feeling more than a little discouraged. She hadn't felt Quinn and she certainly didn't see him. She worked only a few hours on Saturday, then went home and took a nap.

By nine o'clock Saturday night she was back on watch, this time parked on a street where two jewelry stores occupied space across from each other.

By ten o'clock, she caught herself drumming her fingers against the steering wheel and realized she was listening intently.

Listening? Or feeling?

Morgan hesitated, then started her car and began driving. She didn't consciously choose a direction, yet at the same time she felt no hesitation in taking specific roads and turns until she found herself parked about half a block from the rear side of one of the smaller museums in the city. A museum not even on her watch list.

Baffled, she asked herself why Quinn would even bother with a museum containing artifacts that, however valuable, were too large for a single man to roll out with a wheelbarrow, far less tuck into a pouch attached to his belt.

That thought had barely occurred to her when Morgan stiffened, her eyes fixed on a service door of the museum. She couldn't see clearly because of the wispy fog, but it looked like at least three men coming out—and they were carrying a fourth between them.

Quinn.

All the men were wearing dark clothing, and she was too far away to be able to spot any identifying feature. But she knew it was him, just as she knew he had been in her museum more than once watching her. She knew it.

Felt it.

Frozen, she watched a dark van pull up near the men. They tossed the apparently unconscious Quinn into the back of the van, making Morgan wince because of the rough way they treated that limp body.

God, he couldn't be dead?

She pushed that thought away instantly, refusing to consider the possibility. He wasn't dead. She wouldn't be able to feel him if he was dead.

Would she?

No, of course not. In fact, she could probably only feel him now because he was unconscious and so unable to shut her out—or whatever he'd been doing to make sure she couldn't show up inconveniently wherever he meant to burgle.

So he wasn't dead. But he was obviously out cold. And what she should do, she thought as she watched the three other men get into the van, was call somebody. That was what she should do.

"911," she muttered to herself. "That's who I ought to call. Or Max. I could call Max, and tell him to get his Interpol agent out here and rescue— I mean *catch*—Quinn." She automatically put her car in gear as the van pulled away from the museum, and murmured somewhat helplessly, "Why am I not doing that?"

An hour later, Morgan felt the question more intensely. What on earth was she *doing*? She was being an idiot, that's what she was doing. Cautiously, her knowledge purely a matter of cops-and-robbers on television, she was following a van containing three probable bad guys and an internationally famous cat burglar who was either unconscious or dead.

She didn't know where they were going except for the vague notion that it was south, and she was swearing at herself in a monotone for a host of sins beginning with stupidity.

Tailing the van was relatively easy at first; the streets were busy even this late, Morgan had no trouble keeping a car or two between her and the van, and she wasn't stopped once by an inconvenient traffic light. But then traffic thinned, the fog thickened, and she had to get closer than she liked to the van or risk losing it.

It was less than twenty minutes later that it pulled over to the curb, and Morgan barely had the presence of mind to continue on past the van for a full block before turning into a side street. Until then, she'd paid very little attention to her surroundings, and when she did look she reached immediately for her cell phone to call 911.

No signal.

"Shit," she muttered, not at all cheered by the silent reminder to herself that this sort of thing happened to Scully and Mulder all the time. On TV, it was purely a question of cutting off the protagonists from easily accessed help, she knew that. Increased dramatic tension.

In real life, it was the universe giving her a hard time. Probably as payback for this absurd and undoubtedly wrong interest in a thief.

Chewing on her bottom lip, she looked at her surroundings. It hadn't been what anyone would have called a good neighborhood to begin with, and the last big earthquake had made a shambles of most of the buildings Morgan could see. Obviously, rebuilding wasn't high on any landlord's priority list. A dog barked somewhere off in the distance, but other than that there seemed to be no signs of life.

Swallowing, Morgan found her can of pepper spray in her purse, left the bag on the floorboard of the car, and got out. Her cell phone went into a back pocket of her jeans, just in case she was able to get a signal at some point. She locked up the car, then put her keys in a front pocket, reasoning that the police whistle would do nothing except draw unwelcome attention to her here.

The damned thing hadn't been helpful *at all*.

There were a few scattered streetlights casting a weird glow down through the fog, but they provided enough light for Morgan to find her way back to the van. It loomed up suddenly before her, freezing her in her tracks for a long moment until she realized there was no one in it. She checked just to make sure, but it was empty.

It was parked before a building that looked to be ten or twelve stories high, maybe an old office building, she thought. Most of the doors and windows were boarded up, and though she couldn't see it clearly, Morgan had the feeling this building had been condemned for a long time, even before the earthquake had rattled it. There was a smell about it, musty and disused, that said no one had lived here in a long time.

She checked her cell phone, and again the backlit display informed her the device was worse than useless. Unless, of course, she wanted to calculate a tip or play a game.

"Technology," she said under her breath. "Yeah, right."

She nonetheless made her way around the building with the utmost caution, looking for a way in. She found it in the rear—a warped door pulled half off its hinges—and about seven or eight stories up she saw a dim light coming from a boarded-up window. She paused for several minutes, her ears straining for any sound. She thought she heard a couple of dull thuds from up there, and once a ghostly laugh, but mostly what she heard was the frightened pounding of her heart.

She had to take several deep breaths before she could gather the courage to enter the building. It was awfully dark, even after her eyes adjusted a bit, and she had to use her free hand to feel gingerly along the wall.

The floor seemed fairly solid under her feet, and there didn't seem to be any obstructions of old furniture and the like to hinder her, but there were squeaks and rustles in the darkness that made Morgan grit her teeth and move a bit faster. She located a stairwell almost totally by touch, and her relief turned to wariness when she realized that there was dim light spilling down from somewhere above.

She moved with even more caution, her can of pepper spray held ready. Although she couldn't help but wonder how the small can would fare against three large and probably armed ruffians. Telling herself fiercely not to borrow trouble, she continued, always up. By the time she reached the fourth floor, she could see fairly well, and by the sixth she knew the light was only a couple of floors above her.

On the eighth-floor landing, she found a rusted old fire door hanging open, and just inside the hallway a battery lantern sat innocently on the floor. Morgan was tempted but didn't pick it up. Instead, she peered carefully through the doorway. She could see more light coming from a half-closed door at the end of the hallway and, when she strained, hear the indistinguishable sounds of voices.

Morgan checked her cell phone again, hoping she was high enough now, but there was still no signal. Jeez, here she was trying to be a Superfriend, and you'd think the bad guys had put a bubble of kryptonite around her.

It was almost funny. Not quite, but almost.

Now what? she mouthed to herself. After a slight hesitation, she slipped through the door and into the hall. Pressing herself tightly to the wall, she made her way slowly, her eyes fixed on that partially opened door. She was over halfway there when one voice rose harshly above the others and froze her—because it was so vicious and because she recognized it.

"It won't take us long to find out who you are. I'd kill you now, but you might come in handy for something later on. There might even be a price on your head."

And then, almost inaudible but reaching Morgan's straining ears like the sound of sweet, insouciant music, came Quinn's dry reply.

"No honor among thieves? I'm saddened, gentlemen, deeply saddened. To say nothing of being disillusioned."

"Shut up," the harsh voice ordered. "There's no way you're going to get loose, so don't bother trying. You can yell all you want; there's nobody to hear you. I'll be back in the morning when I decide what to do with you."

Morgan remained frozen for an instant longer, then gasped and slid along the wall to the nearest door. Not only was it not locked, it didn't even have a doorknob. She pushed it open and slipped into the room, then closed it again and pressed herself against the wall, trying to control her breathing. Within minutes, she heard footsteps passing the room where she was hiding, the heavy steps of large men.

She counted to ten slowly, then very cautiously opened her door and peered down the hall toward the stairwell. They had left the lantern, which rather surprised her, but she supposed they had flashlights. She debated for a moment but decided she could go back and get the lantern once she found out what Quinn's situation was. She was too impatient to wait any longer, hurrying down the hall toward the now-closed door.

When she neared it, she noticed a large, shiny metal hasp instead of a knob on the door; it was open since there was no padlock or pin with which to lock the hasp in place over the staple. And the door itself was a metal one, set with what looked to be very solid hinges.

Morgan wondered briefly what these very new bits of hardware were doing in this decrepit building—and a few possibilities garnered from thrillers on the late show made her shudder.

She was just reaching for the hasp when she heard the distant thuds of returning footsteps. Morgan looked toward the other end of the hallway, saw the flickering light of someone climbing up the stairs holding a flashlight, and felt a rush of panic. If she tried to move away from this door, she knew she would be seen; he'd be in this hallway within seconds, and the next nearest door was too far away for her to reach in time.

There was nothing else to do.

Swiftly, she opened the door to Quinn's prison and nipped inside, closing it gently behind her.

It was pitch dark and utterly silent in there. Morgan, pressed against the wall by the door, held her can of pepper spray ready as the heavy footsteps neared the door. Then, while she waited tensely, she heard several metallic noises, the faint squeak of a hinge, and then a solid click.

The footsteps went away, leaving Morgan sagged against the wall and filled with a horrible realization. Somebody had come back with a padlock, dammit.

C H A P T E R
THIRTEEN

Wonderful. She and Quinn were on the eighth floor of a condemned building, in a room with a very businesslike locked door barring their way, and even if they could pry the boards off the windows it was doubtful there was a fire escape.

While Morgan leaned there, silently cussing herself and Quinn, she heard a faint rustle and then a conversational voice.

"I seem to be saying this far too often lately, but—Morgana, what the hell are you doing here?"

She took a deep breath, relaxed her death grip on the can of pepper spray, and shoved it in an unoccupied pocket. "I happened to be in the neighborhood," she said, proud of her careless tone. It almost matched his.

"I see. Well, leaving the absurdity of that aside

for the moment, do you happen to have a trusty penknife or pair of sewing scissors?"

"Not on me. I have a cell phone, but no signal. A police whistle—and no friendlies near enough to hear it. My trusty can of pepper spray. And my car keys have a compass on them." She paused and sighed. "The universe hates me. I take it you're tied up?"

"Afraid so. And they took all my tools." He sighed as well, then spoke briskly. "This room is about twenty feet square, and my wretched cot is located about eight feet away from the door. If you could make your way over here and try your hand at untying these ropes, I would greatly appreciate it."

Morgan was surprised at her own calm. The only thing she could figure out was that she was in shock. So she was able to slowly cross the room, estimating the distance, until she felt the cot against her legs, and then kneel down on the hard floor beside it. Now, in which direction lay his head?

Querulously, he said, "What on earth is taking so long? All you have to do is—" He broke off with a peculiar sound.

Morgan hastily withdrew her hands, which had landed rather off target, so to speak. "Um—sorry," she murmured.

Quinn cleared his throat. "Not at all," he disclaimed politely, with only a trace of hoarseness in his voice. "I've always wondered what the attraction was in being held immobile by various bindings and...uh...caressed. There is a certain appeal, I must admit. Though I would, I believe, prefer to have my own hands free should you choose to—"

"Shut up," she ordered fiercely. "It's dark in here, that's why. I can't see what I'm doing."

He sighed. "Yes, of course. Foolish of me to think otherwise."

Morgan reached out again, this time with extreme caution, and encountered the bulky shape of his tool belt. She hoped. With more confidence, she felt the hard flatness of his stomach, and inched upward warily.

In a conversational tone, Quinn said, "You're repaying me for having stolen your necklace, aren't you, Morgana?"

Startled, she allowed her hands to lie flat over the steady rise and fall of his chest. "What?" She'd forgotten the necklace until he mentioned it.

"This torture. Here I lie, helpless and at your mercy, while you amuse yourself with me. If it's ravishment you have in mind, I shall bear it like a man, but please take care how you fondle my poor abused body. Those cretins were not kind."

Morgan grasped the salient fact among absurdities, and leaned closer as she demanded, "What did they do to you?"

"I would rather not discuss it," Quinn replied affably. "I would suggest, however, that you refrain from—Is that...? Yes, I believe so. Even in the dark, quite obvious. Rather prominent, aren't they?"

She straightened hastily. "Quinn, do you want to get out of here alive?" she asked irately.

"I—"

"Yes or no, dammit."

"Yes."

"Then stop making crude remarks."

He cleared his throat. "Admiring remarks, Morgana. Always admiring."

The wistfulness in his too-expressive voice made her want to giggle, but she overcame the ridiculous impulse. "Just shut up about my anatomy, or I'll leave you here to rot. Which is just what you deserve."

"Yes, ma'am," he murmured, not bothering to point out that both of them could rot here in the locked room, tied or not.

Morgan let her fingers resume their progress but stopped when they encountered the warmth of his throat. She swallowed as she realized he wasn't masked, but managed to say lightly, "My kingdom for a match."

He sighed. "Sorry I can't oblige. The ropes, Morgana, please. My fingers are going numb."

She couldn't resist the temptation to glide her fingertips over his face first, feeling smooth skin over his stubborn jaw and high cheekbones, an aristocratic nose, unbelievably long lashes, a high forehead, and thick, soft hair. She tried to be quick, hoping he'd think she was merely feeling her way in sheer indifference, but then he cleared his throat again and spoke in a slightly husky but wry tone.

"If I solemnly promise never to steal anything from you ever again, will you stop doing that, Morgana? At least while I'm bound and helpless?"

She bit her lip to hold back a sudden giggle. "As if I'd believe your promise. Ah—here we are."

His wrists were tied to the very sturdy posts of the cot, and Morgan's amusement faded when she felt how the ropes were digging into his wrists. It was difficult to untie ropes she couldn't see, but she worked at the knots fiercely, sacrificing her fingernails and even a bit of skin from her knuckles.

"What *are* you doing here?" he asked finally while she struggled with the ropes. "I didn't see much of it, but I believe this neighborhood is a long way from yours."

Morgan didn't want to tell him the truth, but she couldn't think of a convincing lie. All she could do was make it sound more casual than it had been. "I was driving by that museum—the one with all the sculpture and statuary—and saw three men throw you into a van."

He didn't ask how she had known it was him. They both knew the answer to that. Instead, he said, "So you followed them here?"

"It seemed like a good idea at the time," she

said, then made a little sound of triumph when the rope around his right wrist finally gave way.

In a judicious tone, Quinn said, "Morgana, that has to be the most reckless thing I have ever heard of in my life."

"Coming from you," she said, "that is praise of a high order. Can you move your—there, like that. Just another second now, and I think—got it!"

Quinn sat up on the cot, and though she couldn't see him she knew he was rubbing his wrists. "Thank you, sweet."

"Are your ankles—"

"I'll get those," he said.

She sat back on her heels, wishing there was just a bit more light so she could see his face. It would be too bad, she thought, if she went through all this and was denied a glimpse of his naked face. She felt she'd earned that much.

"Quinn...the man who threatened to kill you, the one with the vicious voice—that was Ed, wasn't it? One of that gang of thieves who were robbing the museum the night we met?"

Untying his ankles, Quinn said, "You have a good ear."

"Then you ran into them again? Don't tell me you wound up burgling the same place a second time?"

"Ridiculous, isn't it? And unfortunate—this time, they caught me."

A bit dryly, Morgan said, "If you guys keep

bumping into each other like this, people will begin to talk." She was about to ask him what had
interested him in that particular museum when he
distracted her.

He chuckled softly. "Morgana, I've missed you."

With an effort, she ignored that. "You stole my
one good piece of jewelry, you lousy thief. You and
I have a score to settle. That is, if we ever get out of
here."

The cot creaked as he moved, and she felt the
brush of his legs as he swung them to the floor. "I
have no intention of waiting here for the charming
Ed to return. If I did, I've a feeling my next bit of
publicity would be an obituary."

Morgan winced. "You could have gone all night
without saying that. What's the plan?"

"To get out," Quinn replied succinctly.

"There's a padlock on the door—and it's the
one door in this whole miserable building built to
do its job. We're on the eighth floor. How do you
propose to get out?"

"There are windows, aren't there?" He got to
his feet a bit gingerly and caught his breath, mut-
tering, "Dammit."

Morgan heard the note of pain in his voice and
quickly got up herself. She reached out carefully,
relieved when she touched his arm. "Are you all
right?"

He let out a low laugh. "That, sweet, is a loaded

question. Let's just say I'm functional, and leave it at that."

She let go of his arm, sensing rather than hearing it when he moved past her toward the faint chinks of light representing the windows. "The windows must be barred," she offered.

Quinn didn't answer for a moment, but then she heard a low, groaning creak and a satisfied sound from him. "Ah—just as I hoped. This room is designed more to keep things out than in. The metal grating over the windows swings in."

Morgan tried to remember what she'd seen of the building. Precious little, because of the fog. "But most of the windows are boarded up on the outside."

"Yeah." There was a loud thud, then another, and Quinn's powerful kick sent one of the boards flying.

The amount of light that came streaming into the room would have been pitiful under other circumstances, but to Morgan it was a veritable ray of sunshine. She blinked, moving toward it, and didn't realize until he kicked another board loose that she could see him now.

He was fair, which surprised her a bit, his hair thick and a pale color that was either gold or silver. He was also a little younger than she would have guessed, possibly in his early thirties. And his face, his naked face, was visible to her for the first time. Even in the pallid, wispy light it was a good face. A strong face, with plenty of character. It was the face she had touched. Lean and unusually handsome, with high cheekbones, a patrician nose, and those vivid green eyes set under flying brows.

It was a face Morgan knew she would never forget, no matter what happened.

It was also somewhat the worse for wear, boasting what was going to be a beautiful shiner around his right eye and another bruise high on his left cheekbone. Since she knew he'd been unconscious during part of tonight, she thought he probably had quite a headache from having been knocked out. It said something about his nature, she thought, that he could maintain his sense of humor under such conditions.

Unconscious of her scrutiny, Quinn leaned through the opening he'd made and said, "We're in luck. There's a kind of catwalk out here. If it wraps the building, we should find a fire escape or at least an open window to get us into an unlocked room."

The description filled Morgan with foreboding. When he drew back enough for her to see past him, her fears were realized. A "kind" of catwalk indeed; it looked more like one of those rickety things window washers used, except that it was affixed to the side of the building as if intended to be permanent.

Then again, it could just as easily have been intended to be somebody's insane idea of artwork.

"I think not," she said politely. "If you want to

try it, go ahead. And, if you make it, call the police and ask them to come get me, would you?"

Quinn shook his head slightly and looked at her with a serious expression. "Morgana, we have no way of knowing how much time we have here. Despite what he said, Ed could have tossed a lighted match downstairs, or left one of his bullies to do it later. The place could be wired for the sole purpose of getting rid of some nasty little problem—like a witness. We can't waste any time. We have to go. Now."

She wasn't happy, but her common sense told her Quinn was right. The sooner they got out of here the better off they were bound to be. Squashing her fears and keeping her eyes fixed on his face, she said, "All right, but if you get me killed I'll haunt you forever."

He smiled, and if his voice held charm it was nothing compared to that crooked, beguiling smile. "Good girl. Just follow behind me—not too close, we need to distribute the weight as much as possible—and keep your back against the building."

Morgan waited while he climbed through the window and eased his weight onto the catwalk. Then, looking at him and not at anything else, she followed.

For about twenty feet, all went well. Afterward, Morgan was never able to decide if what happened was due to the age of the building, earthquake damage, or some sick joke perpetrated by Ed or someone like him.

All she knew was that their catwalk just sort of disintegrated in midair with an unthreatening little *whoosh* sound.

If she hadn't been obeying Quinn's instructions to walk close to the building, Morgan never would have been able to catch herself. As it was, she was barely able to balance herself well enough to keep from toppling off the treacherously narrow ledge that was all that was left of their catwalk.

As for Quinn, he'd been moving a little farther out, and the sudden drop of the catwalk almost got him. If he hadn't had exceptionally powerful hands with which to grip the ledge, he never would have been able to save himself.

He caught his balance with the agility of a cat and used the muscles of his arms and shoulders to pull himself up. He felt his way by touch alone, his gaze fixed unwaveringly on Morgan. She was pressed back against the wall, her slender body rigid and her head tilted slightly so that she was looking up rather than down.

"All right?" he called softly.

"Oh, I'm fine." Her voice was unnaturally calm.

Quinn frowned slightly but, satisfied that she was in no immediate danger—the section of ledge on which she was standing looked fairly solid, at least for the moment—he turned his attention to their predicament. The catwalk had taken bits of the building with it when it collapsed, depriving them of most of the pitiful ledge on which they were standing.

The ledge had given way cleanly on the other side of Morgan, which made it impossible for them to retreat to their prison even if they wanted to; on this side of her, and between their positions, at least two gaping cracks were mute evidence of instability. Climbing up to the roof would be useless; he knew from the style of what he had seen of the building that the roof would be steeply pitched and covered with slippery, fog-wet tiles. And though he possessed the skill and ability to rappel down, there was nothing to which a rope could be securely fastened—even if he had one.

"Don't move," he told her.

"Don't worry."

He had to smile a little at her tart response, but his sense of danger urged him to move swiftly. Testing each foothold cautiously, he eased ahead toward the corner of the building. At least twice, the ledge beneath him crumbled, and he knew even before he reached it that the corner was badly cracked and unlikely to be able to hold his weight. He paused, still some feet from the corner, and considered rapidly.

"I'm going to climb up to the next ledge," he said finally. "All the windows on this floor are boarded up, but there may be one uncovered above us."

"Great," she said faintly.

Despite his assured statement, Quinn wasn't looking forward to what he had to do. There was no way to anchor himself and precious little to hold on to since there was no catwalk, crumbling or otherwise, for the floor above. Aside from which the building was cursed with jutting bits of stonework guaranteed to do nothing except get in his way. By reaching up, he could grasp the ledge above them, but it was smooth and slippery, offering no purchase for his grip.

It was a long way to the ground.

Quinn closed his mind to that and concentrated on necessity. He managed to turn his body, balancing sideways on the narrow ledge with his feet wide apart to more evenly distribute his weight. He reached up with both hands and carefully explored the ledge, hoping for a tiny projection that would give him a better grip. He had to take a step back toward Morgan before he found what he sought, and the ledge crumbled beneath his foot just as his fingers closed over the sharp projection.

It held. Hardly breathing, Quinn boosted himself up by using the strength of one arm, his soft-soled boots scrabbling for a foothold against the side of the building, until he could get the other arm over the ledge. Moments later, he was lying full-length against the building on a ledge less than a foot wide.

"Quinn?"

"Hmmm?" Still holding to his tiny projection, he rested his forehead on his arm and wondered idly how he got into situations like this one. His head was throbbing from the earlier blow, several parts of his face hurt, his wrists were raw, and he had the suspicion that at least two ribs were cracked.

Not one of his better days.

"Are you all right?" Morgan's voice was beginning to show signs of strain.

"Peachy." He lifted his head and then sat up carefully, looking around. Ah. Just as he'd hoped—an uncovered window. And it was directly above Morgan's position. "Let me get set," he said, "and I'll pull you up."

"I don't think so. I don't want to be a bother," she said conversationally, "but I feel I should mention I have this thing about heights."

Feeling relatively secure on his perch, Quinn leaned out a bit so that he could look down at her. "Now's a fine time to tell me."

"I was hoping it wouldn't come up," she murmured.

"Lousy pun."

She made an odd sound that might have been a laugh on the edge of breaking. "Unintentional, I promise you. Look—why don't you get yourself down and then send for the fire department. They have nice ladders."

Quinn didn't bother to remind her that they

couldn't afford the time. Instead, he slid along the ledge until he was directly above her. He had the window open in seconds, though it took considerable muscle to force the ancient sash upward. He moved as quickly as he could, virtually certain that Morgan's calm was tenuous; she had a great deal of courage, he thought, but phobias could turn even the stoutest hearts to jelly.

The room he found himself in was empty of anything he might have used to help her. He braced himself as well as he was able, then leaned out the window and across the ledge, stretching one hand down to her.

"Give me your hand, Morgana."

"Sorry. I can't move."

"You won't lose your balance. Just reach directly above your head with one hand."

"No. I'll fall."

Quinn's voice remained calm and certain. "Sweetheart, I won't let you fall. I promise. You know I keep my promises."

She was still for a moment, then slowly reached upward with her right hand until her fingers closed convulsively around his wrist. He locked his fingers around her far more delicate wrist, making sure he had a good grip.

"All right. I've got you. Now, I want you to turn around until you're facing the wall. You'll be able to climb more easily if you can use your feet."

"I can't do that."

"Yes, you can. Just—"

"What am I doing here?" she said in a voice of total bewilderment. "I'm on the side of a building. This is absurd. I don't do things like this."

"Of course not. Turn around and face the building, like a good girl."

Irritably, she said, "I'm not a child."

"Then stop acting like one," he told her sharply. He could feel her stiffen, and a jolt of relief went through him when she began to turn around. He had infinite patience as well as genuine sympathy for her feelings and would have hung out the window for hours if necessary—but from this position he could see a crack in the ledge between her feet, and it was widening.

She began to unbalance as she turned, but he was ready for that possibility. It wasn't the first time he'd lifted her weight, and since she was a small woman he had no trouble supporting her, even though his ribs gave him merry hell. And, unfortunately, Morgan's anatomy made it somewhat painful for her to be dragged over the edge of the ledge and through the window.

Several breathless moments later, she was standing inside the dim room with him, half consciously rubbing the parts of her that had been abused.

"Shall I kiss it and make it better?" Quinn asked, entirely his insouciant self again.

Morgan shrugged off his supporting arm and took a pointed step away from him. "No, you shall not." Her retort was more automatic than annoyed, and she followed it by saying sincerely, "But thanks for not leaving me out there to roost."

"It was the least I could do, since you saved my hide earlier. And now I think we should vacate this firetrap before our friends come back."

"You won't get an argument. Lead on, Macduff." She followed him in silence as he moved through the dark hall of the ninth floor toward the stairwell. Her panic out on the ledge had been the frozen kind, and with relatively solid flooring underneath her now, even the ghostly echoes of fear were gone. In any case, she was wrestling with other ghosts now.

Loyalty, for one.

Quinn had, in all probability, saved her life. Perhaps, as he'd said, he had felt that he owed her that, but the fact remained that she probably would have died without him. (Never mind that she wouldn't have been here in the first place if she hadn't gone haring after him.) The ledge beneath her had been crumbling, she knew. He had saved her from certain death; she had merely untied him—something he probably could have done himself, given time.

She owed him. But she owed Max Bannister her loyalty.

"You're very quiet," Quinn noted as he opened the door of the stairwell and began descending with the cautious speed of a man who knows the building's unsafe.

Morgan wrestled the ghosts for two more flights downward, then sighed. Holding her voice steady, she said, "Stay away from Bannister's collection, Quinn."

He was silent himself for another flight, then stopped on a shadowy landing and turned to look at her. "Is there any reason aside from the obvious one why I should?"

"Yes. Because it's a trap." She drew a deep breath and gazed up at him. "There's an Interpol agent working with Max. They want to catch you."

C H A P T E R
FOURTEEN

Quinn looked down at her, expressionless. "I see. The collection is bait."

She nodded. "The only bait virtually guaranteed to draw a world-famous thief across an ocean and a continent." It was difficult to read his face, still an unfamiliar one to her, but she thought his handsome features held a curious sort of admiration.

"Why warn me, Morgana?"

"I pay my debts," she answered stiffly.

"Even if the price is loyalty?"

His soft voice was like salt rubbed in a wound, and she lifted her chin higher as she stared up at him. "I'll make peace with my conscience in my own way," she said. "And peace with Max. Maybe he'll forgive me. Maybe he won't. But I owed you something. Now we're even."

"Not quite," he said, and pulled her into his arms.

In the back of Morgan's mind was the realization that this was no sneaky distraction from a thief who wanted to steal some bauble she wore; this was something else.

It was also insane, and she knew it. She knew it when a strange, feverish tremor rippled through her body, when her arms went around his waist, when her mouth opened eagerly beneath his.

She knew it when she realized he had stolen more from her than a simple ruby necklace.

It was dumb, and reckless, and hopelessly irrational—and Morgan didn't fight it because she couldn't.

He lifted his head at last, and his voice was a bit husky when he said, "We have to get out of here."

She nodded silently and didn't protest when he stepped back, but she felt grateful when he reached for her hand and held it the rest of the way down the stairwell. She didn't want to think at all, because she was coping with the shock of realizing that she was falling for a thief.

Quinn didn't waste any time getting them out of the building, moving swiftly but cautiously. As soon as they were outside, he said, "Where's your car?"

Morgan gestured silently and walked beside him down the block to the side street where she'd parked. He released her hand and waited while she unlocked and opened the driver's side door. Then, softly, he said, "Get out of here, Morgana."

She blinked up at him. "You...?"

"I'll be fine. You go home. And—thank you for charging to my rescue. It almost gives me hope..."

She thought for a minute that he was slipping into his teasing, Don Juan persona, and she thought she would never forgive him if he did.

But then he stepped closer and bent his head to kiss her with a gentleness that made her throat ache. "I think you're going to break my heart," he murmured. Before she could respond, he had faded back into the fog and darkness of the night.

After a long moment, Morgan got into her car and drove away from the shattered buildings.

Wolfe had made an effort to charm Storm's enigmatic cat, scratching him under the chin and feeding him bits of meat from their Sunday night dinner in the suite, but he didn't think he'd made much of an impression.

Until Monday morning. That was when he woke up in Storm's bed, with her cuddled up to his side as usual, and found the little blond cat curled up in the crook of her arm—which was flung across his chest. Wolfe had felt the most absurd sense of triumph as he'd lain there with Storm in his arms and her cat sleeping on his chest.

He didn't want to disturb either of them, but

since neither he nor Storm could afford to spend a weekday away from the museum with the scheduled opening of the *Mysteries Past* exhibit so near, he didn't have much choice.

One discovery he had made was that Storm wasn't a morning person. She was never grumpy, just sleepy and utterly limp—and he was amused to find that her cat was just the same. When he lifted Bear from his chest, the small golden cat hung from his hand as though he were boneless, enigmatic green eyes closed.

"Wake up, you ridiculous cat," Wolfe said, gently shaking the dangling handful of fur.

Sleepily, Storm murmured, "He's not a morning person either."

"Well, he has to wake up. You too; I want to take you out for breakfast on the way to the museum."

She levered herself up on an elbow and peered at him, her green eyes drowsy. "Oh, God, it's Monday, isn't it?"

"Afraid so." He thought about spending eight or nine hours with her at the museum, frustrated by people coming and going all around them, and wondered if he could talk her into returning to his apartment or coming back here at lunchtime.

Storm sighed gustily. "It's going to be a long day."

Wolfe wondered if she meant it the same way he thought, but didn't ask. He slid a hand into her wild, tumbled hair and raised his head to kiss her, absently returning Bear to his chest.

She smiled at him when the kiss ended. "Let's come back here for lunch."

"You're on."

She pushed herself up until she was half sitting, her long hair veiling her nakedness, and Wolfe tried to distract himself before the urge to haul her back down beside him became too strong to fight. The distraction he found was when he realized that Bear was still on his chest, sprawled out now with boneless legs and one ear folded under, snoring softly.

"He's still asleep?"

"I told you, he's not a morning person." Storm reached over and found the tip of the cat's tail, then pinched it gently.

Bear's head jerked up, his eyes blinking sleepily, and his vivid little face was such a feline replica of Storm's that Wolfe burst out laughing. Jostled a bit by the chest moving under him, Bear sort of moaned, "Yahhh," and tumbled off Wolfe to the bed beside him.

Still chuckling, Wolfe said, "I'm glad at least one of us is easy to wake up."

"All he needs is food," Storm said. "And all I need is a shower and coffee."

They shared the shower, and despite Wolfe's good intentions, the steamy heat in the stall had less to do with hot water than with their response to each other. It was the second time he had wanted her so badly that he hadn't been able to wait long enough to get them out of the shower, and since Storm was every bit as urgent, their joining was so explosive it left them drained and clinging to each other.

"Or maybe I don't need coffee," she murmured, rubbing her wet, rosy cheek against his chest.

"If we keep doing this," he told her ruefully, "what I'm going to need is a chiropractor."

"Are you complaining?"

"Hell, no."

He didn't feel like complaining about anything—except the fact that both of them had to go to work. They stopped at a small restaurant for breakfast, and Wolfe amused Storm by saving a piece of his bacon to take to the little cat waiting patiently for them in the car.

"I fed him at the hotel," she reminded him.

"I know. He just looked so . . . woeful when we left him out there."

Storm chuckled. "If you let him brainwash you with those pathetic looks, he'll have you right where he wants you. Cats are the world's worst opportunists."

Wolfe didn't argue with her; he had the sheepish idea that she was right. But he took the bacon out to Bear anyway.

It was after nine when they got to the museum, and Wolfe found himself unusually conscious of the guards' impassive observation as he carried most of Storm's homework in for her. It bothered him only because those same guards had watched him, during the course of the past months, being dropped off or picked up by a succession of blondes, and he wanted to tell them this was something entirely different. Except that it wasn't any of their business anyway.

When she unlocked the door of the computer room, he carried her stuff in and piled it on the desk. "Are you going to be stuck in here all day?" he asked her.

"Pretty much," she said, smiling up at him. "I have to load all the floor plans and security hardware diagrams into the computer to form the basis of the security program, so that means I have to stay close."

He sighed. "I'll be on the phone all morning with Lloyd's. And this afternoon I need to go and talk to the police about that robbery Saturday night." The morning paper delivered to Storm's hotel suite had told them the bare facts of the robbery, but Wolfe believed he could get more information from his police contacts.

Storm had brought the paper with her, since she wanted to study it more carefully, and glanced at it where it lay on her desk. "Did that museum have a modern security system?" she asked, thinking he'd know.

"Yeah, very modern. And I want to find out how they got past it."

"They?" Storm looked up at him curiously. "The article said only a few large pieces were taken and that there was no way to know who the thief was. Do you have some idea?"

Wolfe shrugged. "The way things have been vanishing in this city, you'd think we had a wandering black hole. Do I have an idea? Sure, plenty of them. But all I know for certain is that we have at least one gang of thieves operating in San Francisco and God knows how many independent contractors or collectors."

"And Quinn," Storm said.

"And Quinn." Wolfe frowned. "I've been meaning to ask how you knew he was in town. The police haven't publicly linked him to any theft so far, and neither have the newspapers."

Silently cursing the slip, Storm shrugged and said, "Morgan told me he was in town."

"She would."

"Correct me if I'm wrong, but since he's been in the city for weeks, apparently, and all we can be sure he's stolen is a single jeweled dagger, shouldn't he be pretty high up on our list of concerns? I mean, he must be waiting for something, and if it's the opening of *Mysteries Past*..."

Wolfe looked a bit grim. "Yeah, I know. That's one reason I want to talk to the cops, to find out if they have any suspicions it might have been him

Saturday night. Since only a few choice pieces were taken, it sounds more like him or one of the other collectors than that gang. I need to know."

She nodded. "Makes sense. Let me know what you find out?"

"Of course." He leaned down to kiss her, ending up with both arms wrapped around her when he lifted her completely off her feet, a position Storm clearly enjoyed as much as he did.

Reluctantly, he leaned back down to set her on her feet, and when he released her and straightened he found he'd acquired a passenger.

Obviously surprised that her cat had transferred to Wolfe's shoulder from her own, Storm said, "If it bothers you, just set him on the desk."

Wolfe hesitated, but he liked the slight, warm weight of the little cat and he was still feeling a bit proud at having won over Storm's familiar. "No, it's okay. At least—he won't dig his claws in every time I move, will he?"

"Only if you startle him by moving suddenly. Actually, his balance is pretty good, so he hardly needs to hold on. If he wants down, he'll tell you, and that's when you should bring him back here. I've got his litter box in here, remember."

He knew that; it was over in a corner of the room and matched the one she kept in her hotel suite.

"I'll remember." Still, he hesitated, finally bending to kiss her again, this time briefly.

When he left, she went slowly around the desk and got settled, turning on the computer and trying to arrange the clutter into some kind of order. When the computer was ready for input, she set it up to begin receiving all the data concerning specific details of the museum and the various security hardware. All that was ready to be transferred from disks, which the previous computer programmer had prepared and which Storm had found to be perfectly acceptable.

While the computer began digesting data, Storm eyed her telephone, mentally decided to postpone the necessary call, and drew the newspaper toward her. She was very curious about the Saturday night robbery.

She had just read the short article through for the second time when a light voice said, "Buy you a cup of coffee?"

Her first thought was that Morgan was upset about something, though it was more a perception than a certainty. The brunette seemed both keyed up and curiously calm, as if she had dragged on a surface tranquility to mask a deep turmoil. And it was that more than anything else that caused Storm to agree affably and accept the cup Morgan had brought with her.

"Thanks. Have a seat," she invited.

The computer room's one visitor's chair was shoved over into a corner to be out of the way, so

Morgan casually sat on the edge of the big desk. "Where's your cat?" she asked.

"With Wolfe."

"Oh-ho—is that as promising as I think it is?" Storm widened her eyes innocently.

Smiling slightly, Morgan said, "Listen, I know it's none of my business, but I've got to know. When he went tearing out of here Friday after I delivered your message, Wolfe was madder than I've ever seen him. He looked like he wanted to strangle you. Or something."

Clearing her throat, Storm murmured, "He didn't strangle me."

"So I see. Would I be far off in assuming that you two spent the weekend together?"

"Let's put it this way," Storm said. "When Wolfe woke up this morning—Bear was on his chest."

"Do I offer congratulations?" Morgan asked solemnly.

"Not just yet. We have a few hurdles to get over before anything's settled."

A bit dryly, Morgan said, "Some of his past ladies had pets, and, believe me, Wolfe kept his distance. He didn't want to get involved, and it showed. If he's wearing your cat on his shoulder, it's just a matter of time."

Storm had felt hopeful about that herself, but since the hurdles looming ahead were bad ones, she didn't let herself hope too much. With a slight shrug, she said, "Maybe. But, speaking of his past ladies, did you see Nyssa Armstrong leave here on Friday?"

"No, why?"

"It's kind of a funny thing." Storm hesitated, but she didn't see any reason not to tell Morgan about it. "Wolfe and I went out to the ballpark Saturday night to see the Giants, and I could have sworn I saw her in the crowd."

"Nyssa? At a *baseball* game?"

"Like I said—kind of funny, huh? There was a home run hit just then that distracted me, and when I looked again I couldn't see her. But I'm pretty sure it was her. I didn't tell Wolfe, but I wondered about it."

In a theatrical tone that would have shamed one of those old radio thrillers, Morgan said, "She's obviously following you. Slinking along on your trail, bitter and heartbroken because you lured Wolfe from her bed. She's probably sharpening her knife even as we speak, her serial-killer eyes glittering with insane rage and jealousy while she plots how best to slay you and get away with it."

Storm blinked and then giggled. "Yeah, right."

Morgan grinned at her. "Hey, don't scoff. I read a book just last week where that was the killer's motive. She got away with it too. Better watch your back."

Storm shook her head and tapped the newspaper still lying open on her desk. "This is the kind of crime I'm more concerned with at the moment. Did you hear about it?"

"The robbery? Yeah, I heard about it."

"Wolfe thinks it might have been Quinn," Storm ventured, watching the other woman carefully because she sensed more than saw Morgan tense. "How about you?"

Morgan peered into her coffee cup and pursed her lips slightly, the picture of frowning concentration. "No, I don't think it was him."

"Why not?"

Amber eyes flicked toward Storm, then away again, and instead of answering, Morgan said, "I met him, you know. Quinn. A few weeks ago."

"Did you?" Storm waited a moment, then added quietly, "I'm a good listener. And I don't tell tales out of school."

"I always liked that phrase," Morgan said with a brief smile. "Telling tales out of school...It makes secrets sound like innocent things."

"But sometimes they aren't," Storm murmured. "Sometimes they're dangerous."

It really was a pity he'd lost Carla. He always felt much more in control when his tools knew what the stakes were, even though it was riskier. Having someone on the inside who was completely unaware of being used lacked something, he'd always thought.

Still, there were benefits to using an oblivious tool, and he was fully aware of them. There were also drawbacks, of which he was just as aware; it was a far less direct approach, and he had to be careful how he asked his questions.

But during this pleasant brunch meeting, he didn't have to ask much of anything at all. He just had to listen.

"I don't know about his new security system being installed at the museum. The programmer is supposed to be one of the best, but...she doesn't look the part, for one thing. And I'm not at all sure it's even possible to use the old hardware with all this new software. Bannister is providing some new hardware, of course, but it's still bound to be a patchwork, don't you think?"

"Sounds like it."

"And there are all these thieves in the city. That gang the police can't seem to get close to, for one. I also heard a rumor that Quinn might be here. Have you heard that?"

"As a matter of fact, I have."

"Christ, I hope not. That's all I need."

"Perhaps he's after something besides the Bannister collection."

"Are you kidding? That collection is every thief's wet dream."

"Still, there are plenty of other valuables in the city." As host, he offered more wine.

"Oh, I shouldn't. I shouldn't have had any, really. It's so early, and I have to get back."

He smiled. "If I've learned anything, it's that life is all too short. We never know what might be waiting just around the next corner."

His companion laughed. "Live today, for tomorrow we may die?"

"Exactly." He filled both glasses, still smiling. "Tomorrow we may die."

"Yeah. Secrets can be dangerous." Morgan sighed and set her coffee cup down on the desk. Then, quickly and somewhat tersely, she told Storm about her first late-night meeting with an infamous cat burglar named Quinn several weeks before. About him stealing her ruby necklace right off her neck—though she didn't go into detail about *that*. And, finally, about what had happened on Saturday night. Everything except for what Morgan had overheard here in the museum and those final few minutes with Quinn.

Storm drew a deep breath and murmured, "Wow. You're a braver man than I am, Gunga Din."

"Actually, I was terrified. I don't know what possessed me to do such a ridiculous, dangerous thing." Morgan frowned down at her coffee cup, one hand toying with the handle. "So, anyway, I know it wasn't him that robbed that particular museum Saturday night. I mean, he was obviously *going* to, but that gang got in his way ... or whatever."

Storm leaned back in her chair and folded her hands over her stomach as she watched the other woman. "Sort of reminds me of something I once read about Byron," she said.

Her lazy drawl made the name sound curiously exotic, and it took a moment or so for Morgan to realize her friend was referring to the English poet. "Byron? You're comparing Quinn to Lord Byron?"

Storm smiled. "It's something somebody once said about Byron. Don't remember who, but it must've been a woman. She said Byron was 'mad, bad, and dangerous to know.' That sounds a lot like your Quinn."

"He isn't mine," Morgan denied automatically. But then she remembered his last words, and a little shiver went through her. Absurd, of course. It had just been another of his Don Juan lines designed to throw her off balance. She'd need her head examined if she took anything that despicable thief said seriously.

She was the director of a forthcoming exhibit of priceless art and antiquities, and that was the only reason Quinn kept turning up in her life.

The only reason.

"If you say so," Storm murmured.

Morgan felt a bit startled, until she realized that

Storm was remarking on her own statement that the infamous cat burglar was definitely not hers.

She eyed the other woman, then sighed. "The point is, Quinn's definitely in San Francisco. That's really what I came in here to tell you. I know Wolfe probably told you, but I just wanted to make sure you knew." What she wanted to do was ask Storm if her computer system was being geared toward capturing Quinn, but she didn't dare. Having discovered the plan by eavesdropping, Morgan was very hesitant to betray knowledge of what was going on. Besides that, she couldn't be sure who else—aside from Max and the Interpol agent—was really involved in this.

If Wolfe was involved, he must have decided to take his orders solely from Max rather than Lloyd's of London, because the insurance company would certainly be wild if they found out the priceless collection they insured was being used as bait. But that was possible, because Max and Wolfe were half brothers and blood was thicker than employment.

However, if *Storm* knew, then that must mean that Ace Security was also involved, which seemed unlikely.

The problem was, Morgan decided, she couldn't really ask anybody except Max what was going on. And that meant she'd have to confess her eavesdropping to him. It also meant that, somewhere along the way, she would have to confess to Max that she'd warned Quinn about the trap.

But maybe she could put that off for a while....

"Since he's in town," Storm was saying calmly, "he's bound to be interested in the collection. Is that why you told me? So I'd keep it in mind while I'm writing the program?"

Morgan shrugged. "I figured it couldn't hurt." She picked up her coffee cup and sipped the cooling liquid. "By the way, Max is back from his honeymoon. He stopped by here after hours on Friday to look over the exhibit wing. I haven't talked to him."

"Then I better get busy," Storm said, "and earn my pay."

Removing herself from the desk, Morgan said, "You and me both. See you later."

"You bet." Storm sat there for a long moment after the brunette had gone, then got up and went to shut the door. When she returned to her desk, she paused only to feed another disk into the computer before drawing the phone toward her and picking up the receiver.

He answered on the first ring, and his "Yeah" was impatient.

"It's me," she said.

"We have to meet," he said. "Today."

Storm sighed. "That's not going to be easy. It'll be impossible before lunchtime, I know that."

"How about during lunch?"

She felt her face get hot as she remembered her aroused suggestion that they return to her suite for lunch and Wolfe's prompt agreement. Despite the passionate shower that had followed, Storm had a strong feeling they'd still go back to her hotel for something other than lunch. Food would be an afterthought.

"Storm?"

She cleared her throat. "I don't think so. Look, Wolfe said he'd probably go talk to the police sometime after lunch about the robbery Saturday night. Maybe then. But I didn't drive my Jeep this morning, so I'd have to take a cab."

He swore softly. "I don't know how much time we've got."

Just as softly, Storm said, "I wish I had a little more."

After a moment, he said, "The longer this goes on, the worse it's going to be. You know that."

She knew that. "I'll call you when Wolfe leaves the museum, and we can arrange to meet. All right?"

"Yeah, all right."

She cradled the receiver gently and sat staring across the room blindly. Hurdles—God. They were walls, giant stone walls she couldn't get over or around. She was lying to the man she loved, and she was terrified he'd never forgive her for it.

CHAPTER
FIFTEEN

Morgan returned from lunch to find a messenger waiting for her, with a large envelope sent by Inspector Keane Tyler. She opened the outer envelope, looked at the folder inside, then picked up the phone and called him.

"You got this stuff quicker than I'd expected," she told him.

"Well, it's not like he's anonymous. I mean, we may not know who he really is, but Quinn the master thief is well known to every police force in the West—and a few in the East."

"The East?"

"You haven't read the file yet?"

"No, I just got it. Quinn's committed robberies in the East? As in the eastern part of the world?"

"Definitely in Hong Kong. Possibly Tokyo,

though evidence there pointing specifically to him is iffy. Singapore's a maybe too." Keane sighed. "What can I tell you, the guy gets around."

"I guess so. Um... but this *is* the first time he's hit the States, right?"

"Far as we know, yeah. We don't think it was him Saturday night, if you were wondering."

"You think it was that gang?"

"Pretty sure, just from what was taken. Unless Quinn has started working with a partner, the missing items are too damned heavy for one man to have carted out of there. Even him."

Morgan stared down at the still-closed file lying before her on the desk, wondering at her own reluctance to open it. Because she didn't really want to see the black-and-white facts of the crimes he had committed?

"Morgan? Still there?"

"Yeah. Listen, do I need to get this file back to you?"

"No, everything is copies of what I could get, so keep it. I have another set of copies ready for Wolfe when he gets here. He's been asking about Quinn too."

"I'm surprised Lloyd's wouldn't know at least as much about Quinn as the San Francisco P.D. does," she said slowly.

"Oh, they probably do, at least as far as his history goes. I gather Wolfe is more interested in whether we have any information on Quinn's movements since he arrived here in the city."

"And do you?"

Keane chuckled. "Well, like I told you before, he isn't exactly at the top of our most wanted list at the moment. I'm not saying we aren't concerned with robberies, but we've got half a dozen murders on our plate right now, never mind the assorted other crimes of violence. What you know about Quinn and his activities here is pretty much all we know."

Morgan felt a jab of guilt, but all she said was, "Okay. Well, if you do learn anything new, I'd appreciate it if you could pass it on. And thanks for the file."

"Welcome. See you, Morgan."

"Bye, Keane." She cradled the receiver and drew a deep breath, then opened the file.

Keane Tyler was a good cop, and he had been thorough; Quinn had been a highly successful thief for the better part of a decade, so the file filled with copies of police reports and newspaper clippings was a thick one.

"Jesus," Morgan heard herself murmur at one point as she read an account of an incredibly daring robbery in the penthouse of a Hong Kong highrise. That report was followed by other equally daring, seemingly impossible robberies in various parts of the world. Time after time, sophisticated security systems were breached with almost laughable ease. Time after time, Quinn got in and out without leaving so much as a hair of his blond head behind.

And with literally hundreds of millions of dollars worth of jewelry, gems, and artworks. Maybe even billions.

As she slowly absorbed the enormity of Quinn's career, Morgan understood what Keane had meant about unusually brilliant, talented men needing to push themselves. Because it couldn't possibly have been the money: Quinn had stolen enough long, long ago to live in luxurious style on a tropical island somewhere for the rest of his natural life.

It was the rush.

That had to be it, had to be why he was still active. Still pushing himself, challenging himself with more-difficult robberies, with more-advanced security systems. Taller buildings, tougher safes, riskier goals. Constantly testing his own limits as well as the skills and intelligence of police forces around the world.

And, along with all that, running the almost inevitable risk of being caught, possibly even injured. Or killed.

Morgan closed the file at last and put it away in her desk drawer. She sat there for a long time, elbows on her blotter, chin resting on her raised, clasped hands. She thought, and she did her level best to think logically. Rationally.

Quinn was a criminal. Worse, he was a criminal

who was also a danger junkie. He loved the rush, loved the risk, loved pitting his intelligence and skills against the smartest cops and the toughest security systems in existence. And he was going to go on testing their limits and his own until he ran headlong into a brick wall.

Or a bullet.

He'd retire from robbery only that way. Either he would get caught or he would get dead. It was highly unlikely he'd live to be a roguish old man chasing after nurses in the Retired Thieves Home.

That was the first point. But there were other, equally important points. Robbing only the rich didn't make him Robin Hood, it made him a thief—period. The fact that he had never hurt anyone in the course of a robbery didn't make him a good man, it was just more evidence he was a smart man: Simple robbery carried a lesser penalty than either armed robbery or murder.

The fact that he had saved her from possible death or at least likely injury on two separate occasions didn't change anything.

He was here in San Francisco because he had his eye on Max Bannister's priceless collection. And in a city seemingly filled with thieves, he probably had the best chance of actually getting what he had come here to get.

The fact that he was charming didn't change anything.

The fact that he had kissed her didn't change anything.

The fact that she was already half in love with him didn't change anything.

Anything at all.

When Wolfe finally left the museum to talk to the police, it was much later than he'd planned, largely because his lunchtime meeting with Storm had run well into the afternoon. And also because he had used one excuse after another to avoid leaving the museum. All day he'd gotten the feeling that Storm was, in some subtle way he sensed more than saw, drawing away from him.

It seemed absurd when he thought about her complete physical response to him, but Wolfe had learned to trust his instincts, and his instincts were telling him something was wrong.

Worried but unwilling to take the chance of pushing her for an answer, he finally decided to occupy himself by going and talking to Keane Tyler as he'd planned. He invited her to come along with him, but she said she had at least another hour's work ahead of her and she really wanted to get it out of the way—why not get it done while he was busy with the police? It was nearly six by then; she said if he didn't return to the museum by the time she finished, she and Bear would take a cab back to her hotel.

Wolfe had another uneasy feeling, this one that she wanted him to go away for a while, but chalked it up to paranoia. And he didn't leave before making definite plans with her to go out to dinner as soon as he finished with the police.

But by the time he got out to his car, he was having second thoughts. He pulled out of the side parking lot and over to the curb, gazing toward the museum, trying to gain control over his growing sense of worry. A heavy overcast and creeping fog made it darker than usual for the time of day, which meant he couldn't see a great deal clearly beyond the lighted backdrop of the lobby. Nobody was going into the museum because it was so late, but visitors were beginning to stream out as closing time neared.

When a cab pulled up to the steps, Wolfe didn't think very much about it. He watched idly, drumming his fingers against the steering wheel while he told himself repeatedly that it was probably quite normal for a man in his condition to be filled with the most ridiculous thoughts and worries. He'd have to ask Max one day if it had been this way with him.

When she came out of the museum and went toward the cab, Wolfe felt a moment of simple surprise. A glance at his watch told him he'd been sitting out here no more than ten minutes, which meant Storm shouldn't have been able to finish the work so quickly. He started to lean on his horn to get her attention, but something, some vague suspicion, made him change his mind.

He waited to make certain the cab was moving in the opposite direction—away from Storm's hotel—and then pulled his car away from the curb and began following at a discreet distance. It wasn't a very long trip; less than fifteen minutes later, Storm's cab stopped at a small park that was currently undergoing a renovation.

Wolfe pulled to the curb the moment the cab did and instantly killed his lights and engine. He watched, feeling peculiarly cold, as Storm got out and began walking down a narrow sidewalk that led toward a silent carousel in the distance; Wolfe knew it was there because he knew this park, but he couldn't see it because of the growing darkness and fog. He watched the cab pull away, waited a few seconds, then got out of his car and followed the same path Storm had taken.

In nearly fifteen years in the security business, Wolfe had picked up quite a number of useful things, one of which was the ability to follow someone on foot without betraying his presence. He used that ability now. As silent as a shadow, he glided along after Storm. The building that temporarily housed the huge, silent carousel while it was being renovated was normally locked; Wolfe was close enough to see that Storm entered through a door standing open invitingly.

He hesitated, but the dim light he could see was

coming from deeper in the building, so he felt safe in slipping inside after her. He moved instantly into the shadows cast by the carousel, his gaze fixed past the colorful animals to the two people standing on the other side.

"Where is he?" Storm asked quietly after a quick look around.

"On his way. You didn't give either of us much time to get here." Jared Chavalier shrugged and dug his hands into the pockets of his dark raincoat. There was a battery lantern sitting on the carousel near him, providing decent light for that section of the building.

"I don't have much time," Storm said. "Wolfe's supposed to pick me up in another hour or two for dinner. You have to make a decision about this."

"I know, I know." Jared sighed. "He's asking questions, good ones, and I can't stall him forever."

As he walked slowly around the carousel toward them, Wolfe said coldly, "Then why not try the truth?" His gaze was fixed on Storm, and even in the low light he saw her go deathly pale at the first sound of his voice. She turned slowly toward him, and he could see that the only color in her face was in the darkened green eyes. Bear was on her shoulder, his face as still as hers, and for the first time the sight of the little blond cat riding on the shoulder of the delicate blonde woman had no power to soften anything inside Wolfe.

"Take it easy—" Jared began, but Wolfe ignored him and spoke directly to Storm.

"You lied to me." His voice grated, like a steel file over stone.

She didn't flinch, but though her chin lifted a bit it wasn't with the fearless spirit he'd come to know and appreciate. And her voice held an alien note of hopelessness. Of defeat. "Yes, I lied to you. About the job. About what I came here to do."

Wolfe waited, but she offered no reasons, no excuses. She just gazed up at him with that remote face and those blank eyes. All he could think of was how honest those eyes had seemed to him, and he thought the pain and rage would tear him apart.

"What else did you lie about?" he demanded bitterly. And when she remained silent, he jerked his head toward Jared. "Was it his idea or yours to make the ultimate sacrifice, Storm? Tell me, I'm curious. Did you at least get a bonus out of it?"

Jared's voice dropped deliberately into the awful silence, every word like a stone. "If you say one more word, I swear to God I'll deck you."

But it was Storm who ended the confrontation, walking past Wolfe silently, the remoteness of her face shattered by pain. She didn't look back.

Wolfe swung around and took a hasty step after her but brought himself up short. His heart was thudding sickly in his chest as he watched her vanish out the door, and he couldn't seem to draw a breath without feeling a stabbing agony. The rage had gone, draining away so quickly it left him empty.

Dear God, what have I done?

The silence behind him was so thick it practically touched him. When he turned slowly, he found Jared standing with his arms crossed over his chest, the strange, pale aqua eyes glittering with anger.

"Nice going, pal," he said bleakly.

Before Wolfe could respond, Jared looked past him as a movement caught his attention, and Max walked quietly out of the shadows to join them. His hard face gave little away, but it was clear he was very disturbed.

To Wolfe, he said, "If you want to hit somebody, it better be me. I'm to blame for this."

"Too late," Jared muttered. "He's already beaten up his victim."

Storm wasn't thinking at all when she walked away from the carousel. She'd known it would be bad, but she hadn't expected it to hurt this much. Dimly, she wondered how it was possible to function, to walk and flag down a cab and get inside and give the address of her hotel, all the time filled with this terrible grief. It was like she'd received some mortal wound but her body hadn't recognized it yet because it was in shock.

At her hotel, she walked through the big, quiet

lobby and got on the elevator, more or less blind and deaf. Bear murmured nervously in her ear, but she didn't really hear him. When she got off the elevator on her floor and walked to the door of her suite, she was vaguely aware of claws digging into her shoulder, but she still didn't heed her cat.

It wasn't until she unlocked the door and opened it that Storm was literally jarred from her misery. A hard shove in the middle of her back propelled her into the suite so roughly that she nearly fell. Bear jumped off her shoulder and fled underneath the couch with a hiss of fear, and Storm caught her balance just in time to keep from sprawling out on the carpet.

She turned slowly, the pain inside her pushed aside for the moment by the ancient instincts of self-preservation. Her mind was clear and cold, and the first thing she took note of was the businesslike automatic in Nyssa Armstrong's slender and beautifully manicured hand.

The second thing she noticed was the insane rage gleaming in those wide blue eyes.

Oh, Morgan, you were more prophetic than we could have imagined . . .

Since Storm was a technical specialist with Interpol rather than a field agent, her training aimed at coping with a situation like this one had been rather sketchy. She could defend herself physically quite well—thanks to a father and six older brothers who'd made sure she could handle herself—but she didn't know how to disarm an enemy in a situation like this one, and she wished she'd paid more attention in her few psychology classes.

"Can we talk about this?" she asked, keeping her voice as even and casual as possible.

Nyssa had allowed the suite door to close behind her. She stood just a few feet from Storm, the gun pointed unerringly at the smaller woman's chest. She was smiling. "I don't think so," she said in a reflective tone. "You see, I really do hate to lose. And if I don't stop you, I'll lose twice. First Wolfe, and then the collection."

Storm felt a chill unlike anything she'd ever experienced before. What Nyssa said was scary enough, but the way she said it was terrifying. With absolutely no sign of mockery, she was imitating Storm's Southern accent, her head slightly tilted to one side as if to listen to her own efforts.

Storm wiped the accent from her voice. "As far as the collection goes—"

"No, don't do that." Nyssa frowned at her. "I have to get the voice right. I've seen his face when you talk to him, so I know he likes the voice." She cocked the pistol. "If you don't help me, I'll kill you here." Her tone was so matter-of-fact, almost indifferent, that it told Storm Nyssa would, without hesitation, kill.

Anything for a little more time, Storm thought. Staying alive was the first priority. "Anything you say," she drawled. "Would you like me to talk? My pleasure. Besides, I'm curious. How could you lose the collection because of me? It doesn't belong to me or to Wolfe—it belongs to Max Bannister."

Nyssa had her head tilted again, listening, and when she answered it was with a creditable Southern accent as well as a tone eerily like Storm's. "I could have persuaded Wolfe to let me see the collection. And, after that, it would have been easy to get the security details from him. I could do that, you know. Men tell me all kinds of things in bed. He would have, too, in time."

"Then you would have tried to...take...the collection?" Storm asked, wording the question carefully. She wanted to keep the conversation away from Wolfe if possible, because she had the instinctive certainty he was the danger zone.

"My men would have." Proudly, she said, "I taught them well. The police don't have a clue."

"You mean—that gang of thieves everybody's after is under your control?" Storm was honestly astonished. Interpol had been suspicious of Nyssa, but not for that.

She laughed softly. "It's the perfect arrangement. I find out all the security details, and then they go in. I select a few choice items for myself and give them the rest to sell to a few other collectors on their list. Everybody gets what they want and everybody's happy." She was still drawling.

"It does sound efficient," Storm agreed.

Nyssa glanced at her watch. "I think we'd better

be going. He'll come back here tonight, won't he? To be with you, like he was all weekend. I've been following both of you at different times. I know what's been going on. So he'll come back here soon, won't he?"

Before Storm could reply one way or the other, the taller blonde was going on, her voice beginning to tighten and lose a bit of its lazy drawl.

"That's when I knew for sure that I had to get rid of you. I didn't like the way he looked at you that first night, in the restaurant—as if he couldn't take his eyes off you. But I thought he'd lose interest soon. Then, at the museum on Friday, he gave me the brush-off." Her laugh was high and brittle. "Oh, he was smooth about it, but what he meant was he just wasn't interested in me anymore. It was you. I followed him over here, so I know he spent the night with you. I know he spent the entire weekend with you."

"Nyssa—"

She sort of shook her head, visibly reaching for control, and when she spoke she was drawling again. "He's the first one I really wanted," she murmured, as if to herself. "Don't know why, just something about him."

Desperately, Storm said, "I'm curious again. Did you follow me tonight, or what?"

Nyssa frowned. "No. I had something to do, so I couldn't wait outside the museum for you. I was lucky, though, because I got here just when you did. And when I saw he wasn't with you, I knew I could do it tonight. We're leaving now."

It didn't require any training or special knowledge for Storm to recognize the implacable expression on the other woman's face or the madness in her eyes. All Storm could think of was that she would have to make some kind of move between here and the front door of the hotel; once out of the lobby, her chances of getting help diminished rapidly.

She didn't attempt anything as she walked slightly ahead of Nyssa out of the suite and down the hall to the elevator. The car was deserted when it stopped for them, so Storm bided her time, silently hoping there would be people in the lobby; it was usually pretty active, and there were groupings of chairs and huge planters and other places to hide.

But what if Nyssa began shooting? Could she risk that, Storm asked herself desperately, could she be responsible for this madwoman hurting or even killing some innocent bystander? God, she *couldn't* let that happen. . . .

Frozen inside, her instincts screaming for her to do something and her mind telling her she couldn't, Storm stepped out of the elevator. Nyssa was a half step behind, a scarf draped over her hand to hide the gun that was pressing into Storm's back. They were halfway across the fairly busy lobby when a quiet voice behind Nyssa spoke her name.

To Storm, the next minute or so seemed to drag out until it lasted hours. She flinched away from the gun as Nyssa jerked it away from her back, and she had to turn around just as the other woman did, because it was Wolfe's voice.

He was there, standing very still, looking at Nyssa's face rather than at the gun now aimed at him. Storm wanted to scream out a warning, but a powerful hand was pulling her away. She knew it was Max, because she could see Jared slipping up on the other side of Nyssa, his unusual eyes coldly intent.

"It's me you really want, isn't it?" Nyssa said to Wolfe in that drawling voice uncannily like Storm's. "I'll forgive you, darling, just say you don't want her anymore."

Wolfe never had to respond to that, which was probably just as well; he looked a bit sick. Before Nyssa could take in Wolfe's expression, Jared made his move. He got the gun out of her hand without a wasted second, and before Nyssa could even begin to struggle she found herself in a hold she couldn't escape.

By the time she began screaming, the police had arrived.

* * *

Storm didn't look at any of the three tall men standing in her hotel suite. Instead, she gazed at the nervous little blond cat in her lap and stroked him gently. Max had brought her back to her suite soon after the police had arrived; Wolfe and Jared had joined them up here a few minutes later. She was dimly aware that they had talked, the three of them, but she had no idea what about.

Max had apologized to her quietly and sincerely, saying it was his fault she'd been put into the position of having to lie to Wolfe. It was ironic, he'd said; if she hadn't been so honest and conscientious, she would have saved herself a lot of pain by telling Wolfe the truth when their involvement became personal. Instead, bound by her sense of responsibility to do her job and obey her superior, she had been forced to go on lying.

Storm doubted that Wolfe would see it that way.

With the threat of Nyssa gone, her rush of adrenaline had gone as well, leaving her as numbly miserable as she had been before. She wasn't even interested enough to ask someone how they had known about Nyssa; they must have known, otherwise they wouldn't have been waiting in the lobby, she thought. Not that it mattered.

After an indeterminate while, her frozen senses thawed enough to tell her that Max and Jared were leaving. She looked up, watching them go. Wolfe shut the door behind them. He was staying, she realized. He took his jacket off and flung it toward a chair without looking to see where it landed. He came toward her with a very deliberate tread. She watched him come toward her, and some instinct rather than knowledge told her he was so tense he was on the knife edge of doing something violent.

He bent down, lifted Bear out of her lap and set him gently on the couch beside her, and then he jerked her up into his arms.

CHAPTER
SIXTEEN

For a moment, the breath knocked from her and more than a little dazed by his action, Storm didn't even hear the words he muttered into her hair. When she did hear them, she was afraid to believe what she heard.

"God, baby, I'm *sorry*. I didn't mean what I said, I swear I didn't. . . . I know you never would have lied to me if you'd had any other choice, and I know sleeping with me was never part of the job."

Storm leaned back far enough to look at him when he finally raised his head. There was something wild in his eyes, and she felt hypnotized by it. "I didn't lie about that," she whispered. "What I felt when you touched me . . . How badly I wanted you. I didn't mean for it to happen, Wolfe, but I couldn't help it. And I couldn't tell you the truth about that, about how I felt, when I was lying about why I was here. . . ."

He surrounded her face in his hands, those fierce eyes even wilder. "Tell me now."

Storm didn't hesitate. As long as there was a chance he could forgive her, she was willing to gamble everything she had, every shred of pride and every ounce of dignity. With simple honesty, she said, "I fell in love with you that first day, when I looked up and saw you standing there glowering in *such* a bad mood—"

Wolfe made a hoarse sound and kissed her. "I love you."

She didn't know how much time passed, but gradually she realized that Wolfe was on the couch and she was on his lap, held tightly in his arms. The position was amazingly comfortable, and she cuddled closer with a sigh of contentment even as her mind began functioning with something approaching normality.

Quietly, she said, "I never wanted to lie to you, Wolfe."

"I know." He matched her tone, his own voice still a little strained. "Even before you left the carousel, I knew. Then Max was there, and between them, he and Jared explained why they'd decided to keep their plans from me."

Storm drew back a little and gazed at him gravely. "Jared didn't tell me everything, of course. He just said Max didn't want you to feel torn between loyalty to him and your responsibilities to Lloyd's. He said your job was to protect the collection, and since that wouldn't change no matter what they planned, there was no reason for you to know."

Wolfe smiled slightly, but it was a wry smile. "Both of them knew better."

"I thought they *should* have—but it wasn't my place to say," she agreed. "It seemed to me all they really wanted was to delay you finding out long enough for them to think of a good enough reason to persuade you that using the collection to bait a trap was the right thing to do."

"I think you're right."

"Even so, when I realized how I felt about you, it put me squarely between a rock and a hard place. Interpol recruited me in college—they needed technical specialists, and with a major in computer programming and a minor in law, I was just what they were looking for—and I'd never disobeyed orders. So there was Jared saying he didn't want you to have the chance to look over the program I was writing, and I was falling for you so hard I had all the caution and subtlety of a comet—"

Wolfe kissed her, then said, "I gather your program has one of those doors we talked about a million years ago? Big enough to admit a thief?"

"Well, *one* of my programs does. I'm writing two, exactly alike except one of them has a weak spot—or door. The original plan was to leave one on file at Ace, to be the lure."

"I wondered when we'd get around to Ace," Wolfe said with visible satisfaction. "I always knew there was something fishy about Max's faith in the place."

Storm was a bit startled. "You mean, they left me to tell you all this?"

"They're rotten to the core, both of them," Wolfe said promptly. Then he smiled a bit ruefully. "To tell the truth, I wasn't in much shape to talk about it. I know some, but not all. So tell me—what's the deal with Ace?"

She cleared her throat. "I guess you didn't know Max owned the company?"

He stared at her. "No."

Storm was glad that particular lie (by omission, at least) wasn't hers. And she wondered if this was why the other two men had left her to fill in the blank spaces. Undoubtedly, they felt it best to stay out of Wolfe's reach, at least until he had time to absorb their various stratagems and omissions.

Keeping her voice casual, she said, "Yeah, he does. When they decided to use the collection as bait, Jared put a couple of people inside Ace as a kind of sting. They were supposed to be amenable to bribery, which was how my fake program was going to be available as part of the lure."

"Wait a minute," Wolfe said, frowning. "The

employee who was murdered supposedly broke into secure files—"

Storm nodded. "Nobody saw that coming. See, Jared was still in the process of getting his people settled into the company; nothing was supposed to be happening. Nobody counted on a thief showing interest in the museum before the exhibit was in place."

Including Wolfe. "Yeah. And the fact that an Ace employee was actually murdered, probably after being blackmailed, sent up giant red flags in my mind about Ace."

"Which was the last thing anybody wanted," Storm said dryly.

"Was the computer foul-up deliberate?"

She chuckled. "Actually, no. What was supposed to happen was that the technician was going to get most of the basic programming in place and then admit he was in over his head. He'd leave with abject apologies, and Ace would send me in. I *was* in Paris, by the way, working on another project."

"But not for Ace," Wolfe murmured.

"No."

"So what happened?"

"That poor kid really fouled up," Storm said ruefully. "Then you hit the ceiling and started raining fire and brimstone on Ace, and everybody—I mean Jared and Max—started getting nervous that you were going to throw a spanner in the works and demand a different security company. So I was rushed in and ordered to fix up Ace's black eye in a hurry. I was supposed to convince you I was the best *and* divert your attention away from Ace."

"So your cocky attitude that first day was for show?"

She looked a bit self-conscious. "Well, no. That was really me. When you're little, you learn to talk big—especially with six older brothers."

Wolfe grinned at her. "That's a relief. In case you didn't know, one of the reasons I fell in love with you was that confident, fearless manner."

"You were just happy to have somebody who'd fight with you," Storm said, but she was pleased nonetheless.

"That, too." He concentrated on the conversation. "Let's see now...oh, yeah—the phone patch."

Obediently, she said, "Was supposed to be another diversion for you, if needed. Jared thought I used it too soon, and he was horrified when I pointed you at Nyssa."

"Why?"

"About Nyssa?" Storm sighed. "It's so convoluted. See, one of the inside men at Ace *had* leaked information—to Nyssa. The trap wasn't intended for her, but she's been on Interpol's watch list for years and the agent knew it. He leaked something he didn't think was very vital, intending it to draw her back again later."

It only took Wolfe a moment. "He leaked the information about you."

"Right. So she approaches me in the ladies' room to tell me she knows I'm the new computer technician, and I find myself with a potential problem. Since she also tells me how cozy you two are, I have to assume she might well share her information with you—and, at this point, I don't know what else was leaked to her. No matter what she tells you, it's going to turn your angry attention right back to Ace. So I decide to ... take the bull by the horns. *I* tell you she's somehow found out about me, and at the same time do my best to convince you she couldn't possibly have found that out from anybody at Ace."

"You have a devious mind," Wolfe told her.

"Thank you. But Jared was convinced if your attention was on Nyssa you'd eventually work your way back to Ace, so he wasn't happy with me."

"He also knew she was unbalanced," Wolfe said with a touch of grimness.

"He did? How?"

"Storm, she was on the Interpol watch list because at least three couriers supposedly carrying artworks from her to buyers turned up dead—with the valuables gone. Nyssa was the only common denominator in all three cases."

She shivered. "I'm glad I didn't know that. By the way, how did you guys turn up here in the nick of time?"

"That's the only reason I'm still speaking to Jared. The man he had watching Nyssa radioed that she'd followed you into the hotel."

Storm didn't want either of them to dwell on what had happened, so she said calmly, "Well, I certainly hope all this has cured you of Barbie dolls once and for all."

"You could say that. In fact, I've discovered a new passion."

She eyed him. "Oh, yes?"

"Definitely. I fully expect it to occupy all my attention for the next forty or fifty years."

Grave, she said, "That's a long time. Sure you won't be bored?"

Wolfe started to laugh. "Bored? Jesus Christ."

Laughing herself now, Storm said, "Okay, then the flip side. Sure I won't drive you crazy?"

"I'm absolutely sure you will," he told her. "And I wouldn't have it any other way."

A few days later, Wolfe left Storm at her hotel and returned to his apartment to change because they were going to have dinner with Max and his new wife, Dinah. Wolfe and Storm hadn't yet moved in together, only because they were looking for an apartment or house with a garden where Bear could chase bugs and sun himself; in the meantime, they tended to spend the night in whichever place was closest or most convenient.

Wolfe was in a good mood when he came out of his bedroom dressed for the evening, but he tensed a bit when he saw that he had a visitor—though he might have admitted to feeling a certain amount of relief.

Standing by the open window, which was obviously how he'd entered the fourth-floor apartment, and dressed all in black but unmasked, the visitor said mildly, "Got your summons. Really, though, Wolfe—an ad in the personals column?"

"Last I heard," Wolfe said in a voice of dangerous calm, "you didn't have a permanent address."

"True enough." Quinn's voice was still mild, but his green eyes were watchful—and the open window was close enough for a quick escape if necessary. "But—you're obviously going out. Why don't I come back another time?"

"Don't you move."

Quinn winced at the fierceness in that command. "It was just a suggestion. I wouldn't have vanished off the face of the earth, you know."

"You did in London."

"That was different. I got the distinct feeling at the time that you were about to do something we'd both have been sorry for, so I cleared out. Removed temptation, so to speak."

Waving that aside with an abrupt gesture, Wolfe studied his visitor through narrowed eyes. "You look like hell," he said, taking note of assorted fading bruises and the remnants of a lovely shiner that marred the handsome face.

"Thank you so much."

"Well, what did you expect me to say? Welcome to the States? I don't think so. I want to know what you're doing here. And I want the truth."

After a silence, during which he seemed to be weighing Wolfe's determination, Quinn sighed. "All right, but the answer won't make your life any easier."

On Friday morning of that week, Morgan came into the computer room with something of a flounce and collapsed into the visitor's chair after dragging it out of its corner.

Storm stopped typing her new security program into the computer and rested an elbow on the desk, studying the brunette thoughtfully. "You look a bit aggrieved," she said.

Morgan drew a breath, then began speaking rapidly. "When I woke up this morning, I found a gaily wrapped little package dangling from my doorknob. From the *inside* of the doorknob. The door was double-locked, mind you, with dead bolts. But did that stop him? Oh, no."

"Quinn?" Storm guessed.

Morgan produced a small, ring-sized box, which she shoved across the desk at her friend. "Look at that. A copy, of course, but a damned good one. That lousy thief has taste, I'll give him that."

Opening the box, Storm found a spectacular ring with a huge, square stone that gleamed like moonlight. "It's gorgeous," she said admiringly.

Morgan scowled. "It's a nail in his coffin."

"Why?"

"There's an entire collection of them in an Eastern museum," Morgan said, almost visibly steaming. "He knew I'd recognize it. He knew. He did it deliberately, just to taunt me. And to think I was actually beginning to believe . . . Well, never mind about that. The point is—"

"Morgan?"

"What?"

Storm held the ring box up and tapped the stone with a questioning finger. "Tell me what this is?"

"It's a *concubine* ring!" Morgan all but wailed. "That lousy, no good, rotten excuse for a man gave me a ring they used to pass out in *harems*!"

Storm couldn't help it; she started to chuckle. "I'm sorry," she said penitently to her offended friend. "It's just that he sure knows how to push your buttons, doesn't he?"

"What he knows how to do is piss me off," Morgan said fiercely. "And he's done it. I might have been stupid enough until now to pass up a couple of opportunities to set the police after his ass, but that won't happen again."

"No?"

"No. He's just put himself at the top of *my* most wanted list."

"That could," Storm noted mildly, "be taken another way."

"In the mood I'm in now, I'd slam the cell door shut myself and drop the key into the bay. Thieving bastard."

"Well, you might just get your chance. Once the Bannister collection is out of the vaults, I imagine Quinn is going to be our biggest headache."

"He's the one who's going to have the headache," Morgan promised grimly. "He'll have a headache the likes of which he's never had before. If you're a betting woman, bet on me."

Read on for a special preview of
the next thrilling Bishop/Special
Crimes Unit novel, the first in
Kay Hooper's new
Blood trilogy

BLOOD
DREAMS

KAY HOOPER

Coming Soon

KAY HOOPER

A BISHOP/SPECIAL CRIMES UNIT NOVEL

BLOOD
DREAMS

BLOOD DREAMS

Coming Soon

PROLOGUE

It was the nightmare brought to life, Dani thought.

The vision.

The smell of blood turned her stomach, the thick, acrid smoke burned her eyes, and what had been for so long a wispy, dreamlike memory now was jarring, throat-clogging reality. For just an instant she was paralyzed.

It was all coming true.

Despite everything she had done, everything she had *tried* to do, despite all the warnings, once again it was all—

"Dani?" Hollis seemingly appeared out of the smoke at her side, gun drawn, blue eyes sharp even squinted against the stench. "Where is it?"

"I—I can't. I mean, I don't think I can—"

"Dani, you're all we've got. You're all *they've* got. Do you understand that?"

Reaching desperately for strength she wasn't at all sure she had, Dani said, "If somebody had just listened to me when it mattered—"

"Stop looking back. There's no sense in it. Now is all that counts. Which way, Dani?"

Impossible as it was, Dani had to force herself to concentrate on the stench of blood she knew neither of the others could smell. A blood trail that was all they had to guide them. She nearly gagged, then pointed. "That way. Toward the back. But..."

"But what?"

"Down. Lower. There's a basement level." Stairs. She remembered stairs. Going down them. Down into hell.

"It isn't on the blueprints."

"I know."

"Bad place to get trapped in a burning building," Hollis noted. "The roof could fall in on us. Easily."

Bishop appeared out of the smoke as suddenly as she had, weapon in hand, his face stone, eyes haunted. "We have to hurry."

"Yeah," Hollis replied, "we get that. Burning building. Maniacal killer. Good seriously outnumbered by evil. Bad situation." Her words and tone were flippant, but her gaze on his face was anything but, intent and measuring.

"You forgot potential victim in maniacal killer's hands," her boss said, not even trying to match her tone.

"Never. Dani, did you see the basement, or are you feeling it?"

"Stairs. I saw them." The weight on her shoulders felt like the world, so maybe that was what was pressing her down. Or... "And what I feel now... he's lower. He's underneath us."

"Then we look for stairs."

Dani coughed. She was trying to think, trying to remember. But dreams recalled were such dim, insubstantial things, even vision-dreams sometimes, and there was no way for her to be sure she was remembering clearly. She was overwhelmingly conscious of precious time passing, and looked at her wrist, at the bulky digital watch that told her it was 2:47 PM on Tuesday, October 28.

Odd. She never wore a watch. Why was she wearing one now? And why a watch that looked so... alien on her thin wrist?

"Dani?"

She shook off the momentary confusion. "The stairs. Not where you'd expect them to be," she managed finally, coughing again. "They're in a closet or something like that. A small office. Room. Not a hallway. Hallways—"

"What?"

The instant of certainty was fleeting, but absolute. "Shit. The basement is divided. By a solid wall. Two big rooms. And accessed from this main level by two different stairways, one at each side of the building, in the back."

"What kind of crazy-ass design is that?" Hollis demanded.

"If we get out of this alive, you can ask the architect." The smell of blood was almost overpowering, and Dani's head was beginning to hurt. Badly. She had never before pushed herself for so long without a break, especially with this level of intensity.

It was Bishop who said, "You don't know which side they're in."

"No. I'm sorry." She felt as if she'd been apologizing to this man since she'd met him. Hell, she had been.

Hollis was scowling. To Bishop, she said, "Great. That's just great. You're psychically blind, the storm has all my senses scrambled, and we're in a huge burning building without a freakin' map."

"Which is why Dani is here." Those pale sentry eyes were fixed on her face.

Dani felt wholly inadequate. "I—I don't— All I know is that he's down there somewhere."

"And Miranda?"

The name caused her a queer little shock, and for no more than a heartbeat, Dani had the dizzy sense of something out of place, out of sync somehow. But she had an answer for him. Of sorts. "She isn't—dead. Yet. She's bait, you know that. She was always bait, to lure you."

"And you," Bishop said.

Dani didn't want to think about that. Couldn't, for some reason she was unable to explain, think about that. "We have to go, now. He won't wait, not this time." *And he's not the only one.*

The conversation had taken only brief minutes, but even so the smoke was thicker, the crackling roar of the fire louder, and the heat growing ever more intense.

Bitterly, Hollis said, "We're on *his* timetable, just like before, like always, carried along without the chance to stop and think."

Bishop turned and started toward the rear of the building and the south corner. "I'll go down on this side. You two head for the east corner."

Dani wondered if instinct was guiding him as well, but all she said, to Hollis, was, "He wouldn't take the chance if he had it, would he? To stop and think, I mean."

"If it meant a minute lost in getting to Miranda? No way in hell. That alone would be enough, but on top of that he blames himself for this mess."

"He couldn't have known—"

"Yes. He could have. Maybe he even did. That's why he believes it's his fault. Come on, let's go."

Dani followed, but had to ask, "Do you believe it's his fault?"

Hollis paused for only an instant, looking back over her shoulder, and there was something hard and bright in her eyes. "Yes. I do. He played God one time too many. And we're paying the price for his arrogance."

Again, Dani followed the other woman, her throat tighter despite the fact that, as they reached the rear half of the building, the smoke wasn't nearly as thick. They very quickly discovered, in the back of what might once have been a small office, a door that opened smoothly and silently to reveal a stairwell.

The stairwell was already lighted.

"Bingo," Hollis breathed.

A part of Dani wanted to suggest that they wait, at least long enough for Bishop to check out the other side of the building, but every instinct, as well as the waves of heat at her back, told her there simply wasn't time to wait.

Hollis shifted her weapon to a steady two-handed grip, and sent Dani a quick look. "Ready?"

Dani didn't spare the energy to wonder how anyone on earth could ever be ready for this. Instead, she concentrated on the only weapon she had, the one inside her aching head, and nodded.

Hollis had only taken one step when a thunderous crash sounded behind them and a new wave of almost intolerable heat threatened to shove them bodily into the stairwell.

The roof was falling in.

They exchanged glances and then, without emotion, Hollis said, "Close the door behind us."

Dani gathered all the courage she could find, and if her response wasn't as emotionless as the other woman's, at least it was steady.

"Right," she said, and closed the door behind them as they began their descent into hell.

One

You had that dream again last night, didn't you?"

Dani kept her gaze fixed on her coffee cup until the silence dragged on a minute longer than it should have, then looked at her sister's face. "Yeah. I had that dream."

Paris sat down on the other side of the table, her own cup cradled in both hands. "Same as before?"

"Pretty much."

"Then *not* the same as before. What was different?"

It was an answer Dani didn't want to offer, but she knew her sister too well to fight the inevitable. "It was placed in time. Two-forty-seven in the afternoon, October twenty-eighth."

Paris turned her head to study the wall calendar stuck with South Park character magnets to her refrigerator. "The twenty-eighth, huh? This year?"

"Yeah."

"That's three weeks from today."

"I noticed that."

"Same people?"

Dani nodded. "Same people. Same conversations. Same burning warehouse. Same feeling of doom."

"Except for the time being fixed, it was exactly the same?"

"It's never *exactly* the same. A word changed here or there, a gesture different. I think the gun Hollis carried wasn't the same one as before. And Bishop was wearing a black leather jacket this time."

"But they're always the same. Those two people are always a part of the dream."

"Always."

"People you don't know."

"People I don't know—yet." Dani frowned down at her coffee for a moment, then shook her head and met her sister's steady gaze again. "In the dream, I feel I know them awfully well. I understand them in a way that's difficult to explain."

"Maybe because they're psychic too."

Dani hunched her shoulders. "Maybe."

"And it ended—?"

"Just like it always ends. That doesn't change. I shut the door behind us and we go down the stairs. I know the roof has started collapsing. I know we won't be able to get out the same way we go in. I know something terrible and evil is waiting for us in that basement."

"But you go down there anyway."

"I don't seem to have a choice."

"Or maybe it's a choice you made before you ever set foot in that building," Paris said. "Maybe it's a choice you're making now. The date. How did you see it?"

"Watch."

"On you? You don't wear a watch. You can't."

Still reluctant, Dani said, "And it wasn't the sort of watch I'd wear even if I could wear one."

"What sort of watch was it?"

"It was . . . military-looking. Big, black, digital. Lots of buttons, more than one display. Looked like it could give me the time in Beijing and the latitude and longitude as well. Hell, maybe it could translate Sanskrit into English, for all I know."

"What do you think that means?"

Dani sighed. "One year of psychology under your belt, so naturally everything has to mean something, I guess."

"When it comes to your dreams, yes, everything means something. We both know that. Come on, Dani. How many times now have you dreamed this same dream?"

"A few."

"A half-dozen times that I know of—and I'm betting you didn't tell me about it right away."

"So?"

"Dani."

"Look, it doesn't matter how many times I've had the dream. It doesn't matter because it isn't a premonition."

"Could have fooled me."

Dani got up and carried her coffee cup to the sink. "Yeah, well, it wasn't your dream."

Paris turned in her chair but remained where she was. "Dani, is that why you came down here, to Venture? Not to keep me company while I go through a messy divorce, but because of that dream?"

"I don't know what you're talking about."

"The hell you don't."

"Paris—"

"I want the truth. Don't make me get it for myself."

Dani turned around, leaning back against the counter as she once again faced the rueful knowledge that she would never be able to keep the truth from her sister, not for long.

Paris wore her burnished copper hair in a

shorter style these days—she called it her divorce rebirth—and she was a bit too thin, but otherwise looking at her was like looking into a mirror. Dani had long since grown accustomed to that, and in fact viewed it as an advantage; watching the play of emotions across Paris's expressive face had taught her to hide her own.

At least from everyone except Paris.

"We promised," her sister reminded her. "To leave each other our personal lives, our own thoughts and feelings. And we've gotten very good at keeping that door closed. But I remember how to open it, Dani. We both do."

Dani nodded slowly. "Okay. The dream started a few months ago, back in the summer. When the senator's daughter was murdered by that serial killer in Boston."

"The one they haven't caught yet?"

"Yeah."

Paris was frowning. "I'm missing the connection."

"I didn't think there was one. Which is why I didn't think it was a premonition."

Without pouncing on that admission, her sister said, "Until something changed. What?"

"I saw a news report. The federal agent in charge of the investigation in Boston is the man in my dream. Bishop."

"I still don't see—"

"His wife is Miranda Bishop. Remember her?"

Paris sat up straighter. "It was— What?

Nearly a year and a half ago? She's the one who told us about Haven."

"Yeah. She met with us in Atlanta. You and Danny were one argument away from splitting up, and I was between jobs and at loose ends. Neither one of us was interested in becoming a fed, even with the Special Crimes Unit. But working for Haven ... that sounded interesting."

Absently, Paris said, "That was the last straw for Danny, you know. When I wanted to use my abilities, when I got a job that actually required them. I saw how creeped-out he was. How could I stay with someone who felt that way about any part of me?"

"Yeah, I know. Been there. Most of the guys I've met couldn't get past the fact that I was an identical twin; having dreams that literally came true hasn't exactly been seen as a fun bonus."

"We are unique."

"Well, sometimes I think being ordinary might have been easier."

"Maybe. Less fun, though." Paris shook her head. "Getting back to your dream—are you saying it has something to do with that serial killer?"

"I think so."

"Why?"

"A feeling."

Paris watched her steadily. "What else?"

Dani didn't want to answer, but finally did. "Whatever was down in that basement was—

is—evil. A kind of evil I've never felt before. And one thing that has been the same in every single version of my dream is the fact that it has Miranda."

"She's a hostage?"

"She's bait."